YOU ROCK MY WORLD

CAMILLA ISLEY

B
Boldwood

First published in Great Britain in 2025 by Boldwood Books Ltd.

Copyright © Camilla Isley, 2025

Cover Design by Alexandra Allden

Cover Images: Alexandra Allden and Shutterstock

The moral right of Camilla Isley to be identified as the author of this work has been asserted in accordance with the Copyright, Designs and Patents Act 1988.

Every effort has been made to obtain the necessary permissions with reference to copyright material, both illustrative and quoted. We apologise for any omissions in this respect and will be pleased to make the appropriate acknowledgements in any future edition.

A CIP catalogue record for this book is available from the British Library.

Paperback ISBN 978-1-83633-373-9

Large Print ISBN 978-1-83633-372-2

Hardback ISBN 978-1-83633-371-5

Trade Paperback ISBN 978-1-80635-285-2

Ebook ISBN 978-1-83633-374-6

Kindle ISBN 978-1-83633-375-3

Audio CD ISBN 978-1-83633-366-1

MP3 CD ISBN 978-1-83633-367-8

Digital audio download ISBN 978-1-83633-368-5

This book is printed on certified sustainable paper. Boldwood Books is dedicated to putting sustainability at the heart of our business. For more information please visit https://www.boldwoodbooks.com/about-us/sustainability/

Boldwood Books Ltd, 23 Bowerdean Street, London, SW6 3TN

www.boldwoodbooks.com

To all the readers who rock my world every day and make this job possible for me. Love you.

1

JOSIE

August—Present Time

"Hello, stranger."

The deep, masculine voice rolls down my spine, spreading the chill of an ice cube and the burn of a branding iron. My back stiffens, yet I hold still. I don't turn right away.

I keep facing the desk, surveying the endless shelves in the study. The books belong to tonight's host, someone I've never met—same goes for the rest of the guests. What possessed me to come to this party? I should've told my date no. But he seemed so stoked to be invited to a private Hollywood bash that I reluctantly agreed to tag along. But no good deed goes unpunished, and now I've got my reckoning waiting behind me.

I inhale deeply, exhale, and finally face the owner of that voice. But no amount of controlled breathing can prepare me for the man standing before me, the one who haunts my dreams, turning them into hopeless nightmares.

Rian Phoenix—rockstar, actor, sex icon of my generation.

I fix on a point past his shoulder, not to take him in all at once. Staring at him directly is as dumb as looking at the sun. But my evasive moves are pointless. His charisma assaults me from every direction, pulling my gaze toward him like iron to a magnet.

Giving up, I scan the fitted dark T-shirt that clings to his frame tightly enough to prompt indecent thoughts. The ripped black jeans so worn they might've been through every world tour with him. They fit him as a second skin tailored by time. I take inventory of the silver necklace that peeks out from under the T-shirt, the leather cuff at his wrist, and the chain that dangles from his belt loop, catching the light to reveal its wear and scratches.

His boots are scuffed but expensive. And topping it all off, he's wearing a jet-black leather jacket—lightweight, probably some designer I can't pronounce—that hangs open, making him look even cooler.

His raven-black hair falls past his chiseled cheekbones in untamed waves. But it's his icy-blue eyes, now laser-focused on me, that melt my internal organs a million times faster in person than they do from behind a movie screen or from across an arena packed with thousands of people. Because yes, I'm that pathetic and went to one—*okay, three*—of his concerts.

"Hi," I squawk.

He tilts his head. "Is it my impression, or have you been snubbing me all night?"

I stare at the door that he's blocking with his imposing frame. Yep, we're alone and Rian Phoenix is cutting off my only escape route.

Turns out, hiding in here wasn't the genius survival plan I thought it was. I should've stuck to a "blend in the crowd" approach. Easier to slip away. But now he's found me, and the game is up.

For the first time since I spotted him across the living room, I let myself take his features in, embrace the full force of his burning star. I allow my eyes to roam the planes of his face. The sharp curve of his jawline shadowed by stubble I wouldn't mind nuzzling against. His strong, straight nose that adds to the intensity of his expression, while the cute scrunch of his brows keeps him from being truly intimidating. And then there's that lopsided grin, pointed right at me, fully weaponized and ready to finish me off.

His eyes crinkle, making the whole of him impossible to withstand.

"I... I didn't think you'd remember me," I finally say.

He arches a skeptical eyebrow at that.

"I mean, you must meet so many people. You can't remember all of them."

"I meet a lot of people, yeah." He crosses his arms over his toned chest and leans a shoulder against the doorframe. "I don't get stuck in elevators for ten hours with many of them." A pause, that smirk again. "You made a lasting impression, Josie Monroe."

All I can say for myself is that I keep my mouth shut and don't squawk again, or make any other embarrassing sounds, or faint—even if I'm most definitely swooning.

"Were you really not going to say hi?" he asks in that millions-of-records-sold voice of his.

I give him the slightest headshake.

He narrows his eyes, but he's still smiling as he accuses, "So, you *were* snubbing me."

"No." I cringe in embarrassment. "More like strategically avoiding you?"

His blue eyes widen at the admission. "Why?"

It's a simple question, and I should be able to brush it off nonchalantly, but I can't. I don't really know him, but it feels like I do, and like he knows me in return. Which makes no sense— it's as illogical as it was that night we spent locked up together. And even if it's been a year, it seems like no time has passed at all. As if the intimacy of being trapped alone has never left us even these many months later.

So, I go with the truth, like always for him. "You're still too hot and too married."

His jaw tenses, ticks, but it's only a moment before the clench is released and his entire posture relaxes. "It must be some serious hotness to cause such a flight response."

I smile at that. "Said the world-famous rockstar slash actor who every teenage girl on the planet has a poster of in their bedrooms."

The teasing smile is back. "Every single one? I thought a few still went for Harry Styles, no?"

And now I'm full-on laughing. And see, this is the problem. Because since I got stuck in an elevator with this man a year ago, I've been madly, irrationally, hopelessly in love with him. And not the mega star, Rian Phoenix, who women all over the world fantasize about. No, much worse, because I'm in love with Dorian. The sarcastic, unapologetic, goofy, and still sexy-as-hell man behind the fame. The real him.

"Okay," I concede. "We can settle for half the teenagers on the planet."

"If you're trying to avoid me, why come to a party for the release of my latest movie?" He changes the subject, taking me off guard. As if I needed to be any more off-kilter in his presence.

"I thought you'd still be on tour."

"I'm on a break between cities." His expression gets inscrutable. Now he must think I've been full-on stalking him, which I pretty much did, but he doesn't need to know that.

"Missy mentioned something about Arlington the other day at the general staff meeting."

The company I work for does his public relations. I'm not on his account, my colleague, Missy, is. And thank goodness for that, or I would've lost my marbles a long time ago.

"I wasn't drunk," Dorian says on the defensive, referring to my Arlington comment.

"I know," I tell him. "The press are jerks sometimes."

He studies me, his too-perceptive eyes seeing more than I care for him to see. So, I panic and blurt, "I should go back to my date."

Now both his eyebrows disappear under his unruly fringe.

"You're on a *date*?"

"First date, actually." I cross the room toward him, hoping Dorian will scoot and let me disappear into the safety of the crowds.

No such luck. He doesn't budge an inch, so now we're also standing too close for comfort.

"And how's that going?" he asks in a blank tone I can't interpret.

It's going nowhere. Not after this little reminder of how a man's eye on me should make my skin burn without a single touch and cause my heart to stutter violently in my chest.

But this man—icon, legend, idol?—is already taken and I'm no home-wrecker, so I paste a fake smile on my face and deliver an even more false answer. "It's going great, *super*, in fact."

Without a word, Dorian steps aside, his features carved in stone.

I'm beginning to hope I've made it out of this interaction

alive, with my heart in one solid piece—maybe with only a few small cracks spreading, but still mostly beating fine—when Dorian's parting salvo catches me as I brush past him.

"Do you always hide alone in a room on great first dates?"

2

DORIAN

One Year Ago

I step into the elevator, the leftover adrenaline of another near-scandal not quite gone.

Yesterday, I let my wife rattle me and acted stupid again. Today, the public fallout should be contained at least.

My security detail is waiting downstairs while my team is ironing out the press release that will keep the headlines in check. For how long? At least until the media gets bored and seeks the next fire to fan. I'm their favorite circus monkey.

I push the lobby button just as someone yells, "Wait," and a petite foot in flat sandals wedges itself between the closing doors.

My guard goes up—automatic reaction with strangers—but as the intruder, a young woman, steps inside, the annoyance fades. She's... adorable. Soft, wavy light-brown hair frames her face, half pulled back to reveal a dusting of freckles across the bridge of her nose that makes her seem approachable in a way most people in my life aren't. Her flowing, boho dress flatters her slender curves despite the many ruffles, drawing my attention more than I expected.

Okay, correction: she's not cute. She's stunning. But as her warm amber eyes widen in recognition, I still brace myself. No one was supposed to be around this late—it's the only reason I'm moving without bodyguards. Amateur mistake. I curse my carelessness as I wait for the inevitable fangirl meltdown. Will she burst into tears? Beg for a selfie? Flash me for an autograph on her chest?

None of the above.

Her reaction is a demure, "Good evening," followed by a fierce blush and a fast retreat to the opposite corner, eyes fixed on the carpet.

Most people in this situation would make conversation. Or sneak a not-so-subtle photo. I fight not to smirk as I study her. Curiosity piqued, I return her formal greeting, "Good evening to you, too."

Her blush deepens—impressive, spreading down the elegant column of her neck. I'm oddly captivated by its progress.

"Running late for something?" I ask.

"Oh, no, I..." She stumbles over her words, glancing at me before those mesmerizing eyes dart away again. "The elevator takes forever, and I didn't want to wait for the next one. Long day."

"Fair. But you get extra points for the dramatic entrance." I lean against the wall, angling my body toward her. "The doors are still recovering."

She offers a tiny, close-lipped smile before her gaze skitters away again. I can't decide if she's a nervous fan or just shy. Either way, I'm intrigued.

The elevator begins its slow descent. I'm about to make

another attempt at conversation when the car lurches to an abrupt halt. Then the lights go out.

"Shit," I mutter, reaching for my phone. Before I can flick on the flashlight, the emergency lights kick in.

My companion is wide-eyed in her corner.

"You okay?"

"Yeah?" She sounds unsure.

"Let's give it a minute. I'm sure it'll start up again."

She nods, still looking uncertain. When five minutes go by, and the elevator doesn't budge, I press the emergency button. A chime sounds, but no one responds.

I try again. Still no answer.

I unlock my phone to call for help. But the bars are flat.

I hold up the screen. "No reception. You?"

She fishes her phone out of her bag and shakes her head.

I crack my neck, try the button again. Nothing. "Well, I'm wiped. Mind if I...?" I motion to the floor. When she doesn't object, I slide down the wall to sit, legs bent in front of me, the oldish but clean carpet cushioning my butt.

After a beat, she joins me, fanning out her skirt.

For someone who constantly complains about how noisy my life is, I can't stand the silence and debate what to say to put her at ease. I hate small talk, but also being personal with strangers.

Before I can think of something, the speaker crackles. A technician asks us routine questions: how many inside, any panic attacks or medical issues? I tell him we're fine, and he explains a wildfire took out a power plant and half the grid went dark. We're in a safe zone, but the city's a mess. Emergency services are swamped, and we're a low priority. We could be stuck here for hours. Maybe all night.

I turn to the woman, glad she kicked her ridiculously tiny

foot between the doors earlier and that I'm not trapped in here alone.

She shrugs as if to say, "*What can we do?*"

"Well, at least the elevator is carpeted. We won't freeze our butts."

She finally cracks a smile.

"I'm Dorian, by the way. Figure if we're going to be elevator buddies, we should learn each other's names."

She studies me now. Less shy, more feisty. "Am I supposed to pretend I didn't know that?"

I grin, shrugging. "Up to you. All I ask is that you tell me your name in return. Fair trade?"

She hesitates, then replies, "Josie."

3

JOSIE

September—Present Time

I stride through the revolving door of my office building, gripping my mocha latte—the only thing keeping me upright. Unfortunately, caffeine can't erase the dark circles under my eyes or unknot the tangle of despair in my chest.

I haven't slept well these past few weeks. Running into Dorian at that stupid party a month ago blew six months of therapy to hell. All the work on shutting unattainable fantasies out, setting clear goals for myself, staying rooted in reality... *poof* —undone by a fifteen-minute conversation. Now everything triggers me. Yesterday, it was his new single playing on the radio. After that, I couldn't sleep. Images of him kept flashing through my mind in a relentless onslaught—him on stage, his chiseled features on the big screen, that time I had the sexiest man alive to myself for ten hours. My brain replayed every second we shared that night on a loop.

By 3 a.m., I was still on the couch, eyes bloodshot,

surrounded by KitKat wrappers, streaming his latest album. Each song burned through me like acid.

I shake my head to dislodge the memories. I need to project less "heartbroken walking zombie" and more "adult woman in charge." Not easy when the first obstacle of my day is the same steel trap where this ridiculous crush began. I pause at the elevator bank, eyeing the call button like it might detonate. Do I want to revisit the scene of the crime? Stir up everything again by stepping into the same twenty-five square feet where I first met Dorian? The alternative is twenty flights of stairs. Good for my mental health and thighs, but terrible for composure. I can't sashay into the office a sweaty disaster. With a sigh of resignation, I opt for the elevator of doom and broken dreams.

As I step inside, I half-expect to see his devastatingly handsome smirk again. But it's just me and my tragic reflection in the mirrored walls. I jab the button for my floor harder than necessary, as if the innocent plastic were withholding vital answers I could push out of it.

The ride is mercifully solitary and uneventful, if not a little heartbreaking and panic-inducing. When the doors slide open, I take a fortifying breath and stride out. Confident. Poised. Ready to fake it until I make it.

My positive vibes shatter as Pam, the assistant I share with the other junior associates in the tech division, greets me with a too-bright smile, her eyes darting nervously.

Bad news is coming.

"Morning, Pam. What's with the—"

"Nadine wants to see you. Right now," she announces in a rush, confirming my suspicions.

Nadine Fox is the founder and CEO of the company. A summons from her rarely bodes well.

With a nod, I head for the stairwell, regretting my stilettos.

This morning, the heels felt like a power move against the black hole of my ill-fated feelings. Now, they just feel impractical. But since Nadine is only two floors up, I'll take the sore feet over another elevator ride. Besides, the climb will help clear my head before facing whatever fresh hell awaits me in the big boss's office.

I emerge on the top floor winded but marginally more composed. Nadine's secretary waves me straight through.

The office is minimalist perfection, with sleek white furniture, expansive windows framing a breathtaking view of downtown, and a desk that, for all its simplicity, probably costs more than my car.

Nadine sits behind it, looking sharp in a crisp white blazer. She fixes me with her cold blue gaze, gesturing for me to sit.

"Josie, thanks for coming up." Her tone is polite, but I detect an undercurrent of irritation. "I have some unexpected news."

I feel like a bug about to be squashed. "Oh?"

"Missy was rushed to the hospital last night. Pregnancy complications. She's fine," Nadine adds, seeing my stricken reaction. "But she's been put on bed rest until further notice."

"That's awful. I didn't even know she was pregnant." Missy is in charge of the celebrity division. We're friendly, but not close.

"She hadn't told anyone at the office except for me, she's just finishing the first trimester. We were making plans to cover her maternity leave, but now everything's been fast-tracked."

I process the new info, not fully grasping why Nadine is telling *me*, but not liking where this is going.

"I'm reassigning her clients in the interim."

"To her juniors, right?" I aim for a breezy tone, but it comes out strangled.

Nadine's eyes dissect me like a butterfly pinned to a board. "All but one... who specifically requested you."

Despite being born and raised in LA, I don't know that many celebrities—just the one, in fact. Cue dread.

"Me?" I squeak. I clear my throat, trying again. "But I'm in tech PR. My clients are start-ups, not celebrities."

"I know what division you work in, Josie." Nadine's tone is clipped. "But when our biggest client makes a personal request, I'm not in a position to refuse. Keeping him happy is our top priority."

"*Him?*" I croak.

She steeples her fingers. "Rian Phoenix."

I knew it. I flipping knew it.

My heart is about to explode like a shaken bottle of soda filled with Mentos.

"Did he... did Dorian—I mean, Rian—say why me?" I hate how small my voice sounds.

Nadine's expression is unreadable. "Apparently, you made an impression during your little elevator adventure."

I swallow, dizzy. Did he know at the party last month that I'd be working for him? He must have. From the way Nadine is talking, Missy's emergency scare only sped up things. She was going on maternity leave anyway, and having me fill in must've already been the plan.

Before I can spiral too far, Nadine continues, "It goes without saying, but having romantic or sexual relations with clients is strictly forbidden. It's not just frowned upon—it's grounds for immediate dismissal."

My face bursts up in flames, and I laugh, the sound high-pitched and unnatural. "Of course. I would never sleep with a married man." And I wouldn't. I can be in love with one. But I'd never act on my feelings, regardless of how strong.

"It doesn't matter whether the client is married, single, or a Martian—it's still a fireable offense," she says coldly. "This agency's reputation is everything. I won't have it compromised. Have I made myself clear?"

I nod vigorously, fighting the ever-expanding blush that's now creeping down my neck. "I understand completely. You have nothing to worry about."

Nadine doesn't waste time. She hands me a stack of NDAs and instructs me to transfer my current clients to my head of division because I'm starting on the new assignment right away.

"From now on, Rian Phoenix is your only priority," she says. "Your first meeting is at his place in North Beverly Park at eleven."

"He doesn't come here?" I ask sheepishly.

"No, with clients of his caliber, we go to them for routine meetings. The night you met was an exception as he was flying in from New Orleans and it was more convenient to meet here."

Ah, so celebrities don't darken our doors unless it's a crisis. Duly noted.

"Very well."

I leave the office in a daze. I have two hours to hand off my clients and prepare to face the man who has haunted my dreams, my playlists, and now my career.

4

DORIAN

One Year Ago

"Josie," I repeat, savoring the way the name rolls off my tongue. It suits her—simple, yet charming.

"Yes, *Dorian*, nice to meet you," she says, adding a teasing lilt to my name.

Hearing her say my real name has a tendril of heat coil in my stomach. Most people in my orbit only use Rian. My agent and label had insisted that dropping the "Do" would make me edgier—more marketable. And while it worked commercially, it also chipped away at my identity.

"Nice to meet you, too."

She sighs, then announces, "Listen, since we're stuck here, I'm going to treat you like a regular person."

It's as if a switch has flipped, and her shyness has turned to sass. Outside the elevator, there's a power dynamic. In here? We're just two people equally inconvenienced. Maybe that leveled the playing field for her. Or she comes across as shy at first but opens up quickly once she gets a read on you. Whatever the reason, I'm happy she's not cowering in her corner anymore.

I purse my lips, amused. "As opposed to what? An alien with three heads?"

"You know what I mean," she deadpans.

I give her a small nod, appreciating her frankness. "I've been treated worse. I don't mind." Before the silence creeps back in, I suggest, "We should do an inventory of the resources we have to survive the night."

I set my phone on the floor, pat my pockets, and add a crumpled candy wrapper.

Josie raises an unimpressed brow. "A phone with no service and a candy wrapper? MacGyver would've restored power to LA by now."

She flashes me a goofy grin, and her freckles dance across her cheeks. The motion is hypnotic. I realize I'm staring and avert my gaze, not wanting to make her self-conscious.

I gesture toward her oversized bag. "What are you hiding in there? That thing could double as luggage."

She glances down. "Oh, you know, just the essentials: a grappling hook, a smoke grenade, and a compact rocket launcher. I never leave home without them."

I low-whistle. "Mary Poppins has nothing on you."

Josie smiles and starts unpacking. She pulls out her wallet. A lipstick—which she isn't wearing, but the label makes me wonder how her full lips might look in "forbidden fuchsia." And a tampon. She waves it in the air and says, "We won't be needing this." She goes to put it away but stops mid-gesture and adds, "Unless you're on your period?"

"Not until the full moon," I deadpan.

She studies me and smiles. "You're a smartass."

"Surprised?"

"I *am* a little shocked. Your public persona doesn't exactly scream 'quick wit.'"

I lean in, resting my elbows on my bent knees. "Really? So, what does it say?"

She considers me, then, with the candor of a toddler explaining how they colored on the wall, she says, "More like... cursed sex god."

A deep, belly-aching laugh shakes me, the kind I haven't experienced in months. It's a release from all the crap going on in my life right now. When I catch my breath, I ask, "Why *cursed*?"

Josie maintains a perfectly straight face. "Must be the guyliner. Gives off a tormented vibe." She wields an eyeliner stick. "Don't worry, I've got you covered if you need to reapply after midnight."

I chuckle, shaking my head. "I might be a smartass, but you, Josie, are a sass master."

She pulls the topknot of her hair tighter. The gesture entirely too distracting. "I dabble in the ancient art of sarcasm."

The playful back-and-forth flows naturally, as if we'd known each other for years instead of minutes. It's a distraction from the mess in my head—my crumbling marriage and the uncertainty of the future.

Josie pulls out a small, worn notebook. "My diary."

"Oh? Planning to journal our ordeal?"

"It's a planner mostly, but if we're stuck long enough, I might add a 'survive a smartass rockstar' section."

I nod, mock-serious. "Will that go above or below 'buy cat food'?"

Josie flips through the pages. "Below, obviously. The imaginary cats come first."

I laugh again. "What do I have to do to beat the kitties?"

She taps her chin. "Depends. Do you purr when you're happy?"

The question lodges in my brain, and I consider it more seriously than I should. Surprisingly, I realize that for her, I might actually purr—if I lived in a different universe where I'd never married the wrong woman and my marriage wasn't falling apart.

The thought sobers me, a cold reminder of everything outside of this elevator I don't want to deal with and why I had to rush downtown to do damage control. After getting emotionally hammered by Billie Rae again, I made a scene like an amateur who doesn't know everyone has a phone ready to record what I do. Cue the emergency session at my PR firm and ending up stuck in their elevator. I scrub a hand over my jaw, forcing Billie to the back of my mind.

I look at Josie again. It's weird how a stranger feels easier to be around than the person I promised forever to.

Josie lets out a soft cheer and places a stainless-steel water bottle between us, yanking me out of the mind spiral. "Behold, the elixir of life." She unscrews the cap. "I refilled it right before leaving the office, so we won't perish from dehydration."

"You work here?"

"Yeah, same firm that does your PR, but a different division; I'm in tech." She takes a sip of water, then offers me the bottle like it's the most natural thing.

I drink, hoping divisions don't share info. I suddenly feel more ashamed than ever of my behavior from last night.

"Thanks for the water." I pass it back. "Any other life-saving choices to report today?"

"Never been happier I didn't wait to pee until I got home."

I chuckle. Her knack for saying the first thing that pops into her head no matter how shocking, inappropriate, or perfectly disarming, knocks the rest of the darkness from my brain.

Next, she pulls out a stash of snacks—protein bars, crackers, dried fruit, and a packet of almonds.

"Is that a bag or a vending machine? Do I need exact change?"

She pops a piece of dried mango into her mouth. "When work gets crazy, I don't have time for lunch. This is how I survive."

I nod solemnly. "Ah, the balanced diet of a corporate warrior —stress and pocket pretzels."

"Instead of the healthy rockstar diet of drugs and rock 'n' roll?"

"You forgot sex."

Josie blushes and looks away. Instantly, I feel like a total creep. "I'm not hitting on you. It's a joke about you calling me a cursed sex god earlier."

She meets my gaze head-on. "Don't worry, even if you *were* making a pass at me, I'd never date you or sleep with you."

"Ouch." I mock-wince. "Please, don't sugarcoat it. Be as direct as you can."

Josie smiles, tossing me a protein bar. "Dinner's served."

I catch it, unwrapping the snack as a nagging question loops in my head. I should drop the topic. Not push. But I need to know. "May I ask why you'd never date me?"

I search her mesmerizing eyes, bracing for an answer that's surely going to sting.

5

JOSIE

September—Present Time

In my car, the GPS chirps instructions like this is just another drive—not a slow march into enemy territory.

Having Dorian's home address feels invasive. Not for him, for me. I didn't choose this.

I'm about to lift the curtain on his private life, and it seems *wrong*. Not that I expect piles of laundry in the corner or a fridge covered in takeout menus.

But anything involving Billie Rae might crush me.

My mind races with unwelcome images of Dorian and Billie Rae's picture-perfect life from back in the days when I could still follow it on social media without feeling like my heart was being carved out of my chest with a spoon.

I hope she's out of town. I didn't even check. If I knew for sure, maybe I could stop freaking out. But if she's there, I won't survive seeing them all over each other. Or maybe the sight will cure me of my unhealthy obsession—burn the fantasies in my head and release my heart from the hold Dorian has on it.

The GPS instructs me to keep in the left lane, and I entertain the idea of taking a wrong turn, of getting myself lost in the Hollywood Hills. But that would only delay the inevitable.

With every yard I cover, my car seems to shrink, the air pressing in denser.

As Dorian's gates come into view, the professional in me shouts to treat this like any other client meeting. The rest of me wonders if I'm about to be leveled by a smile. Or will he act differently with Billie Rae present? What if he behaves the same because he's that charming with everyone and I was no one special?

The possibility that the connection I've obsessed over for the past year is nothing more than a standard interaction for him stings. It's a reality check I desperately need, but one I'm not ready to face.

After a routine pass through security, I steer my car along the circular driveway, feeling dwarfed by the sheer size of his estate. The house has a bold geometry and sleek surfaces, easily the size of my entire condo building.

Following the guard's instructions, I pick a random spot in the front yard and kill the engine. Bag in hand, I head to the front door, craning my neck at the stunning architecture and manicured grounds.

A uniformed housekeeper greets me at the entrance, her polite efficiency a stark contrast to the nerves jangling under my skin. She leads me into the foyer—stylish but more lived-in than I imagined—and points me to the living room without speci- fying if that's where the meeting will take place or if Dorian has a dedicated home office. As I cross the hall, I hear the faint strumming of a guitar. I follow the melody, stepping into a spacious, open-plan room the size of a mini apartment—I hesi- tate to call it a mere living room—and there he is. Dorian is perched on a low couch, his guitar balanced on his knee as he scribbles on a music sheet laid out on the coffee table and goes back to playing. Seeing him lost in his creative process steals the air from my lungs.

I stand frozen in the doorway, caught between awe and panic.

This is worse than if I'd walked in on him kissing his wife. Because as of now, I'm not getting cured—the opposite. Seeing him like this, absorbed in his music, with the late-morning sunlight casting a golden glow over his tousled hair, feels far too intimate. My mind goes blank, grasping for the right way to announce my presence without shattering the magic of the moment.

Do I clear my throat? Knock? Or wait for him to notice me? Or do I melt into the walls and disappear? He's alone. Clearly, I'm the first one here and should wait somewhere else while the rest of his team arrives. Fleeing seems like the best solution. I back away, but my bag bumps the doorframe with a soft thud. Dorian's head snaps up, his icy-blue eyes lock with mine, and his face splits into a smile so bright I might actually need sunglasses.

"Morning," he says, his fingers still idly plucking at the strings, like my arrival hasn't thrown his rhythm at all.

I scramble to summon a professional tone, but stammer a weak, "M-morning."

Dorian sets his guitar aside with a fluid motion, like the instrument is another limb for him, and rises from the couch.

I stare as he approaches me, his smile never wavering. As he closes the distance, the walls seem to advance on me, too. Why is every space getting smaller today?

"I'm glad you found the place. The GPS can be tricky around here."

And why does his voice sound so good?

I force a smile, hoping it doesn't appear as brittle as I feel. "Oh, my GPS was in a good mood—it nailed *all* the turns." *Damn it!*

I glance over the room, desperate for a distraction, and my eyes land on the music sheets scattered across the coffee table.

Dorian follows my gaze and gestures for me to sit. "Please, make yourself comfortable. Can I get you anything? Coffee, water?"

I perch on the edge of a sleek armchair, clutching my bag in my lap like a shield. "No, I'm fine, thanks."

As he settles back onto the couch opposite me, I notice the faint smudge of ink on his fingers, from writing lyrics or chords. It's an insignificant detail, but it rearranges something inside me, a subtle displacement I can't explain. This is real. Dorian Phoenix, in the flesh, sitting mere feet away from me, composing the next Favorite Rock Song of the year. And I'm supposed to... what?

Work.

I'm here to work, even if I shouldn't be. Really, I'm not the best person to manage his public image. I open my mouth, ready to suggest that he might be better off working with someone more experienced, more suited to—

"Don't," he says, cutting me off before I can even begin.

I blink, astonished. "Don't what?"

His eyes spear me. "Tell me I should work with someone in the celebrity division. I don't do well with new people."

My stomach flip-flops. So much for finding an escape hatch. How did he know what I was thinking? Am I that transparent?

"I wasn't going to say that," I lie, and the skeptical quirk of his eyebrow tells me he's not buying it. "But you know, I'm not a celebrity PR expert."

"Good. I don't need one. I just want someone who doesn't bullshit me. Besides, Missy speaks highly of you. She says you're quick on your feet and you're not afraid to tell it like it is."

While it's nice to hear a colleague's positive opinion of me, it's counterproductive in my situation. "She said that?"

Dorian nods, leaning back and draping his arm along the frame of the couch. "Yep. I trust her judgment, and I trust *you*. So, here we are."

Here we are, indeed.

I order the butterflies in my stomach to quiet down. "Okay, well, I appreciate the vote of confidence. I'll do my best to live up to it."

"I'm sure you will." His gaze lingers on me, and heat rises to my cheeks.

The sound of loud voices coming from the foyer startles me.

Dorian rises to his feet. "That'll be the team. Come on."

I stand as well, smoothing the skirt of my dress with clammy hands. I've met with clients and their associates countless times before. This is no different. Except it is, because this is Dorian.

A moment later, a parade of people spills into the living room. A man in an expensive suit with a flashy watch and dyed dark hair leads the charge. He greets Dorian with a quick nod, suggesting a long-standing familiarity. Must be his agent, Victor Langston. I identify the others from the brief I was given this morning that I only had time to skim-read.

The next arrival is a tall man with graying hair and an air of perpetual stress. His phone is glued to his ear as he mutters something about tour dates clashing—Grant, the tour manager, then.

Following him is a young woman in a hoodie, ripped jeans, and sneakers, who can only be Bailey, the social media manager. A brunette in a stylish power suit who gives off lawyer vibes.

And finally, another woman breezes in, wearing a blue dress and ankle boots. She seems to hold the reins of the others and must be Dorian's personal assistant, Tessa.

Dorian glances toward the group, then back at me, still smiling. "Perfect timing, everyone. We can move to the office."

I blink. At least he doesn't host his meetings on the couch. That's good. A more professional setting will help me stay focused.

"This way," Dorian says, his words directed at me; the others seem familiar with the house's layout. He leads us out of the living area and into a wide hallway adorned with abstract art.

The group of professionals fall into step behind him, chattering in a low hum. I follow, tightening my fingers around the strap of my bag, resigned to adventure further into Dorian's world. Each layer I peel off causes more trouble for me. At least Billie Rae is nowhere to be seen yet.

As we enter the office, I wish I could stay cool, but I mostly gape at the framed platinum disks gleaming on the walls and the rows of awards lining the sleek bookshelves.

The room is awash in natural light, sunrays pouring through the large French doors that open on to a meticulously landscaped garden with an Olympic-size pool glittering in the distance.

In the center of the room, a massive square white table dominates the space. I wait for the others to sit, not wanting to steal anyone's usual spot, and am relieved when the last free seats end up being not too close to Dorian.

I sneak a glance at him lounging back in his chair, completely at ease, wishing I could feel the same.

The others pull out tablets and laptops. I grab a simple notepad and start scribbling, *Rian Phoenix client meeting* at the top of the page with my mechanical pencil. My hand trembles, ruining my already crooked lettering and sparking a surge of irritation. His proximity is short-circuiting my neurons and giving me actual fucking tremors.

Tessa, seated next to Dorian at what would be the head of the table if it weren't a square, clears her throat and calls for attention. "We all know the priority today." I'm still scribbling when Tessa continues, "How to break the news of Dorian's divorce."

The sound of my pencil lead snapping is embarrassingly loud in the sudden silence. I freeze, staring at the jagged point that's pierced through the next sheet of paper. My heart pounds as I glance up, sensing Dorian's stare on me.

I meet his eyes and his mouth curves into a slow, infuriatingly confident grin. Then he winks. Dorian I'm-Getting-a-Fucking-Divorce Phoenix just winked at me.

6

DORIAN

One Year Ago

"Well, for starters, you're too married," Josie responds to my question of why she'd never date me, popping an almond in her mouth.

"That's fair," I reply. I don't tell her that Billie Rae and I haven't slept in the same room—or house—for a year. I'm not a creep who uses a failing marriage as an excuse to step out of bounds. Whatever's happening with my wife is our mess to clean up—or burn to the ground. But until it's over—legally, emotionally, officially—the line stays where it is. "What about you, are you married?"

The second I ask I know I want the answer to be no. I check her hands as she keeps popping almonds—no rings. Thank f—

"Yes." Her admission hitches my sides like a cramp after exercising too hard. My chest feels tight, burning from the inside out, my lungs clawing for space they can't find. At least until she adds, "To my job, sadly."

I instantly relax but am still shocked by the intensity of my reaction for a total stranger.

"So, is anyone waiting for you outside this elevator? Boyfriend, girlfriend, an army of worried relatives?"

"Hopefully my family won't notice I'm missing. And I have no significant other, I'm unhappily single."

I react with a selfish *phew*. "Unhappily single?"

"Yeah. Sometimes, people claim they're single by choice, I'm not." She sips from the bottle. "But I've also never found someone I wanted to spend forever with. Someone I'd want to share my fries with after they swore they didn't want any."

I laugh at her fast-food representation of true romance. "Or maybe you have incredibly high standards." I grin.

"Nah, I've just been unlucky, never met someone who made me lose my mind. My love life's been one long flatline. Meh relationship after meh relationship. I never felt the spark with anyone. I want to feel the magic just once, you know?"

Yeah, magic is great. At least until it turns into a memory so faded, you start to wonder if it was ever real. "Suppose I wasn't married, would you date me then?"

"No, you're also too hot and too out of reach," she declares, still chewing an almond.

"Too hot? Is that... a thing?"

Josie shrugs. "You're the type women fight over. I've seen those Instagram comments. I'm not volunteering for the Hunger Games."

"See, you have impossible standards."

"No, it's just that people like you are intimidating."

"What? I'm not scary."

"No, not like that," she says, gesturing vaguely. "More... your life. Your fame. Everything about you."

"*Everything?* There must be a little something you'd save."

"Nope. Let's say you were the best man on Earth—looks aside." Josie brushes an invisible crumb off her dress. "You tour a lot, right?"

The question pokes at a sore reality. "Not every year."

"No, but let's assume you weren't married." She crosses her legs under her skirt as if settling in for a debate. "How could you date someone with a normal job? Would you put the relationship on hold?"

Her logic lands like little darts of truth, inching too close to the bone.

"I... I don't know. I never thought about it. Maybe she could join me on the weekends?"

"Right. Hop on a flight to Tokyo for a two-day cuddle break. Super convenient."

I study a spot on the carpet. "I hope that if she loved me, she'd still want to try."

"She probably would. She'd quit her job and become a full-time groupie, which would make being dumped afterward that much more tragic."

Josie means to be funny. But her words hit me like a chord played too sharp. The idea of being loved that deeply stirs something in me that I thought had dulled long ago.

But instead of saying any of this, I ask, "Do you always say everything that passes through your head?"

"No." She stares at the elevator walls. "Must be a side effect of being stuck in a malfunctioning metal shoebox." Josie grins, those freckles of hers turning me into a willing captive.

I should let it go, but I can't. "And in this hypothetical scenario, why would I dump her?"

"Eh. Basic celebrity math. You and Billie Rae are the exception."

Or we're about to become another headline no one will be surprised by.

"Can't argue with that," I say, struggling to keep the bitterness out of my tone.

"You two are one of my favorite celebrity couples."

I swallow back the urge to correct her. What would I even say? Instead, I nod to mask the frustration bubbling underneath.

Before the silence settles too long, Josie pulls her bag into her lap. "Let's see if there's anything in here to keep us from doing shadow puppets."

"What are you looking for? A portable movie projector? A travel chess set?"

"Close. Found them." She holds up a deck of cards.

"You keep the weirdest things in that bag."

"My niece loves card games, I always carry a deck."

I eye the cards skeptically. "Are we playing Go Fish?"

"Go Fish? What are we, five?" She shuffles. "No, we're playing poker."

Teasing her feels like stepping onto a thin patch of ice over a lake: dangerous and unwise. And yet I'm committed to either making the crossing or plunging into the freezing water below as I say, "I don't have any cash on me. Should we make it strip poker?"

"Yes, great idea."

I cough, choking on air at how casually she agreed. My eyes roam over her figure, and I'm not sure I'd survive peeking at what's under that dress. I'm about to backpedal when she adds, "But how about instead of stripping our clothes, we strip our souls?"

"How does one strip his soul?" I scratch my jaw. "Are you part of a cult?"

"No cult, but I'm a proud member of the Cheesecake Factory rewards program." Josie stops shuffling and tilts her head. "The loser answers a question, honestly. No holds barred."

Suddenly, the stakes feel higher. The thought of uncovering some of Josie's secrets is thrilling. But revealing mine? I don't trust easily, and never strangers.

She catches the hesitation on my face and drops the cards to grab her diary. She scribbles on a page that she rips and hands to me.

I scan the text and grin. She gave me a sassy NDA with a one-million-dollar damages clause.

"You got a million dollars?"

"No, and I don't plan to spend my life repaying a debt. Student loans are enough."

I should back out, keep things light and superficial, but I nod. "Deal." I tuck the paper into my jacket. Not because I'd ever use it against her, but because it's a piece of this night I have a feeling I'll want to hold on to.

Josie deals the cards. I study my hand—high double couple. I swap one and stay with my double couple. She swaps three and beats me with a tris of fours.

"Time to pay up, rockstar. How did you become a musician?"

It's a question I've answered a hundred times, but Josie asks it with genuine curiosity instead of formulaic journalism. It makes me want to give her a deeper answer.

I toy with the corner of a card. "It wasn't a grand epiphany. When I was a kid, everything was loud—arguments, slammed doors, life in general. Music was the one noise I could control. Figured if I played loud enough, I wouldn't have to hear the rest. And there was this girl..."

Josie smirks. "There's always a girl."

"She loved this local band, so I joined one too. Turned out I didn't suck with a guitar and I could sing. Then everyone was paying attention. Not just her."

"Bet she still regrets not having your baby in high school."

"What? She didn't even let me get to third base."

"What a shame. They'll put that on her tombstone: *here lies...*" she trails off, waiting for me to supply the name.

"Sandy Parker."

"*Here lies Sandy Parker,*" Josie recites. "*Who went to second base with Rian Phoenix, but never let him get to third—bless her soul.*"

I double over laughing, and something inside me shakes loose.

We play a few more rounds. The questions grow more personal. Josie tells me her biggest fear is ending up alone, that she once stole lipstick on a dare, lost her virginity in the back of a car, and dreams of being an extra in a movie.

In turn, I share things I usually don't talk about: how I sometimes feel crushed by fame, how terrified I am of letting people down, and how I've never felt like I belong anywhere.

Next round, I win. I play it cool, pretending I'm not about to ask the question I've been burning to ask since this game started. "What's your favorite song of mine?"

My music is the one thing I never second-guess, the only unfiltered part of me. But inviting her opinion? It means stripping my soul bare and learning if the rawest parts of me deserve to be heard.

Josie flushes red and covers her face with her hands. "Awww, not that question."

"Why not? I've asked worse." She didn't flinch before telling me how she lost her virginity.

Josie drops her arms and focuses the full power of those amber eyes on me. "Because if I answer, I have to stop pretending I'm so chill about being stuck in an elevator with Rian Phoenix."

My pulse speeds up not for the first time tonight. I've no idea what her answer is going to be, but now more than ever, I'm dying to know. "Then talk to Dorian."

"Alright. But don't say I didn't warn you if you think I'm an unhinged superfan or a stalker." Her eyes get shiny as she whispers, "It's 'Falling From the Same Sky.'"

And yep, a grenade detonates in my chest, leaving nothing but raw, open terrain behind.

7

JOSIE

September—Present Time

A wave of heat rushes through me, and I quickly avert my eyes, pushing the top of my pencil to get more lead. I push too hard and get too much out. As I tap some of it back in, Tessa's voice cuts through the ringing in my ears. "Marcia, the financial side is sorted, right? We're not expecting a legal battle?"

"The prenup covers almost everything," the lawyer says crisply, flipping through her tablet. "Except for the album they co-wrote."

My eyebrows shoot up as I finally get the right length of lead. Of course, *that* album. The one I've grown to loathe after meeting Dorian, despite how beautiful and timeless it is. Every track is a love letter, a reminder of their perfect, untouchable romance. It was an audio scrapbook of why I would never have a chance. Romantic. Brilliant. Forever. They not-so-subtly titled it *Coming Home To You.*

Except now, the needle has scratched the record—literally and figuratively.

I risk another glance at Dorian to reconcile the man in front of me with the devoted husband from the tabloids. His expression is unreadable, his jaw tense. Is he devastated about the end of his marriage? Would he have winked at me if he was? And when did their union fall apart? Who dumped who? Why?

I'm still asking questions in my head when Dorian's agent takes over, waving a hand like this is manageable. "We're already in talks with the label. They're working out what percentages everyone gets from future royalties."

The amount mustn't be insignificant. I don't have a clue how much money we're talking about. I speak burn rates, not music rights.

Tessa steps in again. "What we need to prioritize is controlling the narrative. The public will care less about who owns the album and more about what the split looks like. Whose fault it is. We have to make sure Dorian comes out of this clean."

I nod, even as something inside me recoils. The PR strategist in me knows she's right. Image is everything in this industry, and a messy divorce could tank Dorian's career faster than a bad album. But the hopeless romantic? She's screaming that this is wrong. Too cold. Too impersonal.

My gaze flicks back to Dorian, searching for any sign of emotion, but his face remains frustratingly impassive. Does he even care that we're dissecting his failed marriage like it's any other business deal?

Tessa turns to the social media manager. "Bailey, what should we do for the official announcement, a press release or a simple post?"

"I'd suggest something clean on Instagram," the young woman in the hoodie replies, her focus on her phone. "Everyone's doing the same thing these days." She continues scrolling like she's already crafting hashtags in her mind. "A black-and-white photo, some poetic caption about growing apart but still loving each other. It's bullshit, but it works. I just need the final statement from PR."

All eyes land on me, and I stiffen as I realize it's my turn to speak and I have jack shit to say. I attempt a shy smile, hoping it hides my panic. "Hi, um, hello everyone, I'm Josie. I was put on this account today, so I'll need to get a few more details to craft a proper press release." I keep my tone level, even if the words scrape like sandpaper against my throat. "Is the divorce amicable? Will the statement be a joint one? Should I coordinate with Billie Rae's team?"

I pause, realizing how much I sound like an amateur. I'm used to presenting million-dollar deals, not million-dollar break-ups. I don't deal with hard feelings. Series A fundings are easier to navigate than a series of events that led to marital collapse.

As if to confirm my inadequacy, the room bursts into subtle laughter at my naïve questions. The sound prickles across my skin, making me feel even more like a fish out of water. Victor mutters, "Amicable, that's cute," while the others shake their head.

"No, Josie," Tessa explains, her tone firm but not unkind. "It's anything but civil. And her team? They'll be working against us, spreading lies we'll have to shut down. Don't expect help."

I clench the pencil in my hand as I write:

No help, hostile divorce.

Why is it hostile? She didn't want it to end? Did he cheat? No, he wouldn't do that. I feel ashamed just for having had the thought. My personal feelings are too tangled up in this. And while my professional armor hasn't cracked yet, it's been dented.

It's as if someone repeatedly struck me with a morning star mace spiked in messy emotions that I'm not qualified to deal with or strong enough to repel. Where do I get a bigger shield?

This isn't just another job challenge, it's a war, and I'm on the front lines without a weapon or a plan.

Dorian speaks up. "Missy and I had drafted a statement, but it needs work. It's not polished yet."

I force myself to meet his gaze. His blue irises churn with so much I can't decipher, and it feels intrusive to pry.

"I should have the draft in your file, then," I say quickly, tearing my eyes away. "I'll refine it and give you a few options."

But Dorian shakes his head, surprising me. "Nah. Missy and I used to work through this shit together. Stay for lunch, and I'll bring you up to speed on everything."

Can I even say no? Nadine made it clear I'm at his complete disposal. So apparently, now I'm having meals with Dorian like it's the most normal thing in the world.

The meeting wraps up while I'm still processing. As the team filters out, I gather my things, convincing myself that it's just a business lunch.

Dorian waits for me by the door, guiding me toward the kitchen with an easy stride. "I know the last meal we shared will be hard to top," he says, smirking as he gestures to my bag.

"Are you mocking my vending-machine purse?" I retort, my tone automatically familiar.

"I'd never... but my chef should have something ready soon."

I study him for a beat, a suspicion growing that this lunch wasn't a spur-of-the-moment invitation. Dorian leads me to a table by the pool under the shade of a giant umbrella. He pulls a chair out for me, and I sit, feeling like I'm having an out-of-body experience.

As our plates are served, Dorian leans forward, his eyes locking with mine. "Tell me what you need to know."

I dry my palms against my thighs. He's giving me full access, and I won't be able to keep my interest 100 percent professional —not even 5 percent, I fear. I want to learn everything about him. I can finally explore his relationship without feeling like a stake is being driven through my heart. Even if I shouldn't.

My head is caught between two sledgehammers, cobbling me with opposite messages: Dorian is single. And: Dorian is a client.

Finally available. But more forbidden than ever.

I'm still going to ask everything, because how can I not when he's sitting across from me like an open book that dares me to turn a new page?

8

DORIAN

One Year Ago

"Falling From the Same Sky."

Of all the songs Josie could've picked, she chose that one. A track almost nobody knows exists. It's never been on streaming platforms, it's not even included in the standard version of my third album. Only 2,000 copies of the special edition were ever made, and she has one.

She listened to it and *loved* it. The one song I almost didn't release. Writing it felt like prying open my rib cage and letting the world see every jagged edge inside. Even now, thinking about the lyrics is similar to pressing on a bruise I thought had faded.

I meet her gaze, my throat closing around a question I'm not ready to ask. "Why that song?"

It comes out sharper than I meant, like an accusation, as if she owed me an explanation.

Josie hesitates. "Because it's about loss."

Her answer is a clean hit to the throat; it blocks the air in my windpipe and leaves me speechless. The lyrics were never explicitly about grief—they're abstract, layered in metaphor and symbolism. But I wrote that song after my mother died, each line ripped from a place too painful to revisit. Yet somehow, Josie saw through the veil. She understood.

"I listen to it whenever I need to ugly cry." She says it so matter-of-factly, like she's reminding me to water the plants. This is what sets Josie apart—even when discussing heavy topics, she makes me laugh.

Her admission tugs me in two opposite directions: it's unexpected, strangely endearing, but also unsettling. She's stepped into my private pain and made it her own, without invitation or permission. I feel exposed in a way I'm not used to.

"Do you need to ugly cry often?" I tease to lighten the mood. But I want an answer. I want to learn what makes Josie cry—and I'm afraid I'll also want to maul someone if it's a who and not a what.

Her lips twitch like she might laugh. But then her face crumples, folding in on itself like a piece of paper crushed in a fist. She hides behind her hands, and it takes me a second to realize she's crying. Not the quiet kind of crying either. She's breaking apart in front of me, and I don't know what to do.

I've seen people cry because of my music before—fans overwhelmed at shows, tears streaming down their faces in the front row. It's always moving, sure, but also distant, a step removed. This is different. Josie isn't a stranger in a crowd.

She snorts mid-sob. "Sorry, it's been two years. I should have learned how to control it."

"Two years?" I ask gently. "What's been two years?"

Josie shakes her head, her face twisting as another wave of emotion crashes over her. She dives into that bag of hers, pulling out an old tissue and blowing her nose loudly.

I don't press her again. Whatever she's carrying, she isn't ready to share. Should I say something else, or let her cry it out?

Josie laughs into a sob. "Technically, it didn't even happen to me. I'm not the one who has the right to fall apart every time I think about it."

I have no idea what "it" might be. Doesn't matter. The way she folds in on herself stirs something protective in me. Without thinking, I wrap my arms around her. We hug, kneeling in front of each other on the elevator floor. At first, it's clumsy and unfamiliar. I'm not sure how to comfort her, and I worry I've crossed a line.

But then she leans into me, giving me her weight, and drops her head on my shoulder, crying quietly. Her tears dampen my shirt, but she can soak through a thousand shirts if it keeps her from breaking.

"Sorry," she murmurs against my collarbone.

I drop a hand on her lower back. "Don't be."

The words surprise me. They feel like they're for both of us. For her, permission to let go. For me, permission to be here, to hold her, to care—maybe to let go, too.

It's as if someone turned a key in a lock I didn't intend to open. Something deep inside me unravels, and silent tears stream down my face. I don't wipe them away—there's no room for self-consciousness here.

When Josie finally pulls back, we remain kneeling in front of each other, foreheads nearly touching, our gazes locked. It's not just eye contact; it's a shared understanding, a peek into each other's souls.

Josie sinks back on the floor. "I'm sorry I made you cry."

"It's that damn song." I settle next to her. "I wrote it when I lost my mother."

I've carried this piece of myself for so long in secret, it feels strange to let it out now, to give it to her. I expect to feel exposed or regretful, but despite feeling slightly rug-burned, I'm comfortable—lighter, even.

"I had no idea. I'm so sorry, Dorian."

"It was a while ago, but it still feels like yesterday."

"Yes." She stares at the ceiling, blinking back more tears. "It never goes away."

When Josie looks at me again, she finally gifts me one of her smiles. "Playing strip souls was a terrible idea. We should've stuck to regular strip poker." She wipes her face, and adds, "At least then I could've confirmed how much your abs were retouched on the cover of your latest album."

"You're merciless," I groan. "I felt ridiculous during the entire photoshoot. And I'll have you know"—I pump my chest, Tarzan-style—"that my trainer would be devastated by your lack of faith in my upper body."

She grins wider. "I am amazed you said that with a totally straight face."

I study her grin. It lights up her entire face and eases something restless inside me. For the first time in forever, I let myself exist in the moment, wondering how someone I barely know has cracked me open and put me back together so completely. It's unsettling and oddly freeing, like standing on the edge of a cliff and not fearing the fall.

9

JOSIE

September—Present Time

After leaving Dorian's house, I swing by my niece's dance studio to pick her up from ballet. As I pull into the sun-drenched parking lot, my brain whirls with the tsunami of revelations it has received today. I'm drowning in an ocean of Dorian's secrets —the divorce, the long separation, everything he couldn't tell me in the elevator.

I step out into the cloudless warmth, grateful for the contrast to the storm raging in my head as I join the gaggle of parents milling about the studio entrance. Five minutes later, the doors burst open, and a pink hurricane barrels toward me. Penny bolts past the other kids, her ballet bag flailing behind her. I crouch down just in time to catch her as she flings herself into my arms with the force of a tiny cannonball.

"Auntie JoJo," she squeals, nearly knocking me off balance. Her sweaty hair clings to her forehead, her smile unstoppable.

I hug her tight. "Hey, twinkle toes. How was class?"

"My feet hurt." Penny slumps against my shoulder. "I'm tired."

"Yeah, same. It's been a day."

She frowns. "It's always a day. The Earth spins, and the sun comes up every morning. That's how days work."

I laugh, grab her bag, and ruffle her hair as we head to the car. Once she's buckled in, I ask, "Alright, little astronomer, what do you want for dinner?"

"French fries and a milkshake."

"A true ballerina's menu." I raise a brow. "Wouldn't you prefer something mysterious, like julienne carrots?"

Penny winces. "Nope. I want ketchup."

I kiss her forehead and slide into the driver's seat.

"Fine, but we need to include something green or your mom will fire me from auntie duty."

Penny perks up. "We can buy a bag of M&M's and I'll eat all the green ones."

I can't argue with that logic.

* * *

I strike a dinner deal with Penny for mac and cheese but with the addition of a handful of peas to hit the green quota. We eat at my sister's place, a peach stucco complex with sun-bleached, peeling walls, a central courtyard, wrought-iron balconies dressed in potted plants, and an aggressively chlorinated pool. Over dinner, Penny fills me in on the latest ballet drama involving casting wars for the Christmas recital. Penny launches into a tirade about how all the other girls are fighting over who will get to be Clara in *The Nutcracker*. "I'm not interested in Clara," she declares between bites. "She's boring. I want to be the Mouse King."

I grin, spearing a handful of macaroni. "The Mouse King is pretty fierce. Do you have the evil laugh for it?"

Penny drops her fork and leans forward, scrunching her face into what she clearly thinks is pure villainy, cackling wildly. I pretend to be terrified, clutching my chest and gasping. "Okay, okay, you were born for the role."

After dinner, the bedtime routine is a familiar rhythm: bath, brushing tiny teeth, untangling Penny's hair, and wrangling her into her favorite princess pajamas, complete with a tulle skirt that she insists on twirling in before bed.

Penny climbs into bed, grabbing her favorite bunny plush toy, her eyes already heavy with sleep.

"Alright, sweetheart, what story are we reading tonight?" I ask, smoothing the blanket over her and tucking it around her shoulders. I expect her to grab one of her usual picks—a fairy tale or that book about the dog who loses his sock.

But Penny shakes her head, her curls bouncing against the pillow. "No books. Invent a story, Aunt JoJo, with a dragon."

I arch an eyebrow, sitting on her bed. "A dragon?"

She giggles, clutching her stuffed bunny. "Yes, you're good at telling stories."

"Fine." I sigh as I relax against the headboard. "Once upon a time, a beautiful princess lived in a castle perched high on a mountain with tall spires that pierced the clouds, surrounded by a forest that whispered secrets in the wind. Her father was the king, and her evil stepmother, the queen. The princess was young and beautiful and also in love."

"With who?" Penny interrupts, her eyes wide and curious. "A prince?"

"No, she loved the court minstrel. He sang with the most melodious voice, and even if she'd never seen him, she'd fallen for him just from hearing his songs. But that love was forbidden."

"Why?"

I tap her nose. "Well, the minstrel wasn't a noble, and he was already married to the candy maker's daughter."

"But who did the minstrel love, the princess or the other woman?"

"At first," I say, smoothing the quilt over her legs again, "he loved his wife. But in time, she turned out not to be the woman he desired to spend his life with."

"Why not?" Penny is incredulous, like she can't believe such betrayals exist.

"She only wanted to eat candy and party," I explain with a shrug, "and the minstrel grew tired of it. But they were still married, so he couldn't leave her. Then, one day, he got trapped by accident in a cellar with the princess. He'd never laid eyes on her because the queen was an envious woman and never allowed the princess to attend the court banquets. But the moment he saw her, it was love at first sight. The princess already loved his music, which she listened to hidden on a grand stairwell at every celebration, and now she loved him too."

"Did they kiss in the cellar, Auntie?" Penny holds her bunny up as if the plush toy were as invested in this drama as she is.

I grin. "No, because the minstrel was an honest man, and he was faithful to his wife. But he sang for the princess, keeping her calm and making her feel safe until they were rescued."

"They never get together?" My niece pouts, her bottom lip sticking out in a way that makes me laugh.

"Patience, my darling. After many days of lovesick stolen glances between the princess and the minstrel, a terrible tragedy happened. A fearsome dragon flew over the kingdom while the folks were out in the streets celebrating. He glided low over the crowd, opened his terrifying jaws, and devoured the candy maker's daughter in a single bite."

Penny gasps, clutching her bunny like it might be next. "Why her?"

"Because with all the candy she ate, she was the sweetest of the realm, and the dragon had a fine sense of smell."

My niece's eyes narrow on me, suspicious now. "Are you just trying to tell me I should eat less candy?"

"You're too smart for me, little bug," I admit, ruffling her curls. "But you already know too much candy is bad for you."

"Finish the story, Auntie," she demands, her voice serious now. "Was the minstrel sad his wife was eaten?"

"Of course he was. While he no longer wanted to be married to her, he would've never wished for her to be wolfed down by a dragon."

"But now he's free to be with the princess." Penny's tone lifts with hope, and I feel sorry for what I'm about to say.

"No, he's not. Because the evil queen, Nadine, discovered their secret love and threatened to banish the minstrel from the court forever if he and the princess were caught together."

"But why?"

"The queen was envious. The king was an old man, hunched and shriveled, while the minstrel not only had the voice of an angel but was also the most handsome young man in the kingdom."

"How did he look?" Penny asks, suppressing a yawn.

"He was tall and had dark hair the color of a raven's feathers."

"He sounds very handsome," Penny comments through another yawn.

"He was." I close my eyes, picturing Dorian's face as I caress

Penny's hair backward. "He had the face of a prince—a jawline as sharp as the edge of a sword. His nose was strong and straight, and his cheekbones could've been carved by the most talented sculptors. His mouth had lips so full and soft they promised a true love's kiss. But it was his eyes that made him truly unforgettable. They were the ice-blue of a frozen lake under a winter sun, with a depth that held a thousand secrets."

I pause, trying to figure out how to spin the story into a happy ending, but when I glance down, Penny's head is tilted to the side, her eyes closed, her breathing soft and even. I lean down to press a kiss on her forehead. "Sweet dreams, little mouse."

I flick off the light and leave the door slightly ajar.

I pause in the hallway, pressing my palms into my temples as if that will help clear the image of Dorian's face, in all its chiseled perfection, from my mind. Did I really compare him to a prince—a minstrel, technically—in a bedtime story? It may have worked to put Penny to sleep, but my brain is wide awake and doing its best impression of a hamster on a wheel. I push open the kitchen door and pull out the good tequila from its hiding spot behind the healthy snacks. I grab the blender from the top shelf, set it on the counter, and start mixing margaritas. After the day I've had, I deserve a drink.

10

DORIAN

One Year Ago

The levity from Josie's joke about my need to retouch my abs fades, leaving a quiet that grows heavier by the second. After the hug, we ended up sitting side by side instead of in our corners, and I'm hyperaware of her beside me. I stare at the floor, unsure if breaking the silence would ease the tension or ruin this new, fragile connection.

I glance sideways at her profile. Her lashes are lowered, and her lips pressed into a thoughtful line. She looks vulnerable.

I do my best not to stare, but my gaze keeps drifting back, drawn by the faint crease in her brow and the rise and fall of her chest as she breathes. The urge to smooth that wrinkle, to pull her close and inhale her scent again, threads itself through my ribs, delicate but insistent.

"So, are we going to spend the rest of the night in emotional purgatory?" She might be worse than me at silences.

I fire back a smirk. "Hey, it beats some parties I've been

dragged to where everyone's pretending to have a good time while angling for a photo with me."

My tone is light, but the words taste bittersweet. I'm letting her glimpse the exhaustion I usually hide behind charm.

Josie looks at me with that piercing empathy of hers. "What's that like, being so famous?" Her tone isn't judgmental, simply curious.

My defense mechanisms still lock in place before I realize she's not asking for gossip.

"Most of the time, it's exhilarating," I admit. "Standing on a stage with tens of thousands of fans screaming my name, singing my lyrics back at me... it's a rush like nothing else. A high impossible to replicate." I close my eyes, remembering the sensation of being invincible. "But it's exhausting too. You're always 'on.' Most people around me feel like part of the performance. It's... lonely. They see Rian Phoenix, not me. And sometimes, I'm not sure I even know who Dorian is anymore." I chuckle, not entirely able to shake off the undercurrent of frustration. "It's the little things. The everyday moments most people take for granted. I can't grab a coffee without it becoming breaking news." Guilt sparks in my chest. I have no right to complain. "I know I sound ungrateful."

"No. It's a valid sentiment, no one can tell you otherwise." She grabs my hand, squeezing it once before she lets go. "But you're still not getting the last brownie."

"The last brownie? You've been hiding brownies from me?"

"I wish." She groans. "It's a *Notting Hill* reference. Saddest person at the table wins the last brownie. Julia Roberts says she's been starving for years, and every time her heart breaks, the tabloids make it a punchline. At least you don't have that problem."

She doesn't know how wrong she is—or will be soon enough.

"And she jokes about getting plastic surgery to be so beautiful." Josie studies my face more intently than before, eyes squinting. "You look this good naturally, don't you?"

I laugh because how can I not.

"Yep. Blame my mom, she was gorgeous." I hesitate, then add more quietly, "And I know I don't deserve the brownie. I'm lucky. I really am. I wouldn't trade my success. I get to create and connect with people through my music. And that's worth everything else."

"I get that." Josie nods. "For me, it's the exact opposite. I wish I stood out more." She pauses. When she speaks again, self-deprecating humor laces her tone but it cannot mask the upset underneath. "I've always been terrified of being forgettable. I feel like the human equivalent of the color beige: safe, reliable, and easy to overlook."

She says "forgettable" like it's a fact. It's not.

Her hands fist her dress in her lap as if she's steeling herself for me to agree with her assessment. But nothing about Josie is safe or beige.

I'm talking before I even know I've opened my mouth. "Josie, you're not beige, you're a rainbow. You're color in a world that likes to think in black and white. You're bold when people expect quiet, bright when everything else is gray, impossible to ignore in the best way."

She blinks, stunned, but I forge on, determined to paint the picture I see.

"We're stuck in an elevator with nothing to do and this is the most fun I've had in forever."

I clamp my mouth shut, self-conscious. I've said too much.

She stares at me, wide-eyed, and for a moment, says nothing. Then, "No one's ever described me like that."

"Well, they should. It's the truth."

She ducks her head, shy once more, and I stop myself from adding anything else before I turn into a walking Hallmark card. I'm not being very subtle.

"Did I embarrass you? I'm sorry if I did."

She shakes her head. "No."

Her posture loosens, and her fingers are no longer twisted in her dress.

At least she's not hitting the panic button or scraping to leave this elevator through the hatch on the roof.

Josie tugs her hair behind her ear, smiling. "It's no wonder you're so amazing at writing lyrics. Do you always keep your 'waxing poetics' setting dialed up so high?"

"Default setting," I say. "Can't turn it off."

The truth, one I won't voice aloud, is that it isn't always like this. My "waxing poetics" dial is cranked up to a hundred only because I'm around her.

She's flipped a switch inside me, and I'm not positive I can turn it off.

11

JOSIE

September—Present Time

Half a glass of margarita later, I'm on the gallery patio, watching the sky bleed pink over the rooftops when familiar footsteps echo up the stairwell.

My sister emerges still dressed in her nurse scrubs, hair pulled into a haphazard ponytail. I take Lily in. The faded badge clipped to her collar, the creases under her eyes deepened by another twelve-hour shift. She looks exhausted—not the exhaustion that comes from a long day at work, but a weariness that has taken root in her soul, dulling her gaze and knocking the bounce from her steps.

My problems seem so small compared to hers. I feel selfish for even sitting here wallowing.

But despite the shit hand of cards fate has dealt her, Lily's eyes soften when she spots me. She pauses at the patio railing, her gaze flitting from my face to the drink in my hand, and her lips curve into a small smile. "Why are you drinking and staring into the sunset like you're posing for a reel called *Sad Girl Aesthetic*?"

I snort and wave my glass. "There's a pitcher in the fridge. Join me?"

Lily plucks the cocktail from my hand and sniffs. "Hmm, you used the good tequila. Must be serious."

She has no idea.

Lily shrugs and returns the glass. "Why not? Tomorrow's my day off."

A few minutes later, she comes back with the pitcher and a fresh glass, settling into the chair beside me with a tired exhale. "So, what are we drinking to, or at, or trying to forget?"

I keep my eyes on the sky. "He's getting a divorce."

Lily frowns. "I'm going to need a little more context. Who's 'he'?" I shoot her a look, and her jaw drops. "Nooo, Rian Phoenix?"

I nod and recap everything, swearing her to secrecy until the divorce goes public. Lily sets down her glass. "And the only reason he gave is 'different lifestyles'?"

"He didn't tell me everything." I shrug. "It's obviously painful for him. When he said Billie wanted to keep living the fast life, he mentioned parties, but I can't imagine what 'partying' means in their world. But he got tired of it, whatever 'it' was. He told me that the harder he pulled back, the more she pushed into it. And it tore them apart."

"Drugs?"

"Yeah. One of their biggest issues was her refusing to go to rehab."

"Were they already having problems when you met him?"

"They've been separated for two years." That his marriage was already broken when we met hit me the hardest. It had me rethink everything we shared in the elevator. I cringed at all the dumb comments I made about him and Billie being my favorite celebrity couple. But more than anything, it cast everything he said about me in a different light. I'd assumed those were the compliments of a happily married man, seeing the good in me. Two strangers having a platonic connection in a crappy situation. But since this afternoon, my silly, starry-eyed brain has been churning with a delusional hope that he meant something else, something more?

Lily cuts through the delirium of wishful thinking. "And he never mentioned anything in the elevator?"

"Dorian is a celebrity, he wouldn't tell a stranger he's having marriage problems." I bite the inside of my cheek, chewing on both flesh and thoughts. "And it took them another year to call it quits. I don't know how defined the situation was back then."

"And now that he is single, you still can't date him because he's a client?"

I top off my drink, deflecting, "It doesn't matter. He's probably not interested."

"But he asked for you specifically?"

"He doesn't like new people. I'm familiar. It's practical."

Lily leans back in her chair, crossing her legs, unconvinced. "Okay, but what about *your* feelings, Josie? You okay working for him?"

"It's not forever." I do some quick mental calculations aloud. "Missy will give birth at the end of March. She'll be back by next summer, fall at the latest."

"And you can last that long? Unscathed?"

I meet her gaze, bluffing confidence. "Why wouldn't I?"

"Josie, you were wrecked after ten hours. How can you manage a year?"

She has a point. The thought of being around Dorian day in

and day out is my wildest dream and worst nightmare wrapped into one.

"I'm a professional, Lily. I can handle it."

She drums her fingers on the table. "Can you? Really?"

"I don't have a choice. It's my job."

"I don't want to see you get hurt, Josie."

I force a smile. "I'll be careful. Don't worry."

But the words feel shaky, and I wonder if it's a promise I can keep. My pulse races just imagining being near him. How much Dorian can I take before my heart stops listening to my head?

12

DORIAN

One Year Ago

Josie's still smiling, smug from her "waxing poetics" joke. I should quip something back. Instead, on impulse, I ask, "What color do you see me as?"

Without missing a beat, she says, "Definitely a maroon."

"A maroon?"

Her goofy grin gives her away. She's messing with me.

Josie fires off a playful finger gun. "Gotcha."

After she blows on the tip of her index, her expression turns serious and she destroys my soul a little more. "You're ultramarine, streaked with gold. Full of depth and imperfections that hold a beauty most people don't take the time to see. They stop at the blue and forget to search for the gold."

My knee-jerk reaction is to volley back that her waxing-poetic skills are no joke either—defuse with humor. But something in her tone stops me short. Her words have no trace of irony, no hint of flattery. She means what she's saying. That's really how she sees me.

I settle for, "That makes me sound like a painting no one could afford to buy."

"Maybe you're more like abstract art." She joins her fingers in a square and studies me through the pretend frame. "Misunderstood until you take a closer look."

"I'm too tired to make sense of that analogy."

"Are you calling my analogies confusing?"

I glance at my watch and am surprised to see it's already four in the morning. The hours have slipped by like sand through an hourglass, each grain a flicker of Josie's light I get to keep for myself and steal from the rest of the world.

"I'm saying it's late and my brain is fried."

I stare down at my palm, tracing one of the lines creasing my flesh—is it the life line, the love line? I can never tell them apart.

I don't look at her as I speak next. "Even if you told me half an hour after meeting me that you'd never sleep with me, maybe we should try to get some shut-eye. No one's coming until morning."

Josie gasps, mock-scandalized. "Aren't rockstars supposed to live like vampires, from dusk till dawn?"

I wince. She has a knack for finding all my open wounds and rubbing salt into them. "It gets old after a while."

"Well, I guess even vampires need a break." She kicks out a leg, and in the most casual tone, asks, "Do your feet smell?"

I gape at her. "No?"

"Then take off your shoes."

She slips her sandals off, wiggling her toes, the nails painted in a shade of bright mint green that's perfect for her.

Next, she loosens her topknot. The elastic band slips down her wrist like a bracelet as she combs her fingers through the strands, massaging her scalp in slow, circular motions while her locks tumble down her back in burnished toffee waves.

Once she's done hypnotizing me, she folds her bag into a makeshift pillow and stretches out on the floor, one arm tucked under her head, messy hair fanning out.

I trace the swell of her chest, her collarbones, her mouth, the way her lashes cast faint shadows against her skin. Her beauty is maddening. It doesn't demand attention at first but steals it before you even realize it.

I pull off my sneakers and toss them into the corner, then peel off my leather jacket and lie on my side, facing her.

"Goodnight, rockstar." Josie yawns.

"Goodnight, sass master," I reply, already knowing I won't sleep.

Twenty minutes later, I'm still awake despite being bone-tired. Josie's eyes are closed, but her breathing isn't slow and regular enough for her to be asleep. I suspect she's awake too.

"Josie?" I whisper into the dimness. "Are you sleeping?"

She opens one eye. "Nope. You neither, huh?"

"Must be the five-star accommodations."

"Yeah, the carpet leaves something to be desired." She rolls on her side, facing me. "You should sing me a lullaby."

"A lullaby?"

"Yeah, I have the most celebrated singer-songwriter of our time all to myself, don't I deserve a private performance?"

I'd give her that and more, but I can't tell her. So instead, I go with, "Close your eyes."

And I start singing.

> *"There's a road I've never traveled,*
> *A space I've never known,*
> *It's a dream I can't hold.*
> *Or a voice without a song.*

"I've been chasing the horizon,
But the sky keeps pulling away,
And the closer I get to the answers,
The less I know what to say.

"But there's something in the quiet,
In the way you hold your ground.
Like a song I didn't know I knew,
Echoes that were never found.

"You're uncharted, you're the edge of the earth,
A compass spinning, still finding its north.
You're the gravity I didn't know I'd feel,
Pulling me back to something real.

"Uncharted, untamed, undefined,
But somehow, you're the place I call mine."

She's asleep before I reach the second verse of "Call It Mine."

13

JOSIE

September—Present Time

I have the entire weekend to cool off, but my first official assignment tailing Dorian on Monday is a kick to the groin.

He's doing a photoshoot for an underwear commercial. And it's not subtle. I'm trapped supervising in an airy, industrial loft with exposed brick walls, high ceilings, and strategically channeled beams of light streaming through the windows—great for taking photos, terrible for my mental health.

Dorian is wearing next to nothing, with only white boxer briefs on. He's sprawled over a bed with artfully rumpled sheets, one-upping the sexy dreams I had over the past several months. Too much of his skin is on display, a lot of it covered in indecently sexy tattoos. The ink snakes around his torso and arms, adding a rugged edge to the otherwise minimal setting.

On his chest, sweeping lines coil in patterns that could be vines or waves, the design refusing to be defined. Over his shoulder, petals unfurl from an indistinct center, dissolving into tendrils of ink that sneak out of sight. The transitions are seamless, hypnotic, with no clear start or end.

The closer I look, the more the images seem to change: one moment, they're floral; the next, they ripple like water disturbed by a gentle breeze. Together, they create an enigmatic masterpiece—impossible to decipher, and impossible to ignore.

I can't stop staring.

It's absurd how photogenic Dorian is. But I couldn't care less about the perfect composition or the flattering angles. All I can think about is how much I want to trace those lines of ink with my fingers, then—heaven help me—with my tongue.

But more than that, I crave to learn the stories behind each tattoo. Are they happy memories, moments of triumph? Or are they laced with sorrow? Reminders of things lost? Would he tell me if I asked?

I'm not even sure what answers to that last question would scare me more.

The photographer paces around, calling directions as his camera clicks in rapid bursts. Dorian shifts on the bed accordingly, propping himself up on one elbow. The muscles in his forearm go taut, the ink twisting with the movement. His chin tilts, his smoldering gaze locking on the lens.

His torso is angled to catch the natural light, highlighting the loopy contours of the line of text inked on his ribs. That elusive writing is the perfect metaphor for my mental state: being sure about something that's out of focus. I can tell they are words, but I can't read them at this distance.

I've seen the tattoos before. In pictures, in videos—except for the left side of his chest and that writing that are new... but seeing them in real life is having a strange effect on me. I never even thought I'd be into that much ink. But I clearly am.

If male seduction were a weapon, this ad would be classified as artillery—sleek, provocative, and aimed directly at my professional composure.

To shield myself, I keep my focus on the screen displaying the shots, the diluted grain of pixels easier to bear. As Dorian's PR rep, I'm supposed to make sure the photographer and the publication stay aligned with the image we're shaping for him. But no matter how hard I try, my eyes keep drifting back to the real-life Dorian on that fucking bed.

In the photos, he looks like a marble statue brought to life —detached, flawless, untouchable. In reality, there's nothing cold about him. He sizzles. I'm surprised those sheets haven't caught fire yet. And through it all, I feel like I'm being deep-fried.

If the goal here is to market him as the eighth deadly sin, they might as well call it a day. Mission accomplished.

"Okay, that's a wrap," the photographer announces, echoing my thoughts. He steps back, lowering his camera and checking the last few shots with a satisfied smile.

Dorian swings his legs off the bed, stretching his arms overhead and hopping off with feline grace. His movements are unhurried and languid, showing too much comfort in his near-nudity as he strolls toward me. At his approach, I force myself to keep my gaze locked somewhere above his shoulders, hazing out the defined lines of his torso or the tattoos that seem even more vivid up close. And I'm most definitely not looking at his crotch region where those tight briefs are leaving little to the imagination.

I'm about to combust from sheer proximity when a production assistant mercifully swoops in with a white satin robe. Dorian takes it with a casual, "Thanks," shrugging it on, still looking incredibly masculine despite the shiny fabric. As he ties the sash around his waist, I track the motion of his hands—his long fingers tugging, knotting, cinching the strap in place, somehow more sensual than the act itself.

Heat creeps up my neck as I get a whiff of Dorian's scent. I fold my arms to withdraw from it and lean away. Before any of us speak, the photographer and a production assistant huddle behind the monitor next to me to review the shots. I jump at the opportunity to put more distance between us, stepping aside and leaving space for Dorian to check the screen. He glances at the preview images with a nod of approval.

"Looks great." Then he turns his piercing eyes on me. "What do you think?"

"Uh..." Words fail me as my brain scrambles for something insightful, witty—anything to make it seem like I haven't spent the entire shoot drooling. "Classy but seductive. Right on target."

The photographer harrumphs in agreement. "I'll start post-production once I get back to my studio."

They shake hands and then the photographer and his assistant scurry off to pack their equipment.

Once they're far enough not to hear us, Dorian leans in, his robe shifting at the collar, deepening the V in the middle, and whispers, "Finally got to test your retouch theory. Still convinced I need much?"

I glance back at the screen, forcing a casual tone. "Oh, I don't know, isn't the lighting doing at least 50 percent of the heavy lifting?"

Dorian's eyes narrow playfully. "The lighting, uh? Give me an answer elevator Josie would've given me."

"What do you want me to say?" I throw my arms up in exasperation. "Your abs are perfection, and I hope they won't put this ad on a billboard overlooking a street because it's going to cause accidents?"

Dorian tosses back his head and roars with laughter. I should be embarrassed, but I'm strangely not. When he's done laughing, his focus slams into me. "That's the Josie I know. Anything else?"

I pat his chest and add, "Nice tattoos." The touch is meant to be casual, but the moment my palm makes contact, it's anything but. My hand brushes against the satin of his robe—soft, deceptively delicate—while under it, his pectoral is solid, unyielding. The warmth radiating through the cool fabric catches me off guard, the contrast sending a jolt straight to my nerve endings.

Under my palm, his heart beats at a maddeningly steady pace, as if this isn't affecting him at all. But then his gaze lowers to the spot where my hand rests. I freeze in that position, pinned under the weight of his attention. The intensity in his stare makes everything else fade away—the bustling studio, the chatter of assistants... the world narrows to this single point of contact between us, and I realize it's the first time we've touched since the elevator.

When his gaze lifts, the smirk he usually wears is nowhere to be found. His eyes are smoldering, that brilliant blue darkened with something I can't name but feel deep in my stomach, sharp and twisting. My pulse thunders in my ears, and I drop my hand as if burned, taking a step back.

"On a different note"—I smooth a non-existent wrinkle on my dress—"the divorce announcement goes live this afternoon at four. I'll see you tomorrow morning at your house for the debrief with the team."

Without giving him time to respond, I turn away and head for the door with brisk strides.

The feel of his chest under my fingertips still tingles. When I reach the exit, I don't dare turn back—not because I fear being caught, but because I won't be able to mask what I'm feeling if he's watching me.

14

DORIAN

One Year Ago

A static crackle intrudes into my dreams. Even before I open my eyes, I know something's off. I shouldn't be this comfortable, this warm, but I can't pinpoint why it's wrong to feel good. Then a voice fizzles through the elevator's speaker. "You still okay in there?"

Reality crashes into me. I'm sleeping on an elevator floor—that's why I shouldn't be comfortable. When I open my eyes, my heart stutters. I'm curled against Josie, my head resting on her chest. My arm is flung over her waist as if it belongs on her.

I freeze as horror and reluctant delight course through me. Her left boob has become my personal pillow, and I never want to sleep on anything else.

The speaker crackles again, snapping me fully awake. I sit up carefully, easing out of Josie's warmth, and press the button. A new technician informs me the fire department should reach us within half an hour. I thank him and close the conversation, not sure how I feel about the impending rescue.

Josie stirs. Her eyes flutter open and widen when they meet mine—not in the awestruck way they did when she first stepped into the elevator, *Shit, that's Rian Phoenix.* But with sleepy surprise, the kind that says, *Oh, it's really you, last night wasn't a dream.*

"Morning," she mumbles, yawning as she sits up. Her hair's a mess, her cheeks flushed, and she's stupidly adorable.

Her gaze flicks to my unruly hair and crumpled shirt, and I wonder what she sees. With her usual lack of filters, Josie asks, "So... did I drool on you?"

I huff a laugh. "Not that I noticed, but thanks for asking."

As she smooths her hair and yawns again, I share the good (?) news. "The cavalry is on the way; they should rescue us any minute now."

Her expression falters. I swear I catch a flash of disappointment, fleeting but unmistakable. Maybe she was enjoying this forced closeness as much as I was and doesn't want it to end.

But then she smirks. "Good. I was starting to need to pee."

It knocks me off balance all over again. Just when I kid myself I have her figured out, she surprises me. She's upfront about the mundane stuff, but I can never tell what's going on deep down. Josie is full of wonderful contradictions, and a mystery. And the longer I am with her, the more I wish to keep solving the clues.

But our time's almost up. The realization hits me like a sucker punch. I steal a glance at her to memorize the way her hair frames her face, the curve of her lips, the golden flecks in her eyes. I want to remember it all, just in case I won't see her like this again—sleep-tousled, unguarded, and beautiful.

"This has been incredibly fun." Josie swipes her fingertips over her cheeks as if to iron the creases. "Same time next week?"

I wish. "I'm in, but only if you bring more survival veggie chips."

Josie laughs, and the sound turns the fluorescent lights into sunshine. "Sure, but don't expect me to be this entertaining again. This was peak awkward charm, I can't top it."

I'm done with the surface-level banter. "Last night was the most normal I've felt in years."

Josie's eyes widen, but then she smiles. "I'm glad. You're not too bad for a celebrity," she teases me, even as a quiet intensity seeps into her gaze. And, again, I can't pin down what's the sentiment behind that look. Is it friendship, admiration, or something else entirely? But she continues, "For someone who could live a hundred feet off the ground if they wanted, you stay close enough to touch the world and make it bigger."

First, she teases me, and then she floors me with something like that. I blink at her, unsure if I'm supposed to agree, argue, or laugh it off.

She lets me off the hook with another grin. "Last night is going to go in my top ten life experiences."

My heart thumps as I unwillingly follow her down the road of teasing retorts. "Only top ten? I'll have to do better next week."

A loud thud interrupts us. I grab Josie's hand as the hatch on the ceiling creaks open and a firefighter's head appears, upside down, peering at us with a grin.

"Josie Monroe, is that you?"

She lights up and waves. "Hey, Mitch, took you guys long enough."

A strange pang squeezes my chest at their easy interaction. If she hadn't told me she's single, I suspect that pang would've been a sledgehammer smashing into my ribs. I shake off the irrational feeling as Mitch adjusts the harness slung over his shoulder and gestures for us to clear some space.

He hops down with the agility of a superhero. "Alright, folks, we're getting you out. Ladies first."

Josie puts on her sandals and flips me a mock military salute, before stepping forward. Mitch helps her into a harness, tightening the straps around her waist and shoulders. His hands linger a moment too long, and I clench my jaw, fighting to ignore the urge to slap his grubby paws off her. I put my sneakers on instead, pretending I'm not glaring at them.

"You're in expert hands, Josie." He winks at her. "The boys won't drop you."

Josie laughs, a breezy sound that I want to catch and keep. "They'd better not."

As she's hoisted up through the open hatch, she flashes me a quick grin before disappearing above. Her voice echoes down the shaft. "Don't look up my skirt, Phoenix."

I smirk despite myself, her playful jab breaking through my irrational jealousy. This woman gets under my skin, and I'm not sure I mind.

Mitch straps me in a second harness. "Hold on tight," he advises, then adds, "My wife loves your music, man."

The tightness in my chest eases. Looks like Jositch isn't happening after all.

I joke, "Meaning you don't?"

Mitch makes a sheepish face. "I'm more of a country buff."

"Fair enough."

As Mitch pulls on the line, I'm yanked up half a floor to the forcibly opened elevator doors, where more firefighters wait to pull me to safety.

I stumble onto solid ground, my legs feeling unsteady despite the short harness ride.

Shaking off the vertigo, I scan the upper floor, desperate to lay eyes on Josie. She's hugging a firefighter, beaming. I grit my teeth at the sight.

She moves on to fist bump the next firefighter in line, then hip bumps the last guy. They're all ruggedly handsome, clearly familiar with her in a way that makes my blood simmer. I'm an outsider looking in, and I don't like it. I want back into our circle of two.

Just as I'm about to go to her, in typical Josie fashion, she spins around and gives the firefighters a theatrical bow. "Thank you again for the rescue, boys," she announces grandly. "But I'm two seconds away from peeing myself."

She vanishes down the hall, leaving me gaping after her.

Before a firefighter can pull out their phone and ask for a photo with me, I cut in, "Yeah, same here, thank you."

Then I head after her, fueled by a desire to hold on to our connection and a gnawing unease that whatever last night was, it's over. But I need to catch up with her, to... I've no idea to do what.

I just know I'm not ready to lose her.

15

JOSIE

One Year Ago

I'm already washing my hands when I realize that once I come out of the restroom, Dorian might be gone. I should've squeezed my bladder harder and waited to pee until after saying goodbye to him.

I scowl at my reflection in the mirror above the sink. A red crease slashes across my cheek from using my bag as a pillow. But the real problem is my eyes—the unhinged, maniacally bright light shining in them. I splash water on my face, but when I check again, the look is still there, and it only means one thing: I'm fucked—forever. Because in the most incredible night of my life, I have fallen in love with a man I can never have. I wanted a spark, I got a blaze that's going to burn me to cinders.

I grip the sides of the sink, my knuckles turning white as I glare at myself.

How did it happen so fast? I did my best to play it cool with him, not to let it show how much I found him attractive and what a ridiculous celebrity crush I had on him. Then the next moment, I was coming undone in his arms, and he was describing me as a rainbow... and I went from being star-struck to a total eclipse of the heart.

I dry my face and hands on a paper towel and exit the bathroom, not sure what I'll find. I fear Dorian will be gone. I hope he'll still be in the atrium. But I don't expect to find him in the darkened hall, leaning with one shoulder against the wall, waiting for me.

Something sharp stabs at my chest, violent and unforgiving. His gaze, earnest but sad, cuts me open. But what breaks me is how unmistakably his attitude looks like a goodbye.

Heart thumping like a jackhammer, I approach him. "Hello, stranger."

"Hey," he says, jaw tight.

I don't know what to make of the situation, so I resort to my default setting of using humor. "I thought *I* was supposed to stalk *you*."

But he's not in the mood. His stare is serious, almost mournful. "I wanted a moment of quiet to say goodbye."

I nod, understanding so much more of what he isn't saying. "Thank you."

The words are wholly inadequate to express the magnitude of what I feel. I want to say more. *Thank you for coming back for me. For acknowledging what we've shared. For making me feel seen for once. And for not making the goodbye harder than it already is.*

He opens his arms to me, and I, like it's the most natural thing in the world, go to him. We hug. I breathe him in. He smells like a patch of sunlight in an otherwise dark forest, and leather and skin. His scent is now somehow mixed with my perfume. My floral and watery notes blend with the dark woods of his essence, creating something new and entirely ours—brief and fleeting, yes, but still unforgettable.

He doesn't pull away and neither do I. We hold on... to what, I'm not sure. Perhaps to the possibility of what could have been in another life. Or perhaps to the undeniable connection we've forged in such a short time. I don't want to let go. Not yet. Not ever.

It isn't until a commotion starts back where my brother-in-law's ex-squad team waits, that we pull apart.

"Those are my people." Dorian smiles apologetically. "I'd better go."

I nod, not trusting my voice.

"It was great meeting you, Josie." I can't decipher his tone.

I swallow the knife lodged in my throat and force myself to reply, "Same, Dorian."

With one last wave, he turns the corner. I lean a palm flat against the wall for support and double over as another sharp pain lodges between my ribs—an arrow dipped in the sweetest poison. It's a bittersweet ache, knowing I met someone who touched my soul in ways I never expected, but also understanding that our time together was never meant to last.

Later that day, when I'm at home and can't sleep despite having only dozed off for a few hours, I go on an Instagram stalking spree. His profile. Billie Rae's. Each photo of them together that I scroll past is a little death. My finger hovers over the *"unfollow"* button, but I can't bring myself to cut that last tie.

Instead, I search for Dorian's next concert dates in LA and almost go broke buying tickets for all three nights on the secondary market since they sold out within an hour of sales opening. But I'm determined to see him again, even if it's from a distance.

* * *

The four-month wait until his first concert lasts forever. Yet the moment the concert begins, I realize the waiting was a mercy compared to the pain of seeing him again. Night one, I stay until the end, my heart a flame that burns higher at every song. Night two, he plays "Call It Mine" for his surprise song—a track he wrote before Billie and the one he chose for me. When he reaches the chorus, I break down so completely I have to leave, the memory of him singing it just for me as a lullaby hitting me too hard.

I still come back for night three. But when Billie Rae makes an impromptu appearance on stage and they sing one of their love songs together, something inside me shatters. I leave the venue, tears streaming down my face, vowing to let his voice fade from my heart, to let it become an echo I won't chase anymore.

As I step out into the night outside the stadium, I inhale the fresh air and tilt my head to the stars. They seem to wink at me, as if to say, *It's fine, you'll be fine.* And maybe they know that letting go is the only way to move forward, to find the love and happiness I deserve somewhere else. In a place where Dorian can't come.

Sometimes, the greatest love stories are the ones that remain unfinished...

16

DORIAN

September—Present Time

I'm in the home office, sitting at the large meeting table with my team. Sunlight pours in from the French doors, pooling on the polished white surface. Everyone's here except Josie. Her unoccupied chair across from me a gaping hole.

Victor, my ever-impatient agent, leans forward, glancing at his watch. "Should we start without PR and catch her up later?"

I check the time on my phone. "Let's give it a few more minutes."

I drum my fingers on the table, wondering why she's late. Josie doesn't strike me as someone who'd be tardy without a reason. Did something happen to her? Was she in an accident?

Just as my mind conjures increasingly absurd possibilities, Tessa's phone buzzes. She glances at the screen, then at me. "The gate guard just pinged me. Josie has arrived."

Relief sweeps over me in an oddly physical way, like stepping into the shade after hours under an unforgiving sun. But it's joined by an aching anticipation that presses against my ribs.

Footsteps in the hallway make my pulse trip, and when the door finally opens, gravity forgets its hold on me for a beat, everything inside me suspended and weightless.

Josie rushes in. She tugs at the strap of her bag, wrestling it over her head in a flurry of movement.

She's wearing one of her floral milkmaid dresses, flowy, kind of old-school but in a trendy way, with a blue floral pattern over an off-white soft fabric. The sleeves are puffed up, and the neckline dips enough to be interesting without trying too hard, with these little strings tied in a bow in the middle that are as innocent as they're maddening.

Her hair is half-up, half-down, same as the night we met. But unlike that night, when her skin was a constellation of freckles and flawless perfection, she has a black curly mustache drawn on her upper lip.

My own lips twitch as I trace the lines of the doodle with my gaze, both smooth except for the right curl that's smudged at the end. At once, I'm intensely curious about the story behind the mustache.

Has she taken up morning theater lessons? Maybe it's a new viral trend I'm not cool enough to know about. Whatever the reason, I'll never guess because it's Josie—delightfully chaotic, a riddle wrapped in humor and heart, impossible to pin down yet always what I need.

"Morning," Josie says, out of breath. Her cheeks are flushed, and a few stray wisps of hair cling to her temples. "Sorry I'm late. Did I miss anything?"

Tessa shakes her head. "We were about to start."

Josie nods, acting as if everything is perfectly normal with her circus-chic look. She slides into her chair, setting her bag on the floor. "Great. Go ahead, then."

Glances dart around the table, a silent game of chicken to

see who will address the elephant—or rather, the mustache—in the room.

Victor, predictably, caves first. He gestures vaguely toward his upper lip, his voice hesitant as he brings it up. "Are you aware that you have—"

Josie doesn't let him finish. "A curly mustache drawn on my face, yes, I'm aware." She doesn't offer any explanation.

Tessa clears her throat, clearly hoping to steer the meeting back on track, but it's a futile attempt; all eyes remain fixed on Josie's mustache. I lean back in my chair, fighting not to grin.

I follow the outline of that imperfect curl again before speaking. "What Victor meant is that we're all going to have a hard time focusing on anything else unless you could maybe share why the mustache?"

Josie closes her eyes, taking a deep inhale in a sort of "finding my inner peace" way. When she reopens them, she takes her notepad and pencil out of her bag and, without looking at anyone in particular, tells the group, "I had to take my niece to school this morning and learned last minute it was Bring Your Dad to School Day. Since Penny doesn't have her dad, she asked me to go."

Josie doesn't specify what *doesn't have her dad* means, but that moment in the elevator when she broke down slams into me with vivid clarity. Josie must mean that Penny's father is dead. Was he Josie's brother? Her brother-in-law? From what I remember of her saying how she didn't have the right to break down because technically, whatever caused her pain hadn't happened to her, I guess brother-in-law.

I will her to meet my gaze, but she doesn't. She studiously keeps her head down as she fights a slight tremor in her voice. "Of course, I agreed to go. But Penny decided I looked too pretty to play the part of a dad."

I silently agree. Josie is too pretty for everything. Too pretty to make sense of, too pretty to keep my sanity as she sits across from me, impossibly beautiful even with a silly doodle on her face, too pretty and so fantastically unaware of it.

"So, Penny insisted I let her give me a mustache as camouflage. Only instead of using what she promised was washable ink, the little monster thought it'd be funny to use a permanent marker." Josie beats her pencil nervously on the notepad. "Once I realized, I could either spend hours removing the damage and miss the meeting, or arrive mostly on time and keep the mustache."

I'm equal parts charmed and gutted. I admire her for going to such ridiculous lengths to make her niece happy, for letting herself become the person a little girl can count on. I can picture Josie in that classroom, standing tall with that absurd mustache, playacting. She has to carry not just her grief but someone else's too, to hold herself together while making space for another's sadness. Stepping in where a parent should have been, keeping the smile on a little girl's face through a sure-to-be-hard day. It takes strength to fill that absence, and it's as beautiful as it is devastating.

I give Josie what I hope is an encouraging smile as I thank her for sharing with the group.

Turning to the others, I ask, "Any more questions?"

They mutter negative responses, so I nod at Tessa, asking her to go ahead with the day's agenda.

But as the meeting progresses, I don't listen to a single word of what anyone says. My focus is on Josie bathed in the sunlight streaming through the windows. In this setting, her amber irises are so much more striking than they were under the fluorescent lights of the elevator. Yeah, those neons didn't do them justice, and yet, her eyes were already stunning enough to bring me to my knees. Now, I'm not even sure where I stand. In a puddle on the floor?

Every additional detail I discover about her is a prize worth more than all the Grammys I have in this room. It's not only her beauty that captivates me, more the essence of who she is. It's the way she fills the space without even trying, how her presence electrifies the air, making every word anyone else says irrelevant.

I finally recognize the emptiness I've been carrying these past months: I've missed her.

Ever since that night, there's been a Josie-shaped void I couldn't fill no matter how hard I distracted myself with work or music. And now that I've got her back in my life, it's all I can do to keep from grinning like an idiot. I'm giddy, downright light-headed, my entire body is buzzing knowing that she's mere feet away from me.

Her laugh, her quirks, her ridiculous fake mustache—they're everything I've been starving for in the past year. And like a man breaking a fast, I'm terrified of overindulging, of rushing her with too much too soon.

I yearn to touch her, to brush that stray tendril of hair from her cheek. But I clasp my hands tighter under the table, reining myself in.

Slow and steady, Dorian. Don't spook her.

When I met her, a barrier stood between us, a truth I wasn't ready to share. But now, I've finally razed that wall. I'm done with my failed marriage, with the shambles of my old life... She knows I'm unattached. And I'm free to go after her.

But that freedom is still laced with fear.

Fear of saying the wrong thing, of moving too fast, too slow, of letting her slip through my fingers again. I don't even know if she's seeing someone. Fuck, if she has a boyfriend I'm going to lose my shit. How did I wait an entire year? Would've been more if Missy hadn't had her medical emergency.

I feel stupid for having wasted all this time. But Josie has told me more than once that I was too married for her. I needed the relationship with Billie to be over in every sense— emotional, legal, public—before approaching Josie. I just hope I haven't waited too long.

My first instinct is to leap over the table and kiss her, but I need to tread carefully.

Josie isn't someone I can chase recklessly. She's the breakout song in an album, one I have to compose with intention, every note considered, every lyric meaningful. She's a melody that got stuck in my head, and I have to take my time, let each chord fall into place naturally, with the care I'm still learning how to give after my marriage imploded so spectacularly. Still, as I watch her in my house, with my people, the need to prod overcomes everything else. I'm only human, and today, I won't let her slip away like she did at the photoshoot yesterday. Not again.

This time, I'll give her a reason to stay.

17

JOSIE

As the meeting at Dorian's continues, Bailey, the social media manager, pulls her sleek ponytail tighter and begins her update.

"The Instagram post announcing Dorian's split from Billie Rae is doing well. Close to forty million views, five million likes, and over a hundred K supportive comments flooding in. Of course, Billie's die-hard fans left a few salty remarks, but that's to be expected." She scrolls through her phone, her long, pointy nails clicking against the screen. I wonder how she types, let alone avoids spelling disasters, with those claws. "Oh, and the usual gossip about who Dorian will be dating next has started."

I keep my pencil gliding across the notepad, feigning intense concentration on my notes, but my ears prick up at the mention of Dorian's romantic prospects. And I swear I can feel the brush of his gaze on me as he smoothly declares, "I'm not seeing anyone."

It's embarrassing how relieved I am. I fight the urge to kick my feet under the table.

Bailey nods, her ponytail bobbing with the motion. "Got it. But remember, we need to be in the loop ASAP if that changes, okay? Any rumors of you dating someone new might put Billie Rae's fans in a tailspin."

I dare a peek as Dorian confirms with a silent dip of his head. But it's his agent who talks next, addressing his question to me. "Josie, given Dorian's history as half of a music power couple, what's your take on shaping his image post-divorce?"

"Mmm, what do you mean?"

"Do we make him America's sweetheart, market him as a sexy bad boy, keep him a dark horse?"

I'm appalled by how they discuss him—*to his face*—like he's a piece of meat to sell at the butcher shop to the highest bidder.

I part my lips to respond that we should market him only as the best singer and songwriter of this century, but Dorian's voice cuts through the air. "Hold your horses, Victor. I'm not interested in crafting some new persona." His tone is resolute. "I want to be myself. My only concern is steering clear of bogus rumors and handling any potential backlash from Billie's fanbase."

He seems ready to shed the past and determined not to be boxed into a future that isn't on his terms. Dorian wears his confidence like an invitation, pulling me in and making me want to be a part of that journey, even if only as his publicist.

I clear my throat, drawing the attention of the room. "I agree with Dorian. Authenticity is key here. We don't need to reinvent his image, just protect it from any unwarranted attacks or false narratives."

"The fallout has been minimal so far." Tessa nods. "A few snarky tweets, but nothing alarming. Both your fanbases are mostly sad about the end of an era, not out for blood. If Billie Rae doesn't pull any stunts, we're good."

Dorian gives a skeptical glance at his assistant, as if asking, *What are the chances of Billie not pulling stunts?*

Tessa meets Dorian's questioning look with a wry smile. "I know, wishful thinking. Billie's not known for staying quiet. We'll keep monitoring social media and news outlets. If something concerning pops up, we'll be ready to do damage control as needed."

I nod, scribbling a few last notes. No one has anything further to add, so everyone packs their laptops and tablets.

I gather my notepad and pencil, tucking them into my bag, already thinking ahead to how I'm going home to scrub my skin raw if that's what it takes to get rid of the mustache. And tonight, Penny and I will talk about which pranks are acceptable and which aren't when Auntie has to go to work. I still can't believe I had to sit through an entire meeting in front of Dorian with doodles on my face. The thought has been needling me for the past hour, small and persistent, a splinter under my skin that refuses to work its way free.

Like a sudden gust of wind, Dorian's voice sweeps away my circling thoughts, cutting through the noise and leaving no room for anything else. "Josie, could you hang back a minute?" He gestures for me to follow him. "Leave your stuff. You can grab it later."

Nervous, curious, and bewildered, I trail after him, my heart rate picking up speed with each step. He leads me out of the office, down the hall, and up a grand staircase. A million questions swirl through my head as we ascend. What does he want? Why the mysterious trek? Where is he taking me?

We arrive at what I can only assume is his bedroom. It must be. A king bed dominates the space, the sheets are still rumpled and Dorian lives alone, right?

A stack of worn paperbacks sits on the left nightstand, covers dark, spines creased, and the titles unreadable. I squint, desperate for this tiny glimpse into his inner world. Is he into thrillers or does he secretly enjoy mafia romances? I need to know. But the shadows and the distance keep his secrets.

I give up on the bookish quest and take in the rest of the room.

In the corner, a burgundy electric guitar catches the sunlight near a desk cluttered by crumpled music sheets.

Enormous, unwise feelings balloon in my chest as I picture him, scribbling down chords and testing them on the guitar. The scene feels intimate, personal, like I'm peering behind a curtain Dorian usually keeps drawn.

Why did he bring me here? My eyes flit to the bed, its rumpled sheets suddenly taking on a new, enticing meaning. Heat rushes to my cheeks at the thought.

But before my imagination can run wild, Dorian pivots, heading for the en suite bathroom. I follow—and nearly choke. It's the size of a New York apartment and looks like a spa: warm stone, rainfall shower, soaking tub, and a suspiciously well-stocked skincare line-up.

He grabs one of the containers, a sleek white one with gold lettering, and squirts a dense, milky liquid onto a cotton disk. "My stylist swears this is the best makeup remover on the market."

I quirk an eyebrow, lips twitching. "You wear makeup often?"

He flashes me a grin, the kind that makes standing upright complicated. "Gotta get rid of the guyliner somehow."

I laugh, the sound echoing off the stone walls. But my laughter chokes in my throat as Dorian steps closer, too close, the heat of his body warming the air between us. He raises the cotton disk, hovering it halfway to my mouth. "May I?"

My breath catches. "I can do it myself."

"I know."

Dorian doesn't step back, and his gaze, piercing yet gentle, has me nodding a silent permission.

His free hand comes up, cupping my chin with a tenderness that contrasts the calluses on his fingertips. Musician's hands. Now I understand what the fuss is about in romantasy novels about callused hands.

He holds me still as he brings the cotton to my lip.

The disk grazes my skin, and it's nothing—a faint pressure, a fleeting contact. And yet, somehow, it's everything.

It's not a sexy act, not really. But the intimacy, the reverent care in his touch, makes me feel like I'm free-falling. I stiffen at first, every survival instinct screaming at me to pull away, to deflect with a joke, to do anything but let myself fall for him any harder.

But how can I not?

His hand doesn't waver, and neither does his gaze. Gosh, I'd forgotten what it's like to be the sole focus of Dorian's attention. It amplifies my existence while simultaneously locking us up in an invisible cage, cutting us off from everything else.

He finishes dabbing the cleanser. "Now you have to let it sit for a few minutes." Dorian sets the bottle aside on the counter but doesn't step back. We stay facing each other in his personal bathroom, too close, in a space that's too private.

"I'm sorry, by the way." I feel compelled to apologize. "About the mustache. I know it's unprofessional, but I didn't have a choice. I promise it won't happen again."

"Don't apologize." His jaw tightens as if he's wrestling with what to say. "Your niece's dad, he's...?"

I don't answer right away. Instead, I use a technique I've learned in therapy to talk about my grief without breaking down. To stay present and reduce emotional overwhelm, I focus on five things I can see—the frosted windows, stone tiles, the tub, the moisturizing jars, Dorian. Four things I can touch—the counter, a towel, my dress, Dorian. Three I can hear—a leaf blower in the distance, the faint hum of the air conditioning, any of Dorian's songs that I can play in my head as clearly as if streaming them at top volume. Two I can smell—the cleanser and Dorian—and one I can taste. No Dorian here, I've no idea how he tastes. All I have is a trace of this morning's coffee to focus on.

"His name was Daniel," I finally say, my voice steadier than I expected. "He was a firefighter. We lost him three years ago."

Dorian's eyes soften with genuine sympathy. "I'm so sorry, Josie. That's devastating. How old is your niece now?"

"She's seven. She was only four when it happened."

A slight frown creases Dorian's brow as if he's just grasped a memory. "Is that why you knew the firefighters who rescued us that day?"

I nod, a sad smile tugging at my lips. "Yes, those were Daniel's old squad mates. They're still like family to us."

Dorian's fingers graze my arm in a comforting gesture that has goosebumps breaking over my skin despite the heaviness of the moment. "Is he why you cried in the elevator?"

I nod. "The last time I listened to 'Falling from the Same Sky' was when my sister, Lily, asked me to help her clear the house of his things. It had been a year since he'd passed." I swallow against the twisting emotions. "We put it on repeat and ugly cried the entire time we were collecting his stuff."

"I'm sorry." Dorian works his jaw. "And your sister? How is she doing?"

I take a shaky breath, voicing the worries I usually keep tucked away. "Honestly? I don't think she'll ever be truly okay again. Daniel was the love of her life, her soulmate. Losing him... it shattered her in ways I can't even fathom. But she has

Penny to live for, and so she pushes through..." Guilt seizes up my chest. "You know, I used to be so jealous of her. Of their whirlwind romance. They met and were married within a year, had a gorgeous kid the second my sister graduated from nursing school and had a stable job. I used to think how lucky she was..." I don't know why I'm baring the darkest parts of myself. "And when she lost him..." I blink rapidly, glancing at the ceiling, willing the tears not to fall. Turns out my coping strategies still need work.

"Hey." Dorian's fingers slide down to give my hand a gentle squeeze. "We don't have to discuss it if it's too much."

Grateful for the out, I nod. "Can I take this cleanser off now? My lip is going numb."

Dorian's lips quirk into a smile. "Let's check."

He reaches for a fresh cotton disk and carefully dabs at the corner of my mouth. Every brief touch from him is like taking a direct hit from a bolt of lightning.

"Looks good," he confirms. "I'll get the rest."

With gentle motions, Dorian wipes away the remaining cleanser. I focus on keeping my breathing even, but it's a losing battle.

When he's done, I stare in the mirror, needing a moment to collect myself. My upper lip is pink and tender, but the mustache is gone without a trace.

"What magic potion did you use on me?" I turn back to Dorian with a raised brow. "That's not an off-the-counter cleansing milk."

Dorian grins. "Busted. It's a professional-grade makeup remover I use on movie sets. Basically a chemical peel."

"Apparently so. Thank you." I touch my lip, marveling at the smoothness. "Now that I'm presentable again, I should head back to the office."

"Stay."

I'm taken aback by the intensity of the single-word request. It doesn't sound like a casual offer, it feels like a plea for connection.

He sounds so alone. How many people does Dorian interact with who aren't on his payroll? I wonder if he has any friends. Or if his world has narrowed down so drastically post-divorce that the only interactions he has are transactional. Or maybe I'm grasping for an altruistic excuse to give myself permission to stay.

Before I can reply, he adds, "If you go, I'll picture you eating a protein bar while driving and I can't have that." His tone is playful but sincere. "You have to eat anyway, and purse food doesn't count."

I should refuse, jump in my car, and get to work. But my other clients have been shifted to colleagues to clear my docket for Dorian. And while I'm sure I could find something to help with if I went back to the office, I'm not really needed there. Still, the professional thing to do would be to leave.

But he's watching me with that world-blurring, cocoon-making gaze I can't say no to. I'd say yes to matching tattoos if he looked at me like that and asked, and I'm terrified of needles.

"Okay, I'll stay," I relent. "But only for a quick bite. Then I really need to head back."

Triumph brightens his face as he smiles, but it's the relief in his eyes that rasps against my rib cage, demanding to be let in.

"I'll take it." He beckons me. "Come on, we can raid the fridge and eat outside."

I hope the fridge is the only thing he plans to raid because my heart can't withstand the assault.

18

DORIAN

I walk at a lazy pace as I lead Josie downstairs, prolonging my quiet elation that she agreed to stay. She's here. With me. A little less guarded perhaps now that we're alone. And we're having lunch. We'll finally talk—and not about my divorce.

In the kitchen, Josie perches on a stool by the island, her fingers absentmindedly toying with the hem of her dress. The midday sun spills through the windows, catching the lighter strands in her hair and the golden flecks in her eyes.

It's the first time I've seen her a bit more relaxed since stepping back into my life. The guarded expression on her face has eased, and I want to keep her like this forever, untethered from the outside world and its responsibilities.

Crossing to the fridge, I tug open the stainless-steel door, cool air whooshing over my face as I grab what we need for sandwiches: turkey, cheese, veggies, and a jar of mayonnaise. I spread the ingredients on the island next to a cutting board and pluck a chef's knife from the magnetic holder in the corner.

"Do you prefer tomato duty or mayo spreading?"

Josie's lips quirk. "What, no personal chef today?"

"Nah, it's Alfred's day off." I shrug, trying for nonchalance when I'm feeling anything but. I sent the entire staff home, hoping for a chance to look a little more... normal in Josie's eyes. "Figured we could handle a couple of sandwiches on our own."

"Oh, I see, that's why you asked me to stay. You needed the manual labor!" Josie teases.

I grin, handing her the sliced bread. "I had my heart set more on the company."

The words slip out, uncontrolled. *Shit.*

I check her reaction.

Josie blinks at me, but she recovers quickly and reaches for the mayo. "I'll spread, you cut."

I nod, smiling as I busy myself with slicing the tomatoes. We work in companionable silence, layering meat, cheese, and veggies onto the bread. It's such a simple, mundane task, but doing it with Josie sets a wonderful warmth burning behind my breastbone.

When the sandwiches are assembled, I grab a pitcher of water, fill it with ice at the fridge, and pick up two glasses from the cabinet while Josie carries our plates. On our way out of the kitchen, I make a quick detour to the hall closet to snag a blanket.

Outside, the sun is shining, bright but not too hot for a meal in the garden. Josie starts in the direction of the patio tables by the pool, but I stop her.

"Do you mind a change of scenery? There's a spot I want to show you. Best view from the property." I nod toward the lawn. "If it's okay to eat on the grass."

Josie's gaze darts from me to the plush expanse of green, a slow smile spreading across her face. "Wow, we're really roughing it, huh?"

I grin back at her, exaggerating an eye roll. "Relax, it's artisanal grass. Hand-trimmed. Very exclusive."

She laughs at that, and it strikes somewhere low in my chest, spreading more heat that coils tight in my stomach.

Swallowing past the sudden dryness in my mouth, I lead the way across the garden. Josie trails behind me. Her steps are light, but the sound carries over, reassuring me I'm not dreaming. The yard slopes downward as we move away from the pool, heading toward a shaded patch framed by a line of old sycamores.

I set the pitcher and glasses on the lawn and flick the blanket open, spreading it over the grass. Straightening, I catch Josie pausing, plates in hand, her gaze lost on the horizon.

It's the same view I've admired countless times, but today, it feels clearer because she's here. The rolling hills stretch before us, houses tucked discreetly among the trees, their rooftops catching shards of sunlight. Beyond them, the city opens up, a shimmering grid of glass and movement. The downtown skyline rises faint and distant, softened by a golden haze.

"I've always appreciated how North Beverly Park feels both connected and apart from the world." I watch Josie's profile as she takes the view in. "High enough to keep the chaos at bay, but not so far as to feel detached."

She turns to me then, her eyes shining with wonder. "It's beautiful, Dorian."

Say my name again. Say it a million times. Whisper it, moan it, scream it.

I duck my head before she can read my thoughts on my face and flee. "If we're going to have a picnic, might as well do it right." I don't mention how often I've sat here alone, guitar in hand, letting the city hum in the distance while I string together broken lyrics.

Josie sets the plates down and kneels across from me, smoothing her skirt under her as she sits. "Not bad," she jokes, glancing up at me. "For roughing it."

I smile and pour her a glass of water. Josie takes it as her hair is caught in the breeze, wisps dancing around her face. I'm struck once again by how beautiful she is.

I grab a sandwich. "Shall we test our culinary efforts?" I need to fill my mouth before I blurt out something I'm not sure she's willing or ready to hear.

Josie accepts the challenge with a grin. "Let's see if you're as skilled in the kitchen as you are on stage."

We both take a bite, chewing thoughtfully. The flavors meld together perfectly. Crisp lettuce, juicy tomato, and savory turkey complemented by a tangy aioli. But something is missing...

"Hmm, good. But my chef makes them tastier." I frown. "I swear we used the same ingredients."

Josie laughs. "It's better than purse food anyway, and the view compensates."

I raise an eyebrow. "What of the company?"

She blushes. "Can't complain."

I take the win home with a smile and don't push her. Between chews, I tell her more about why I brought her here. "This is a place where I can hear myself think." I glance sideways at her before turning back to the cityscape as if the comment were casual. It isn't. It never is with her.

"What are you thinking about right now?"

A ripple of heat skitters over my skin at her question, because the answer is always the same. "You." I can't think of anything else.

Her cheeks gain more color, and she looks away. I've made her uncomfortable. Quickly, I add, "How's the last year been for you?"

Josie swallows a bite, considering. "Same old, same old."

She's pretending a catch-up is all I meant after admitting I'm thinking about her. But then a shadow of sadness crosses her face as if something had clouded the months we weren't in each other's lives. I wonder what could've made it worse than when we met. And I can't play it cool anymore. I have to ask. "So, still unhappily single?"

Her gaze flickers over the blanket and then back to me, guarded.

I stretch my legs out. A casual gesture on the outside as I wait for her answer. But inside, I'm caught between bracing for impact and hoping for a soft landing, like a diver suspended mid-air, unsure if the water will welcome or shatter me.

She swallows a bite before finally asking, "Why do you want to know?"

I shrug, keeping my tone unbothered. "Why not? Just curious."

Josie sets her almost-finished sandwich down on her plate, her focus narrowing on me in that discerning way she has. It's not an innocent question, and we both know it. "We shouldn't discuss my personal life, Dorian."

I recognize the line she's drawing, the careful barrier she's erecting between us. It frustrates me more than it should. Still, I push back. "The other day, we dissected my divorce down to the bones."

Josie flinches faintly, something she tries to hide as she reaches for her water glass. "That was work," she counters, her tone measured.

She's holding the line, or trying to, but I'm not having it. I lean back on one arm, my gaze steady on her. "You asked me all those questions just for work?"

A long moment passes as she studies me with a troubled expression. "What's happening here?"

I sidestep the question. "Want to play a game?"

Josie stares at the view, stalling. Then, keeping her focus on the skyline, she asks, "What game?"

My mouth quirks. "Let's play Truth or Truth."

Josie huffs, a strangled sound that might've been a laugh if she'd let herself mean it. "That's not a real game."

"We can make it real. We take turns asking questions, and the other has to answer honestly," I propose.

She angles her face toward me, her small frown carrying a dozen silent questions of its own. I fear she might leave it at that, decide I'm not worth the effort.

Instead, she mutters, "Now I'm curious about what you'll ask."

I want to rock her boat, to know she has skin in the game, too. So, I destabilize her. "The first question is yours."

Josie doesn't speak right away. She fixates on a spot somewhere past me, her fingers absently tracing the rim of her water glass.

Then, as casually as if she were asking me what I thought of the weather, she says, "What's your biggest regret?"

The question punches me straight in the solar plexus. A dozen possible answers rush through my mind—choices I've made, paths I've taken, things I've lost. But as I look at Josie, there's only one true answer.

19

JOSIE

The silence stretches endlessly, each second folding into the next as I wait for his answer.

"Not getting divorced sooner," Dorian replies, blue eyes on me.

The admission carves into the stillness between us. The words settle in my soul like an uninvited guest I've no idea how to greet. Keep quiet and pretend not to be home? Bar the door and send them away? Or throw it wide open and let them in?

A high, invisible pressure vibrates in the space separating us.

Heart thumping, I ask him, "Why?"

Dorian smirks, eyes crinkling. "You already used your question, Josie."

"What?" I blink, taken aback. "That's ridiculous. I don't get a follow-up?"

My muscles tense, the need for answers coiling in my stomach painfully tight. But Dorian seems entirely unfazed by my protest. His smirk lingers as he calmly shrugs. "I'm only following the rules."

I scowl. "You mean the made-up rules of your made-up game?"

He watches me squirm with infuriating ease, as if this is just another move in a match he already knows he'll win.

"Rules are rules."

"Go ahead, Rule Police, ask your question." I gesture impatiently.

"Have you thought about me this past year?"

I cross my arms, straightening my posture, and meet his gaze, keeping my answer minimal. "I have."

A flicker of satisfaction warms me, knowing the simplicity of my response will frustrate him right back. But instead of conceding, he appears more satisfied than before, his grin broadening, making me second-guess my advantage.

"Touché."

It's my turn again, and I don't hesitate. "Why did you wish you'd gotten divorced sooner?" I drop the question and wait for an answer that could change everything.

This time, he doesn't deflect. He pins me down with a stare as he tells me, "So I would've been unattached when I met you. So, I could've kissed you that night."

The words detonate in my mind, scattering every carefully stacked barrier, dragging me back to the hours in the elevator in vivid detail. The press of the metal walls boxing us in, the flicker of the emergency light, the faint scent of leather and forest that was undeniably his.

But more intense than anything else are the memories of his silences, how he'd looked at me like he had a secret he couldn't share. Only now do I realize that the suspension between us hadn't been indecision; it had been restraint.

The memory isn't soft; it's a jagged pull, cutting me open

with everything we didn't do, didn't say. I grasp the blanket, crushed by what-ifs. I don't know what to do with this new knowledge, this revelation that's repainting the edges of what I thought was possible. My heart is doing painful kung fu moves in my chest, torn between the thrill of his words and the fear of letting myself believe them.

I tap my foot on the ground. It's the only movement I allow myself while I fight the tide of uncertainty so it won't swallow me whole. "You wanted to kiss me?"

Dorian's expression hardens, not with restraint but with intent. "I did. I still do. And that's two questions."

It doesn't matter how many questions because we're no longer playing a game.

But before I can protest, he asks, "How often have you thought about me this past year?"

I glance away, not able to hold his gaze. "Dorian, I can't go there."

"Why not?" he demands in a measured tone.

I force myself to look at him again. His face has changed; the smirk is gone, replaced by a seriousness that makes my breath shallow.

I pick at a loose thread on the blanket, unraveling it, same as his words are unraveling me as I give him the truth. "Because I've thought about you every single day." The admission spills from me in a rush. "I went to your concerts in Inglewood."

Dorian leans in, his attention so fixed on me, it feels like the blaze of headlights cutting through a dark road: sudden, blinding, unescapable. "Which night?"

"All of them," I confess in a whisper.

His eyes widen, my answer seeming to stagger him. But now that I've started, I can't stop. "The last night, when Billie Rae came on stage, I... I fled the stadium in tears. I told myself I had to get you out of my head, that it was crazy to be so hung up on someone I met only once."

I drop my gaze to my hands, twisting them in my lap. The memory of that night is still raw, the pain of watching him singing with her.

Dorian is silent for a long beat. I don't look at him, afraid of what I'll see in his eyes. Pity? Regret? Confirmation that I'm nothing more than another crazy fan?

"Josie." His hand covers mine, stilling my restless fingers. "Look at me."

I do as he asks. His gaze on me is soft and intense at the same time, calm and churning.

"Billie showed up that night on stage only to rattle me," he explains. "We were already negotiating the divorce settlement at that point. I had to roll with it not to make a scene. I had no choice."

I let his words sink in, but they do little to ease the knot of emotions sitting heavy in my chest. "Even so," I say, my voice quieter now, "there are a million reasons we shouldn't be having this conversation."

Dorian's eyes bore into mine. "Name them."

I want to ignore the rational arguments and tell him he can kiss me now if he still wants to. But I can't. So I don't back down. "For one, you're fresh out of a divorce."

"My marriage has been over for two years," he counters. "When I met you, it was already over."

"But it still took you another year to formally end it," I argue. "And rebound relationships are called that way for a reason."

A protest rises to his lips, but I barrel through, unwilling to lose momentum. "And even if I disregarded that, the unknowns of your world are daunting for someone like me." His jaw ticks, like he's holding himself back. And I take advantage, voicing my doubts. "But most importantly, I'm not sure what we felt that night was even real." My voice softens as I add, "We've spent a few hours locked up together, and it feels like we've known each other for a lifetime, but we really don't. It was a cocoon, an unreal situation with heightened emotions. Like being on *The Bachelor*."

Dorian scoffs and leans back, studying me with eyes that want to stay serious but sparkle with amusement. "How is being trapped in an elevator comparable to being on *The Bachelor*? Shouldn't there be more screaming women?"

Despite myself, I smile. "Be serious," I scold him playfully. "Don't make me laugh when I'm making a point."

He raises his hands in mock-surrender, a smirk playing on his lips. "My apologies. Please, continue."

I pluck a blade of grass, gathering my thoughts. "It's like being on a TV show because it's easy to feel infatuated while on a hot-air balloon ride, followed by dinner in a vineyard surrounded by twinkling fairy lights and sharing roasted marshmallows by a firepit for dessert with only the moonlight as a companion."

Dorian's smirk widens. "You're really romanticizing our captivity in that elevator."

I shoot him a look but can't entirely hide my own smile. "Because those ten hours felt more exhilarating than any scripted date could ever be. But real life isn't like that." My smile fades as I meet his gaze head-on. "We don't really know each other."

Dorian's expression sobers. "That isn't entirely accurate. I know that you're kind, fun, and sarcastic. What song you listen to when you need to ugly cry. That you hold yourself together for everyone else, but sometimes, you just need someone to see through it. You have a tell when you're about to cry. The way you blink fast, like you can will the tears away before they have the chance to fall. Because you want to be strong enough that no one ever has to worry about you. And you deflect with humor when you're uncomfortable. Sarcasm is your armor to hide everything you're afraid to show."

Gosh, why does he have to be so—so *him*? So into my very soul. I can't even process everything he just told me.

I sigh, conceding the point. "Okay, yes, we shared some deeper truths that night. But we also missed so much." He opens his mouth to protest again, but I hold up a hand to stop him. "Be honest, Dorian. Until an hour ago, you didn't know I lost my brother-in-law in a fire. You don't know where I went to high school or what foods I hate. You don't even know where I live." He frowns, but he remains silent as I continue. "And what I assume I know about you must be mostly untrue, cobbled together from gossip sites and social media. Only last week, I thought your marriage to Billie Rae was picture-perfect."

Something in Dorian's expression shifts, vulnerability flickering in his piercing eyes. "What if I wanted to learn all of that about you, Josie?"

Yearning wars with the stark reality of our situation. "I'm working for you now, Dorian. Even if I was willing to overlook the other risks, I can't date you. My boss made it clear that if I so much as look at you with anything other than total professional detachment, she'll fire me."

Dorian sighs heavily, regret evident in the set of his jaw. "Is it too late to request working with someone else?"

"Yes, it would make me look terrible."

He runs a hand through his dark locks, his gaze meeting

mine with a rueful intensity. "Then I'm changing my original answer. My biggest regret is requesting you to be on my PR account."

I stare at him, confused. "Why did you approach me this way? You could've asked me out like a normal person."

His response is a frustrated, "I wasn't sure how you'd react. When you saw me at that party, you avoided me."

"Because I thought you were married," I protest, my hands flailing.

"I didn't know that was the only reason," he counters earnestly. "You were on a date. It was a month ago. You could be in a relationship by now. What if you were no longer single?"

"Would you still have wanted to work with me if I wasn't single?" I ask on impulse.

Dorian's answer is immediate. "Yes, because I trust you, and I don't trust people easily."

I absorb his last words. He trusts me. That means something. Maybe more than I'm willing to admit right now.

"What was your big plan, then, having us work together?"

Dorian studies me like he's deciding how much to reveal. "The plan was to show you that my life, while not normal, is manageable. That I'm not too out of reach. I thought that it'd be for a shorter period and temporary, and that... I don't know, signing a module with HR would be enough if something happened between us..." A small smile tugs at the corner of his mouth. "If I managed to woo you a little in the process."

Woo me. The phrase is so old-fashioned and charming that it makes my heart do an uncomfortable flip. I stare at the distant horizon as I bare even more of my soul. "You don't need to woo me, Dorian, consider me thoroughly wooed."

Dorian raises an eyebrow, his lips curving into that familiar, teasing smile. "Well, that was easier than I thought. Here I was, ready to pull out all the stops."

"Yeah, like what?"

"Sorry." He pretend-zips his mouth. "I can't reveal all my moves, I might still need to use some."

Curiosity gets the better of me, and I can't resist asking, "When was the last time you even dated someone normal? You know, after Sandy Who-Didn't-Let-You-Go-To-Third-Base Parker?"

Dorian laughs, his eyes crinkling at the corners. "I can't believe you remember the name of my high-school girlfriend."

I lock eyes with him. "I remember everything."

He nods, serious again. "Post-Sandy, it was mostly celebrities. Not because I'm a snob, it's more that I don't run into non-famous people that often." Dorian reaches for my hand again, tracing a distracting pattern on my palm with his thumb. "What matters now is whether you'd be willing to risk the fallout, the fans, the tabloids, and everything else you mentioned that night, to date me."

Frustration bubbles inside me, and I pull my hand away, breaking our contact. "Even if I could manage all that, I can't risk my job, Dorian. I'm not a gazillionaire. My savings are almost non-existent and I have rent to pay, student loans." I swing a hand at the mansion surrounding us. "I know it must seem peanuts to you. But I can't put everything on the line for something that won't last."

"Ah." His eyes flash. "Your statistics about celebrity relationships."

I pin him down with a pointed look. "Tell me they aren't accurate."

Dorian considers my words carefully. "Fair enough. But don't write us off on principle. I hear you, I know this isn't just about feelings. You've got real risks, real consequences, and I'd never ask you to gamble everything just because I can afford to." Then, in a gesture that is confident yet careful, as if testing the boundaries between us, he takes my hand again and presses a soft kiss to the palm. "How about this?" he proposes, his words unadorned, simple, genuine. "We're going to be around each other a lot until Missy comes back. We can get to know each other outside of the balloon ride, see if it's still real. You can get a behind-the-scenes peek at what my life is really like: the security, the paparazzi, the crazed fans, everything. And then you can decide if it's too much for you."

I bite my lip, considering his offer. "And then what? Where does that road lead? To me quitting my job and becoming a full-time groupie?"

Dorian doesn't flinch at my blunt question. Instead, he holds my gaze steadily, his eyes filled with a determined intensity that feels like a tether, binding us. "I can't quit being famous, Josie. Even if I wrote no more music, I can't control my fame." He speaks matter-of-factly, stating a reality, not using excuses. "But my commitment to you? That's something I can control. I can do fewer concerts, fewer tours after I finish this one." His thumb brushes over my knuckles as he collects his thoughts. "If this thing between us is real, Josie, it could be more important than a job. You could move to a different PR firm. Or I'll simply go back to Missy when she returns and then your conflict will be gone."

"She won't be back for another ten months, a year most likely," I point out, wanting to be realistic despite the sensation that I might burst into confetti at any second.

Dorian smiles then, a sweet, open smile that has my heart tripping over itself. "Plenty of time to discover more about each other."

I'm stunned. He'd wait an entire year for me? Is he serious? "Wouldn't that be too long for you?"

He tucks a stray lock behind my ear, his fingers brushing my cheek and leaving a trail of tingles in their wake. "I've already waited a year without you, Josie. Dreaming of all the things I'd do with you, to you..." His voice is low, intimate. "Being near you will make the waiting easier... and a hell of a lot harder. But totally worth it."

"So you want to get to know me platonically?"

"No, I want to get to know you *romantically*," Dorian replies, his eyes locked on mine, "but if we need to take things slow while we figure each other out, we'll do it. If, with your job, you can't be in a full relationship with me, we can leave the physical stuff out—no chances of being caught. Pretend we're Elizabeth Bennet and Fitzwilliam Darcy and live in an era when sex before marriage is not accepted. We'll be courting each other without any of the naughty stuff."

I groan, shaking my head. "You did not just use *Pride and Prejudice* against me." He grins, and I lose the resolve to resist him. "So no sex and no kisses?"

Dorian seems outraged. "Not even first base, Monroe? Be careful of what will be put on your tombstone."

I laugh, and I'm not sure it isn't giddy, or hysterical. "You'll have to work for that home run, Phoenix."

He leans in just a little, heat simmering in his voice. "Then let me earn it. All I ask is that you don't see anyone else while we figure this out—and I won't either. I want to explore this connection properly. Just us."

As if there could ever be someone else. "Just us," I echo. "I like the sound of that."

Dorian stands up, his tall frame towering over me. He offers me his hands with a boyish grin on his face. "Are hugs allowed?"

I beam back at him as he pulls me up. "Yes, hugs are allowed."

He steps closer and opens his arms. I go to him, and he pulls me into a warm embrace that has me melting into his chest as I inhale his forest scent.

I'm confused as to what I've agreed to, but I know I never want to let him go.

20

JOSIE

I never imagined a hug could be the most satisfying sexual experience of my life, but here I am.

At first, Dorian's embrace is chaste. His arms anchor me to him, firm but careful. But then his hands begin to roam—up my back, down my arms, resting on my hips. His thumbs press into my flesh, igniting my skin, while my face burrows into his chest, soaking in his scent and the steady rise and fall of his breathing.

He draws small circles on my sides through the thin fabric of my dress, sending waves of electricity through my body. I sigh, my eyes fluttering closed as I savor the sensation.

Dorian's hands travel upward, and he tilts my chin up, his gaze locking onto mine as he reaches up and undoes the topknot in my hair. He steals my elastic and loops it over his wrist. He never looks away, even as he smooths my disheveled locks, trailing his fingers between the strands. Every touch sends fire licking down my spine.

"Dorian." My voice is unsteady, my mind reeling. "You hug a little too hard."

A slow smile unzips across his face, his hands still tangled in my hair. "Am I being sanctioned?"

I move my hands from around his back, letting my fingers graze up his chest with featherlight strokes. His T-shirt does a poor job of hiding the hard muscles underneath, compelling me to explore. When he trembles at my touch, it's a silent acknowledgment of my power over him that sends a thrill through me.

"I don't think this amount of touching would've been acceptable in the Regency Era." My lips brush close to his ear.

"Should I stop?"

I should tell him, yes, but it's the last thing I want. My body betrays me, leaning infinitesimally closer, drawn to him as if magnetized, but I plead, "Please," saying yes when I mean no.

He steps back, creating a sliver of distance between us, his hands still working through my hair. "I'll be good, I promise," he says, before placing a soft kiss on my forehead and letting go.

The gentle touch of his lips burns me, fire propagating from my hairline through my scalp, searing down my neck and shoulder blades, and then frying my nerves all the way down to my toes.

Dorian steps away completely, leaving me breathless and stunned. The sudden absence of his touch is a bucket of ice water dumped over my head, a numbing shock. I'm in a daze as he walks me to my car, holding my hand. The gesture feels both silly and meaningful. I glance down at our intertwined hands. His palm—dry, warm, reassuring—fits mine with a strangely familiar ease, as if we've done this a thousand times before. His hold on me is not possessive, or demanding, but certain. It's nothing, and yet everything.

As we reach the patch of gravel in the front yard that his guests use as a makeshift parking lot, it's clear neither of us wants to say goodbye. I reconsider all my wise choices—

deciding not to kiss him, not to explore this attraction physically until we're both sure. But certainty is a distant concept when my mind is a haze of confusion. One moment, I'm convinced I know what I want—*him*; the next, I doubt everything. Am I star-struck? Is he? Like not star-struck but high on some sort of Stockholm syndrome from that night? Is he too good to be true? Will he tire of me in no time? Will this intensity fade, leaving me with nothing but regrets? The questions pile on top of each other, making me unsteady and unsure. Yes, waiting is the smart thing to do.

As if reading my thoughts, Dorian cups my cheek, his touch gentle yet electric. "It sucks to have to wait, and it's my fault. It's going to be brutal—but I'm fully prepared to suffer dramatically and often if it is for you—for *us*."

And then he kisses my forehead again, short-circuiting the last functioning neurons in my brain. I'm grinning like an idiot as I get into my car, but I can't find it in me to care.

Dorian is holding the car door open for me. "See you tomorrow. Drive safe."

He steps back, eyes intense, as he closes the door.

I drive straight to Lily's place, hungry for the kind of comfort only family can offer. She's making dinner when I arrive—I can't believe my lunch break with Dorian lasted the entire afternoon. We eat together like always, but I barely taste anything. I mostly listen to Penny chattering. Lily's eyes track me, probably sensing I'll need to vent later. After dinner, Penny begs for an original mermaid story, so I tuck her in and weave a tale about a princess of the sea who lives in an enchanted coral reef and swims between two worlds.

Once Penny is asleep, I tiptoe out of the room, leaving her to dream of turquoise seas and magical adventures. Ah, if only real life could be as simple and enchanting as a bedtime story.

I find Lily on the patio seated at the table with two steaming mugs of red berries tea waiting. I settle in the free chair and grab the mug closest to me.

Lily doesn't ask me anything. She waits for me to break. And it's not long before the thoughts swirling in my mind demand an outlet. "I don't know what I'm doing."

My sister watches me, her sad eyes filled with understanding and a hint of concern. She sips her tea, waiting patiently for me to continue.

And so, I spill everything. I tell her about my day with Dorian, the mature conversation we had about our feelings, and the hug that left me breathless and longing for more.

Lily listens, her expression neutral as she absorbs my words. Until I voice the doubt that has been torturing me all night. "Do you think I'm making a mistake? That I've picked an impossible man to love, and I'm only going to get my heart broken?"

My sister doesn't answer immediately. Instead, she gazes out at the horizon, where the last streaks of sunset are being swallowed by darkness.

"You could have picked the most regular man." My sister's tone is measured when she finally speaks, "And he could still leave you. Even if he didn't want to." Her voice catches as she turns to me, her eyes soft but serious, holding a wisdom born of experience and heartache. "The heart wants what the heart wants."

The words sink deep into my chest, heavy but undeniable. They aren't the reassurance I had hoped for, but maybe they are better—brutal and unflinching like truth often is.

"You never fall for anyone," Lily continues. "When your last boyfriend asked you to move in with him, you broke off a two-year relationship without batting an eyelid. Then you spend a few hours locked in an elevator with Rian Phoenix and are heartbroken for a year. You can't un-love him, Josie. And if you don't at least try, you're going to regret it. But it's smart that you're taking things slowly. And it's promising that he's okay to wait."

We finish our tea in the growing darkness, the bond of sisterhood speaking louder than any words ever could. As the night settles around us, I find a strange sense of peace in the uncertainty. Love isn't about guarantees or safe choices. It's about taking a leap of faith, even when the landing is uncertain. And maybe the heart really knows best.

* * *

As I step into my apartment, it's late, but I'm not tired—more restless. The excitement of today coalesces into a fidgety energy that buzzes under my skin.

I get behind my laptop and polish my CV that I haven't updated in years and set up various job alerts for positions in my field. Dorian is right, I can change agencies. I like my colleagues, but I'm not close to anyone in particular at work. And I don't love Nadine. We coexist well thanks to the hierarchical levels separating us, which allow me to forget she exists.

When I'm done, I curl up on the couch, too jacked up for TV. Instead, I grab my tablet, unhook my pen, and open my favorite design app. The familiar interface soothes me, tugging me back to college, when I discovered digital design. My major was communications, but my minor in visual arts unlocked a deeper hunger in me to illustrate my ideas. Tonight, that need bubbles up again. I start sketching the mermaid kingdom from Penny's bedtime story: swaying seaweed forests, coral castles, and glowing jellyfish. When I reach the merman prince, he somehow ends up looking like Dorian—powerful jaw, intense eyes, an air of mystery. I give him tattoos, inked dark against bronzed skin.

Time slips away. When I resurface, the screen glows with the start of a storybook. It's exactly how I saw it while telling Penny her tale.

I hug the tablet to my chest. Penny will love it. I smile at the handsome merman prince—bet Dorian would love this, too. I stare out the window, picturing him in his mansion. Will he be in the garden, stargazing? In his living room, composing? Is he thinking about me? I wish I had the freedom to hop in my car and drive to his place, but I can't. I can only hope the heart *gets* what the heart wants. "Soon," I promise the night and get back to drawing.

21

DORIAN

I recline in a patio chair, feeling unusually light as I stare at the stars. The conversation with Josie lingers in my mind, infusing me with optimism. I hate that I put her in a position where we can't openly date, but I'm sure we'll find a solution. We only need time.

Despite the complications, the idea of a slow courtship is exciting. It feels romantic to take it slow. I want this relationship to work, and an unhurried approach makes me feel calmer. I'll have fewer chances to screw up. It'll also spare me the scathing, he-replaced-his-wife-in-a-week headlines, the fans thinking I moved on too fast, and Billie from having the truth dragged out in front of the world before she's ready for it. Not that my ex is ever going to accept my new relationship.

I pick up my guitar, my fingers dancing over the strings as I experiment with new chords. A melody begins to take shape, soft, hopeful, and entirely inspired by Josie.

I play until my phone rings, but it's only front gate security trying to reach me, not a real call.

I balance the guitar on my knees and pick up. "Yeah?"

"Mr. Phoenix, sorry to disturb you, but we have a situation at the gates."

"No worries, what's up?" I ask, imagining it could be a crazy fan or rogue paparazzo—wouldn't be the first time.

"It's your ex-wife, sir. She's demanding to be let in, and she seems... agitated."

My shoulders tense as I set the guitar aside, already bracing for the emotional storm Billie brings. I sigh, knowing it's no use denying my ex when she's in this state. "Let her in. I'll handle it."

As I make my way across the house to the front yard, acid burns in my stomach. What could Billie want? Our divorce has been finalized, and we've said everything that needed to be said. Her showing up like this can't be good.

My gut feeling that trouble is coming is confirmed when Billie parks haphazardly in the front driveway, leaving the car at a slant with the engine still running. She stumbles out of the driver's seat, her movements unsteady. My ex-wife is wearing denim shorts, a white tank top, and cowboy boots. Billie is thin, too thin. And her speech is slurred as she shouts, "You backstabbing bastard."

I flex my fingers, steeling myself for the onslaught. "What are you doing here?"

She storms up to me. Her blue-streaked blonde hair falls into her face as she jabs a finger into my chest. "You know damn well why I'm here. You've been sabotaging my career, haven't you? Telling everyone in the industry that I'm unstable, that I'm difficult to work with."

I hold up my hands to placate her. "Billie, I haven't said anything like that. I—"

"Don't lie to me," she screams, her face inches from mine. "Producers, agents, our label, they're all turning their backs on me, and it's because of you."

I step back and pinch my nose, gathering my patience. "The only thing I've told anyone is the truth, Billie. That you need help."

"Help? *I* need help?" She lets out a harsh laugh. "That's rich coming from you. You're reveling in my misery, aren't you? Relieved that we're fucking divorced so you can move on with your perfect little life while I'm left to deal with the fallout."

Her words strike a nerve and are met by a surge of anger that I push down, refusing to engage with her on that level. "I never wanted things to turn out this way. But our divorce was for the best, for both of us."

"The best for you," she spits out. "Admit it, Dorian. You're seeing someone else, aren't you? You couldn't wait to replace me."

She's thrown the accusation at me before, but tonight, for the first time, it's true. My thoughts drift to Josie, with her sweet, honest face and her pure heart. A wave of protectiveness washes over me. Billie Rae will never accept my new relationship, and I'm grateful that Josie and I will have time to explore our feelings in private before facing the world's scrutiny and my ex's wrath.

I'll have to keep Josie a secret from Billie Rae for as long as possible. My ex is already teetering on the edge, and the truth would push her over. But more than that, I need to protect Josie from this drama.

"Billie," I start, choosing my words carefully. "This isn't about replacing you. It's about moving forward. You and I—we were stuck. Unhappy. You know that."

She crosses her arms. Her posture is defiant, but her eyes show regret—sadness? Is it real? Is she playing me? "We could have worked it out. We could have tried harder."

Guilt gnaws at me. But the endless fighting, the emotional

exhaustion, watching her destroy herself... it had become too much. "I tried, Billie. For years, *I* tried. You're the one who never—"

"Oh, please, not that again." She scoffs, her lips curling in disdain. "Don't try to feed me more crap about rehab. You think I don't know what those places are like? I've seen friends come out worse than they went in. I'm not checking myself into one of those looney bins."

"Billie—"

"I can handle my shit, Dorian," she cuts me off, her voice rising. "A drink here, a pill there—it's nothing I can't control. You always blew everything out of proportion. You never believed in me."

Her stubbornness is a brick wall, impenetrable and unyielding. I once admired that fierce determination, but now it just makes me tired. Deep down, I know she's just scared, but admitting that would mean acknowledging the depth of her problems. She's not ready for that, and maybe she never will be.

"Billie, there's nothing for you here, you need to go."

She sways on her feet, her eyes glassy and unfocused. I search for a glimpse of the vibrant, creative woman she used to be, now buried under layers of anger and intoxication. It breaks my heart to see her like this, but I can't fix her. She has to want to fix herself first.

"I'm not going anywhere until you admit it," she slurs, her voice rising again. "Tell me you're fucking someone else."

I ignore her. "Why did you drive in this state?"

"I'm in no fucking state, you self-righteous prick." Her face twists into an ugly sneer. "And stop acting like you're worried about my safety."

"I *am* fucking worried."

"You never gave a damn about me when we were together. It was always about your music, your career, your fucking ego."

Billie stomps into the nearest flower bed, the heels of her boots snapping stems and crushing the buds into the soil. Broken petals fly everywhere. A good metaphor for what she did to our life together. "Your music is as fake as you are." She spits more venom. "The same old boring chords, the same tired themes."

I let her insults wash over me. It's not the first time she's attacked my music, my character, my soul. But engaging with her when she's high is pointless. It's like trying to reason with a hurricane.

Instead, I discreetly pull out my phone and text her manager, praying he's nearby.

DORIAN

> She's at my house—drove here wasted. Can you come get her? I'm worried she'll hurt herself

As I send the text, Billie is still ranting, her words blurring together in a drunken haze. "You think you're so much better than me, don't you? The great Rian Phoenix, always the fucking saint. Well, guess what? You're as messed up as I am. You're just better at hiding it."

More bushes get destroyed until her manager's car finally pulls up behind hers. As John approaches, Billie whirls around, her eyes wild.

"You called my manager on me? How dare you?"

"You need someone to take you home."

"I don't need your pity," she screams. "I don't need any of you."

She shoves John away, but he takes her arm, guiding her

toward his car. She fights him, her protests growing more incoherent by the second. Finally, he manages to wrestle her into the passenger seat, restrain her with the seat belt, and close the door. He looks up at me.

"She needs help," I say. "It's getting worse."

"I'm trying, man. But until she decides to help herself, there's not much I can do. If you couldn't convince her, how can I?"

John doesn't mean to be accusing or confrontational, but hearing that I wasn't able to help my wife slashes an old wound open in my chest. I'm about to retort that sometimes the people closest to us are those we're least willing to listen to when Billie cranks the car radio of his car to an earsplitting volume.

Her manager sighs. "I'd better take her home before she wakes up the entire neighborhood and we face charges."

I nod, rubbing my temples. "I'll have my driver bring her car back tomorrow."

As John slides into the car beside Billie, I remain rooted on the spot, torn between guilt and a strong sense of relief. But it's a Catch 22. The more relieved I am Billie is no longer my responsibility, the guiltier I feel. I watch until their taillights disappear down the dark road. She's in good hands with her manager, but the sight of her so broken tugs at memories I'd rather forget.

I go to her car and turn it off. My gaze catches on the beads she has wrapped over the rearview mirror. My heart squeezes with the flashback of our first concert in New Orleans when we were still happy. A fan had given the beads to me, I had them over my neck, and she wanted them. I remember her teasingly lifting her top to get them once we were alone in our hotel room. Us making love all night. I shut my eyes against the memory. That person is gone. Doesn't exist anymore.

I seal off my brain before it can go back to the other time we stayed in a hotel in New Orleans. No point in torturing myself.

I slam the door of the car shut and text my driver to take it away tomorrow, then head toward the house, each step heavier and lighter simultaneously. At the front door, I pause and glance down the driveway, half-expecting Billie to reappear—maybe with another desperate plea, an apology, or fresh accusations. But the night is silent, and the only movement is the rustling of leaves in a gentle breeze.

Back out on the patio, I pour myself a bourbon. The amber liquid catches the faint glow of the garden lights as I swirl it in the glass. The color reminds me of Josie's eyes.

Sinking into a chair, I stare out at the glittering cityscape below, willing the alcohol to dull the sharp edges of my emotions. As the tension ebbs away, my thoughts drift more insistently to Josie.

Is she right? Am I on the rebound from Billie? Am I looking for someone who's the exact opposite of my ex-wife as a reaction?

Billie would say I'm after someone plain, someone simple that I can handle while I could never handle her. But there's nothing simple in the way I feel about Josie. It's equally thunderous, only in a positive way. One that makes me happy instead of miserable. That has my heart palpitating with joy instead of despair.

I shouldn't feel guilty for wanting happiness. But I wonder if Billie will ever let me go. If she'll seek to destroy whatever I rebuild.

I take a long sip from my drink, savoring the smooth burn as it slides down my throat. I'll have to protect Josie, whatever it takes. She doesn't deserve to be dragged into the mess of my past. When our relationship finally goes public—and I pray it will—Billie Rae is bound to lash out. Her anger and accusations will be fierce, and the tabloids will eat it up, turning it into front-page news.

I swirl the remaining bourbon in my glass, watching the liquid create a tiny vortex. The thought of Josie being thrust into the spotlight makes my stomach churn. She's a private person, unaccustomed to the relentless scrutiny that comes with being involved with someone like me. Can she handle it? More importantly, can we handle it together?

As I take a last sip and set the empty glass aside, I vow to myself that no matter what Billie Rae does, I won't let her drive away the woman who's brought joy and hope back into my life.

I crave to hear Josie's voice, but I don't want to wake her if she's sleeping. What time does she go to bed? I've no idea whether she's a night owl or an early bird.

I grab my phone and type out a message.

DORIAN

Hey, you awake?

My phone pings right back.

JOSIE

Yep, still up. What's going on?

I grin, picturing her curled up on a couch with a book in her lap. Just the thought of her calms my frayed nerves. I text back.

DORIAN

Mind if I call you?

Instead of a reply, my phone starts buzzing with an incoming call. I smile as I answer, "Hi."

"If this is a booty call, you're about 364 days too early," Josie jokes, her voice warm and light.

I chuckle because even on a night like this, she makes me smile. "Hey, *you* called *me*, so we're both bad at self-restraint tonight."

I keep my tone playful, but something in my voice must give me away.

"What's wrong?" Josie asks, her lighthearted tone replaced with concern.

"Billie Rae showed up at my house. Drunk, high, I don't even know. She was a mess."

The words start pouring out of me, every bitter accusation Billie hurled, every biting remark. I don't hold back, letting Josie see the ugly reality of what I'm dealing with. Of what she's getting herself into.

As I talk, I realize how freeing it feels to confide in someone without worrying about ulterior motives. Josie listens, really listens, without judgment or an agenda. She won't sell my secrets to the press or twist my words against me.

"I'm so sorry you're going through this, Dorian," Josie says when I finally fall silent. "I can't imagine how difficult it must be."

"I feel better already, just being able to talk to you about it. I trust you, Josie. Completely. And that... that means everything to me right now."

A beat of silence follows, then Josie's voice filters through. "I'm here for you, always. We'll get through this together."

Together. Her promise wraps around me and holds me.

I'm tempted to tell Josie everything I feel, to pour out my heart and lay it all on the line. But I don't want to overwhelm her, not when we're both still navigating this new connection between us. Instead, I force a chuckle.

"Well, if we can survive a blackout and an elevator Armageddon, we can handle anything, huh?"

Josie laughs, and the sound washes over me, soothing the jagged edges of my soul like a balm. "You're right. We make a pretty good team."

I hope we do because what's coming won't be easy. But I don't want to think about that now. I need positive vibes, so I change the subject. "What were you up to before I so rudely interrupted with my late-night texts?"

"Oh, I was sketching. I had a random burst of inspiration and had to get it down."

This catches me by surprise. "Wait, you draw? I had no idea."

"More illustrate, digitally. See, this is what I'm talking about," Josie teases. "We still have so much to learn about each other."

"I can't wait to discover all your secrets, Josie Monroe," I reply, meaning it with every fiber of my being.

"Easy tiger. You just used your seduction voice on me," she accuses, but I can hear the smile in her tone.

"My seduction voice?"

"It's the one you switch to in movies any time you're about to kiss someone. All low and husky and sexy as hell."

Now I lower my tone on purpose. "How many times have you watched my movies?"

"I can't answer that."

"Why not?"

"It wouldn't be dignified," she huffs, and I can almost see her biting her lip, her cheeks flushing.

"You get a pass, but only this once." I glance at the time on the screen, stifling a yawn. "Speaking of movies, we should call it a night. We have to be on set early tomorrow."

I'm recording a cameo for a fantasy TV show in Burbank. What I don't mention is the surprise I have in store for her.

"Can't wait to see you in armor."

"Wish I could say the same, the costume is a pain to wear."

"Mmm, but you look wonderful in it on TV. I'm looking forward to a live show." Josie stifles a yawn of her own.

"You're falling asleep on me. I'll let you go. Night, Josie," I murmur, wishing I could pull her close and whisper the words against her hair.

"Night, Dorian," she replies softly before the line goes quiet.

I don't get up right away but linger on the patio, picking up the guitar again, the melody from earlier flowing. I close my eyes and let the music wash over me as I dream about a future where loving someone has no catch. Where a relationship is a two-way street of giving and taking, and not a one-sided drain that sucked away at me until nothing was left but a hollow shell.

22

JOSIE

I show up at the studios early and makeup-free, following Tessa's oddly specific instructions. Good thing, because security takes forever—just like she warned. My ID gets scanned, photocopied, and inspected like I'm here to rob the place, but I keep smiling until they finally wave me through. A studio golf cart whisks me across the lot, weaving past soundstages and trailers.

As we round a corner, another electric cart approaches from the opposite direction. My breath catches when I spot Dorian lounging in the passenger seat next to Tessa. Suddenly, I become self-conscious of my makeup-free face while my body forgets how to regulate, my temperature running hot and cold as everything in me pounds erratically in response to seeing him. I try to rein in my smile, to stay chill. I fail.

Our carts slow, and Dorian's gaze locks with mine. Every detail of him sharpens—his blue eyes, tousled hair, his fingers drumming on his thigh. My senses are heightened. I've turned into a vampire, only I'm not starved for his blood, but for his attention. It's the way he looks at me that keeps me alive.

Even if I wouldn't mind sinking my teeth into his neck and getting a small nibble.

The carts roll to a stop, and Tessa hops out, eyes glued to her phone.

She waves at me. "I'm going to check with production that everything's on schedule. Catch you two later."

Dorian unfolds himself from his seat with the poise of a jungle cat, all lean muscles and coiled energy. I stumble out and don't face-plant at least.

The drivers wave and drive off, leaving us alone in the shade of the massive stage buildings.

Dorian steps closer, a warm smile spreading across his face that makes me forget my insecurities about the lack of makeup.

The urge to run into his arms, to bury my nose in his neck and breathe him in, is overwhelming. But we're in an open space where anyone could spot us. I need to stay professional. So I clench my hands at my sides, resisting the temptation.

"Hey," I pant.

"Hey, beautiful." His voice is honeyed velvet. "First time on a movie set?"

I nod, suddenly shy. "Yes."

"Allow me to do the honors."

With a flourish, he opens the studio door. As I brush past him, my gaze snags on the hair tie around his wrist—mine, the one he stole yesterday. A thrill spikes through me—he's still wearing it.

Dorian catches me looking and winks. Confetti explodes in my belly, and I bite my lip to keep from grinning too wide. I duck my head to hide my smile and walk in.

Inside, the studio buzzes with activity. Crew members dart between rigs, actors rehearse off to the side, producers shout into headsets. The air fizzes with the smells of coffee, paint, and the sharp bite of sawdust. "Overwhelming, isn't it?" Dorian's hand grazes my lower back, his breath tickling my ear.

I nod again, leaning into his touch. We're toeing the line and it's so dangerously thrilling. "It's incredible. I had no idea so much effort went into the show."

"This is only a glimpse." His fingers trail up my spine, leaving goosebumps in their wake. "Wait until you see the rest."

Right. Work. I step away. "I have to meet with the behind-the-scenes director." If I don't move away from him, I'll do something rash. I turn, heading in a random direction, confident I'll find my way once his proximity won't scramble with my brain.

But Dorian's hands drop on my shoulders, stopping me. He stands behind me, his warmth perceivable, even at a distance. It's like my entire back has been flayed, my skin left exposed, burning. He leans in, his breath fanning my neck. "Slight change of plan. You have somewhere else to be."

"I'm pretty sure I have to talk to the director."

I feel his smirk against my ear. "I've asked Tessa to cover that."

"Why?" I tense. "That's my job."

Dorian spins me to face him, his hands gripping my upper arms. I lose a breath at the sudden movement as I find myself staring into his mesmerizing blue eyes. "Because you need to report with the other extras in the costume department."

I blink. "I'm sorry, what?"

"You're going to be in the episode. Surprise."

My jaw drops. Why would he—? *He remembered.* In the elevator, I told him my dream of playing an extra in a movie. That's why Tessa said no makeup.

My rib cage cracks open, and instead of a heart, fireworks shoot sparks through every vein.

"You remembered?" I ask.

He nods. "Production's happy for the free labor, you just have to sign a waiver."

I smile so big I'm afraid my cheeks might split. On impulse, I throw my arms around him, knocking us into a dark corner in a tangle of limbs and need.

It's clumsy, but I don't care, and neither does he seem to. The hug is anything but innocent. If hugs could bite, this one wouldn't just have teeth, it'd have venom-tipped fangs.

My fingers tangle in his hair, and I finally breathe him in, his scent a new addiction I can't resist. Dorian's arms pull me impossibly closer until our bodies are pressed together so tightly that every point of contact is electric with tension. Our noses brush, I can smell the coffee on Dorian's breath. I stare at him, then at his mouth, wanting to drag my teeth over his lower lip. His eyes darken in response.

He leans in closer and his nose grazes my cheekbone before his lips brush against my ear. "Careful, Josie, you look like you're about to kiss me. That's against the rules."

I groan. "This is against the Geneva Convention."

His breath is hot against my skin. "The sweetest torture."

Dorian squeezes me closer before he steps back. My body aches with the absence.

"Go, or you'll miss your big moment."

I nod, chest tight. "Thank you."

I turn to leave, but his hand catches my wrist. Dorian spins me back, his eyes searing into mine.

"Josie, I..." He hesitates. "Break a leg."

I nod again, not trusting my voice, and hurry down the hall before lust frays me like a rope dragged over rough edges, one pass away from snapping.

23

DORIAN

In the dressing room, I shift restlessly as the makeup artist blends smudges of dirt around the fake scar glued to my skin.

A cameraman is filming the behind-the-scenes special, so I pretend the process doesn't bother me.

After what feels like an eternity, she steps back, inspecting her work with a critical eye before nodding in satisfaction. "You're ready."

I thank her and stand.

The costume crew straps me into armor and chain mail that squeaks and tugs in all the wrong places. I adjust the sword strapped to my side and march on set like an armored penguin waddling through medieval hell.

I push past the discomfort, smiling for the ever-present camera and focusing on the scene. Acting is about owning the uncomfortable, right? Still, by the time I reach the main studio, I'm ready to toss the entire outfit into a funeral pyre.

The set for today's shoot is a grand banquet hall. Long, wooden tables, goblets, tapestries, iron chandeliers.

The air is thick with the mingling scents of leather, a whiff of glue from freshly assembled set pieces, and the faint tang of sweat from the bustling crew—or maybe it's me who smells. I'd lift my arm to sniff my armpit, but the armor limits my movements. Hoping my BO is under control, I sweep the room, searching for Josie.

The extras are milling to one side in their period attire. I check each face until I find Josie, blending in yet standing out. She's acting casual, but her excitement shows in the way her eyes dart around the set, soaking in every detail.

She hasn't seen me yet, giving me a precious few moments to drink in the sight of her.

Half her hair falls in soft waves down her back, while two thick braids frame her face and cross on top of her head. Her gown is a deep-purple velvet embroidered with gold and leaves her shoulders bare. My fingers curl around the hilt of my sword as my eyes settle on her pale collarbones that stand out against the dark color of the fabric. I study her face next. Her lips are painted a muted pink. That is the same mouth that almost kissed me earlier.

The knowledge that I can't touch her—not yet—hurts more than the chain mail digging into my shoulders.

When she finally spots me, her smile pierces straight through my breastplate and stops my heart. I grin back, nodding in what I hope may appear as a casual greeting and not the look of a drowning man gasping for air.

I want to go to her but the director's voice booms through a megaphone. "Alright everyone, gather around."

I reluctantly tear my eyes from my damsel, focusing on the instructions for the upcoming takes.

When the scene starts, I wait off-camera, blind to the hall and everything unfolding inside. Until an assistant director hisses, "Go."

I storm into the studio, cloak billowing, armor clanking, and stop on my mark, bowing. "Your Grace, we were led astray," I begin in an urgent tone as I bow respectfully. "The enemy is on the march. They'll reach the gates by dawn."

The hall erupts into choreographed chaos, but it barely registers. I have eyes only for her. Josie sits quietly as her role demands, but her eyes betray her. The poised, modest mask her character should wear slips as her eyes burn for me.

I lose my next line.

"Cut," the director snaps. "Focus, Phoenix. Take it from the top." He twirls his finger in the air.

The others reset, but Josie keeps her eyes downcast as she smooths her skirts.

Her expression has shifted, the hunger replaced with something smaller, tighter—remorse? I will her to look at me. She must sense my plead because she finally meets my gaze, guilt etched all over her face. I shake my head almost imperceptibly. *It's okay*, I want to tell her. I can't blame her for looking at me like that, not when it's exactly how I feel.

She nods, and I smile, striding out of the set, ready to get back into character.

The next take, I don't let myself look at her. I deliver my lines with precision, and when the director yells, "Cut," he sounds satisfied. But as the scene wraps, Josie rushes to me.

"I'm so sorry. I didn't mean to mess up your first take. I just" —I hold up a hand to stop her, but she continues, her words rushing out in a torrent—"got caught up in watching you and didn't think you'd notice."

"I always notice." I lower my voice. "But don't worry, you were the best distraction."

She starts to reply, but the assistant director calls, "Extras back to first positions." Josie has to stay also for the next scene.

Before she goes, I tuck a strand of hair behind her ear, letting my fingers linger.

As I step out of the set, I glance over my shoulder. She's watching me, hand pressed to her cheek.

Then she's swept back into the scene, and I walk away, already counting down the minutes until I can steal another moment with her.

24

JOSIE

The hallway outside the women extras' dressing room is a tangle of actors and crew. I'm exhausted but still thrumming, as if I'd plugged myself into an open socket and got charged by the surreal experience of being on a TV show.

My phone vibrates with a text.

DORIAN

Have you forsaken your knight in shining armor?

I smile, amazed that he's already washed off the fake mud and blood. It feels like I just got to the studio, but it's been hours. The scene Dorian wasn't in dragged on.

JOSIE

Isn't patience a knightly virtue?

His typing bubbles pop up, but I reach his dressing room before his reply is delivered.

I knock, and Dorian opens the door, freshly showered and relaxed in a plain T-shirt and jeans. His damp hair falls in tousled waves, so sexy the lust fairies themselves must've styled it.

He looks maddeningly good, the kind of handsome that short-circuits my brain.

Despite his undeniable charm also in civilian clothes, part of me mourns the armor. Earlier, when he stormed into the hall, he was a hero straight out of a fairy tale—or a smutty romantasy novel. Even the fake scar carved into his cheekbone turned me on. I would've kissed him in a heartbeat, mud and all.

He leans against the doorframe. "Why are you still looking at me like that? The armor's gone."

I plant my palms on his chest and push him into the dressing room, kicking the door shut behind me with my foot. We're finally alone, protected from prying eyes. "But the memories are not."

He catches a loose lock from my medieval updo and lets it fall through his fingers. "Is that why you've kept your hair like this? To torture me?"

I smile, still jacked up with adrenaline. "I would've kept the gown too, but they made me give it back." I turn serious now. "Thank you, Dorian. Today was a dream come true. Being treated like a royal, even if it was all pretend... it felt surreal."

He mock-bows. "I am your loyal subject, my lady. Here to serve." He straightens, opening his arms. "Come here."

I go to him, the contact growing more familiar yet no less exhilarating. I press my cheek to his chest, listening to the steady rhythm of his heartbeat.

"If the elevator was in the top ten of your life experiences, how does today rank?"

I pull back my head, fisting the soft fabric of his T-shirt. "You're in a solid top eight."

He beams down at me. "What gets me in the top five?"

Without hesitation, I bury my face into the crook of his neck again. "Just keep holding me."

Dorian kisses the top of my head. "I can do that."

After soaking in his warmth and filling my lungs with his scent, I reluctantly pull back.

"I've already missed too much work today." I flash him an apologetic smile. "I have to prep the press for your interview and check in with Tessa about the behind-the-scenes special." I frown as a sudden thought strikes me. She must've thought it was weird to do my job today. I hope she doesn't resent me. "Does she know about us?"

"Tessa's chill. She knows you're a friend from the elevator. And we all cover for each other sometimes."

"Okay, I'll go thank her and tell her I owe her one."

Dorian tilts his head. "Of course, go be responsible. But." He pauses as he grabs another lock of my hair and lets it flow through his fingers. "Have dinner with me tonight?"

"I can't." I sigh. "I have to be at my mom's. The Monroe women get together once a week."

He quirks an eyebrow. "Are men banned from these sacred gatherings?"

A sudden, all-consuming sadness grips my heart. "There are no men left." I swallow, fighting the familiar lump in my throat. "Daniel died. My parents have been divorced for twenty years. I call us the Monroe women, but I'm actually the only one. Mom went back to her maiden name five minutes after signing the papers and has refused to live with another man ever since. Aunt Moira doesn't believe in marriage. She's still living in the seventies and isn't seeing anyone right now. And Lily has kept Daniel's name and given up on romance after losing him."

Dorian's hand finds my elbow, his touch grounding me, steadying me.

"My family is not a beacon of happily ever afters," I add with a faint, self-deprecating laugh.

He gives my arm a gentle squeeze. "I'm sorry, Josie."

I shrug. "It's life. We're doing okay, all considered. These dinners help."

He's thoughtful for a beat, then says, "So, let me come."

Something pinches in my heart at the eagerness in his voice. "You want to meet my family?"

He juts out his lower lip in a pout that's both cute and devastating. "Why not? I'm great at meeting the parents. Sandy Parker's mom still sends me a card every Christmas."

"That's adorable. Do you send her a signed headshot in return?"

He grabs me by the hips and nuzzles my neck. "Always with the sass."

I laugh at the tickling sensation while also going hot in several places. I flash him a goofy grin. "And yet, here you are, asking for more."

"I am."

Dorian is so blunt, so unapologetic. His directness makes my heart trip all over the place. "My family is intense. Are you sure you want to meet them?"

He doesn't even blink. "Yes."

I'm about to say okay, but then I frown. "Wait, how can you go to a regular person's house?"

Dorian's eyes crinkle. "I'm not a vampire, Josie, I won't even need to be invited in to cross the threshold."

I scold him, suppressing a smile. "Be serious. We can't have paparazzi swarming my mom's house. Or anyone know about us."

"If you want me to come, I can manage that part." He gives

my sides a little squeeze. "I'll just need some basic information about the layout."

"Of course I want you to come."

His gaze turns searching. "Can your family keep a secret?"

I consider it, then nod. "If you handle the security side, I'll take care of my family's big mouths."

"Then it's settled." Dorian grins in a way that makes my insides melt. "I'll be there."

I extricate myself from his arms but don't make it halfway across the dressing room before he grabs my hand and pulls me back.

Pop Rocks light up in my belly as he presses a soft kiss to the pulse point on my wrist.

"I can't wait."

"Me too," I breathe back, my vocal cords not cooperating.

On impulse, I get up on tiptoe and stamp a quick peck on his cheek, then flee the dressing room before I kiss him again, and not so innocently this time. As I walk down the hall, I rub my wrist where his lips have left an invisible brand. If mere hugs and pecks to the wrist have this effect on me, what will a real kiss do?

* * *

A few hours later, I'm marching in front of my family like a lieutenant before her battalion. Mom, Lily, Aunt Moira, and Penny sit lined up on the couch, watching me with varying degrees of amusement.

For the third time, I repeat, "You cannot tell anyone I'm sort of dating Rian Phoenix."

Aunt Moira huffs as she turns to my mom. "Betty, darling, show me a picture of this man."

Mom pulls out her phone and shows Moira. My aunt lets out a low whistle. "I don't understand, sweetie. If he wants to bang you, and you want to bang him, why aren't you two banging?"

Lily covers Penny's ears, but my niece wriggles free. "Mommy, what does banging mean?"

"It means... Aunt Josie's boyfriend is a musician, and they'd like to play the drums together." Lily shoots Moira a disapproving look.

Moira waves that off. "Josie, you're wasting your prime. If I had a man like that—"

"You'd scare him off before the appetizers," I mutter.

"Appetizers? Honey, I'd skip straight to dessert."

Penny perks up. "Can I skip to dessert, too?"

Lily sighs. "Not until you're eighteen, sweetie."

Moira taps her chin, still eyeing the photo. "Does this gentleman have a brother? Or better yet, a father?"

The doorbell saves me from having to reply. I shoot them a look. "Be good," I warn and head for the door.

I can't believe I'm about to introduce Dorian to my crazy, lovable, unpredictable family. Taking a deep breath, I paste on a smile and open the door.

25

DORIAN

Ned drives me to Josie's childhood house while I lie flat in the back seat not to be spotted. I straighten up only when we park in front of the attached garage and pull a baseball cap low on my head as I exit the car.

The yard is neat—trimmed lawn, potted plants, and two flowerbeds at the end of the concrete driveway. Unbidden, my mind flickers to the trampled flowerbeds at my place. The ones the gardeners still have to fix after Billie ravaged them last night. I push the thought away. Tonight isn't about my ex-wife. It's about Josie, about showing her we can have normal things.

As I take in the house, I wonder what it was like for Josie to grow up here, what parts of this place shaped the woman who's waiting inside.

I close the car door, eager to find out. I wave at Ned as he drives away and head to the front door. I linger on the porch, as jittery as a teenager about to confess his first crush, and finally ring the bell.

Josie comes to open it with her hair still in the medieval braids from this morning—*damn her*—but she's now wearing one of her milkmaid dresses. The style makes her a cross between a fairy-tale princess and the girl next door. And I'm afraid I can't resist either version.

She glances past me, presumably scanning for any sign of cameras. "You weren't followed?"

"No, we were careful. No one knows I'm here." I give her a reassuring smile.

"Hurry in before someone sees you." Josie steps aside to let me in, warning, "And brace yourself, Moira is springy tonight."

I step inside, and the house envelops me in its cozy warmth. Family photos line the walls, a small table holds a bowl of keys and a stack of mail, and the savory scent of home cooking wafts in from the kitchen.

Josie leads me into the living room where her family is gathered. Eager to make a good first impression, I remove my cap, rake a hand through my hair, and put on my most charming smile.

A lady with long white hair dressed in a colored kaftan approaches me, enveloping me in a hug so enthusiastic it's alarming. Aunt Moira, I suspect. Her hands linger on my lower back, skating dangerously close to inappropriate territory. She doesn't quite squeeze my ass, but it's a narrow escape. I suppress a smirk at the borderline groping as Josie rolls her eyes.

"Easy, Moira," Josie says, exasperated.

Her aunt winks and pats my cheek. "He's even better looking in person," she declares, eyeing me appreciatively.

One vote in my favor.

Josie introduces me to the others.

Her mom, Betty, greets me first with a firm handshake, her no-nonsense demeanor softened by a friendly smile. "It's wonderful to meet you, Dorian."

"The pleasure is all mine."

Lily's hug is short but kind, her hazel eyes assessing.

While Penny looks up at me with wide eyes. "You're very tall," she states matter-of-factly.

I crouch down to her level, grinning. "And you're very observant." I tap her nose lightly.

Penny beams, pleased with herself, while Josie's eyes shine at seeing me interact with her niece. And her admiration makes me feel a bit like I also am a kid being patted on the head.

As we take our places at the dinner table, Moira insists on sitting next to me, claiming she has to "inspect the merchandise" more closely. Penny pipes up, securing the spot on my other side. I'm caught between amusement and mild apprehension as I settle into my chair with the youngest and oldest women flanking me.

Lily pats my shoulder as she passes me on the way to take her seat. "If you can keep up with my daughter's questions, you'll be her new favorite person."

I grin in response, silently noting the unspoken sadness that lingers behind her eyes. Across the table, Josie slides into a chair opposite me, leaning forward to whisper, "Blink twice if you need rescuing."

I suppress a grin, feeling oddly at ease despite being in a room filled with new people.

Dinner begins with Moira passing me a dish of roasted corn. "Careful, it's spicy. I hope you like chili powder. It's an aphrodisiac."

I manage a straight-faced, "Ah. Good to know."

Josie smiles, mouthing, "Blink twice."

Being with her family feels like stepping into a past life, one filled with home-cooked meals and warmth I haven't known in years. They all welcome me. Betty beams when I compliment the food, and the banter flows easily. Penny asks me to cut her chicken and not-so-subtly brings up my tattoos, telling me the princes in Josie's stories have ink, too. I catch Josie staring at my forearms, and Moira notices too. She almost tells us to quit with the eye-fucking, but Lily stops her in time, playing referee. I've missed this dynamic, this sense of being part of a loving family. My mom was the glue that kept me and my dad together. Since she's passed, we've been drifting further and further apart.

As the meal winds down, the lively chatter fades into the satisfied silence of full stomachs. A wave of nostalgia hits me. This is the kind of evening I didn't realize I missed—warm, affectionate, unfiltered.

I help Lily clear the plates, deftly dodging another of Moira's thinly veiled innuendos. In the kitchen, Josie's sister surprises me by saying, "You held up well under fire. For someone who sings to screaming crowds, you're surprisingly laid-back."

I smirk. "Don't tell anyone, though. It'll ruin my brand."

"Your secret's safe with us." Lily's eyes hold mine, and I know she's really referring to keeping my relationship with Josie private. "Just don't break her heart, please."

The tentative trust in her stare strikes me harder than the words themselves. I nod in response. A silent promise I intend to keep.

Ten minutes later, I'm hugging everyone goodbye. Moira doesn't let me go until Josie comes to the rescue and maneuvers us to the back porch for a private goodbye. As we walk out, Josie's hand finds mine, our fingers intertwining as she smiles radiantly. I'd attend a thousand family dinners, answer a million awkward questions, and manage as many handsy aunts to keep that smile on her face.

"Thanks for inviting me," I say, leaning against the railing. "I know it was a leap to do it so soon."

She smiles. "You invited yourself over, rockstar."

I tug the ribbon at the top of her dress, undoing the bow slowly. Josie goes still, breath catching as the bow slips free. "Wish I hadn't?"

"No, you were perfect. Everyone's charmed."

I grin, stepping closer. "Including you?"

Her eyes meet mine, sparkling brighter than the stars above. "Yes, including me."

The urge to close the distance between us and taste her lips is overwhelming. But the sound of my car pulling up in the yard breaks the spell. I hesitate, then step back with a soft, "Goodnight, Josie."

She puts my baseball cap on my head. "Night, Dorian."

We circle the house together, but can't even hug in a space so exposed.

She mouths, "Drive safe."

I nod and climb in the back seat, watching Josie as she stands in the driveway, her arms wrapped around herself against the cool night air, as the car pulls away.

Once we're on the road, I lean my head back against the seat, closing my eyes. Tonight was a glimpse into a life I never thought I could have—messy, loud, *real*. And now, more than ever, I want it. I want her.

But I'm not the one who has to put everything on the line to make it happen. When the time comes, when Josie will have to choose between me and her career, between me and her anonymity—her family's privacy—will she think I'm worth the price?

I hope she will because I'd give it all up for her.

26

JOSIE

The day after Dorian meets my family, I drive to Inglewood, where he has a rehearsal for the VMAs. *The freaking VMAs.* He has to perform for the opening ceremony next Wednesday, and I'll get to be backstage. I only ever watched the awards on TV, and now I'm dating—sort of—the major star. Whenever I remember how famous Dorian is, it blows my mind.

The giant indoor arena looms ahead as I pull up in the parking lot and kill the engine. I check my watch. I'm earlier than I need to be. Should I wait in the car? Nah. Dorian is performing in there, and I don't want to miss a single note.

The hot concrete radiates through my sandals as I approach the massive building. Getting inside is disorienting, the blazing sunlight snuffed out in dim light, the air instantly cooler. And the backstage corridors are a confusing tangle of dead ends and identical doors. It's a maze. After a few wrong turns, I finally stop to ask a staffer for directions.

The young woman, wearing a headset and holding a clipboard, gives me a once-over, and I suddenly feel conscious of my outfit—jeans and a T-shirt with Dorian's first album cover on it. She could assume I'm some crazed fan, but instead of calling security, she eyes my pass and smiles.

"Follow me."

She leads me through the labyrinthine hallways, and I take mental notes of the turns so I don't get lost again. We pass various backstage areas, until finally, the staffer opens a door and gestures for me to enter.

I step through and my breath catches. The auditorium is massive, with endless rows of empty seats that circle the stage. The arena floor is a good hundred yards away, but as I hop down the steps in the center aisle, I can pick out Dorian on the platform, joking with the band.

I take him in from a distance as I keep walking. It's impossible to reconcile the easygoing man who had dinner with my family last night with the legend standing on stage now. He's wearing an intricately embroidered black velvet vest, left open over his muscular chest and abs, paired with fitted, leather pants detailed with side lacing that crisscrosses along his thighs. The outfit is edgy, rebellious, and so far removed from the Dorian I'm getting used to, it leaves me momentarily stunned.

He looks different up on set. Taller, more imposing. The spotlights give his dark hair a glossy sheen, and his trademark smirk is in full effect. This is the Rian Phoenix the world knows —the rock god. It's a little surreal because to me he's just... Dorian. The guy who keeps a stack of worn paperbacks by his bed and gives great hugs.

Dorian turns mid-laugh, as if sensing my arrival, just as I hop off the last step. When his gaze lands on me, the warmth in his grin shifts into something more intimate, only mine. My heart was spinning like a wheel while I watched him unnoticed.

But his sudden focus is a crowbar in the spokes that brings the poor organ to a jarring halt and sends it slamming into my ribs.

Dorian waves me over, gives a nod to the band to take five, and steps to the edge of the platform, squatting down.

"Hi," I breathe, hesitantly stepping forward until I'm looking up into those icy-blue eyes from under the stage.

Dorian leans down, resting his forearms on his knees. "Hey, beautiful, did you come to steal the show? Should I warn the band to pack up?"

A grin breaks across my face, wide and unrestrained, making my cheeks ache in the best way. Gosh, he's so cheesy sometimes—and I love it.

"Only if stealing the show involves tripping over a mic cord. The band can stay."

Dorian tilts his head. "Does the idea of tripping on cords always make you smile like that, or am I having an exceptionally good hair day?"

His hair is intentionally disheveled like always to give him that just-rolled-out-of-bed sexy vibe he "rocks" so well. But today, my gaze drifts lower to the tantalizing strip of skin visible between the lapels of his vest and the waistband of his low-slung pants. Then back up, taking in his broad shoulders and muscular, bare arms. "It's more the display of muscles and bad-boy leathers than the hair..."

When I meet his gaze again, I notice his eyes are rimmed in black, the eyeliner accentuating their unnatural brightness, making the crystalline blue of his irises seem otherworldly. I swallow my initial reaction, determined not to look completely smitten. And fight to keep a straight face as I tease him about it. "Uh, and I finally get to see the guyliner."

Dorian hops off the stage, landing in front of me with a soft thud. "Glad you approve." He widens his arms, letting the vest fall open a little more as he flexes his abs. "Though, let's be honest, it's hard not to."

I shake my head, still beaming. "I don't know what's worse, that you said that or that you can get away with it."

His smirk deepens as he takes a slow step closer. I feel like prey being stalked. "Something else I can get away with today?"

I lift my eyebrows in mock-suspicion. "Like what?"

Dorian shrugs, feigning nonchalance. "I'd take anything... how about a good-luck kiss before the show?"

I shift my stance at the fluttering in my stomach as if I could physically sidestep his suggestion. "That's against the rules, and this is a rehearsal."

"Always so strict." His voice is velvet—pure temptation. It lands somewhere deep in my core where someone must've started melting honey, a warm gooeyness spreading everywhere. "Weren't you supposed to get here after the sound check? You're early. Couldn't wait to see me?"

I narrow my eyes, determined not to let him fluster me further. "Actually, I was hoping Harry Styles would show up."

Dorian's bark of laughter echoes through the empty auditorium. "Aww, below the belt, Josie."

Before I can reply with another witty comeback, his drummer hollers, "Rian! We're ready when you are!"

Dorian turns his head, nodding at the band, before glancing back at me. "Duty calls. They never let me have any fun."

With a gallant gesture, he motions toward the front row. "VIP seating for my number-one critic. Try not to be too harsh, yeah?"

I point at my T-shirt. "I'm more your number-one fan."

Dorian covertly blows me a kiss and hops back on stage. And I sink into the seat he gestured to. The music starts with a jarring crash of drums and a bold guitar riff that immediately demands attention. Dorian grabs the mic and his eyes land on me. He's making me his sole focus in a stadium meant for thousands.

When his voice cuts through the music, it's a shock to my system. His timbre is rough but controlled, deep, a visceral blend of gravel and heat. No softness here, only intensity and grit, and yet it feels vulnerable in its boldness, as if he's laying himself bare through his art. The sound vibrates in my chest, rattling something loose inside me, and I'm left clinging to every word, entranced as he keeps singing just for me.

Without the added confusion of an audience, his raw talent is too much for me to take. The stripped-down performance leaves me even more awestruck. More in love, if that's possible. The way he pours his heart into every lyric, how his body moves with the rhythm—it's mesmerizing.

The fact that he keeps singing every soul-baring note while looking straight at me doesn't help. But it's not just about how beautiful he is or the way his voice curls around my spine to wring me tighter and tighter. I'm captivated by the discipline of his team and the way the band works together as they cycle through multiple repetitions of the medley until every note is perfect. What may appear as an effortless performance is a carefully honed craft built on repetition, mutual trust, and a grind so impeccable it becomes invisible.

As the last notes of the song fade, Dorian's eyes remain locked on mine. I can't take any more, but I also can't look away.

My heart races as he jogs off the stage and strides toward me. "So, what's the verdict? Did I pass the audition?"

I play it cool, despite the butterflies wreaking havoc in my stomach. "Hmm, I don't know. I might need to hear a few more songs before I make my decision."

Dorian smirks. "Love a challenge, Monroe." He glances back

at the platform, where technicians are switching over the staging. "We're rehearsing the last part of the number soon. In the meantime, want to check out the snacks table? It's pretty lavish."

I nod, getting up on legs that are still shaky from watching his performance. We approach the sawhorse table covered with a paper towel, and I snag a couple of mini-donuts. Dorian, meanwhile, pours himself a cup of coffee, basically inhaling it.

"Thirsty much?" I joke.

"Caffeine is the only thing that keeps me standing during these long days."

I chuckle, taking a bite of my donut. "I thought rockstars thrived on chaos and sleep deprivation."

"Not really."

His eyes are wary. I'm not sure if it's because of what happened with Billie and her choice of lifestyle. But I hope his love of music will never be soured because when he performs, he's a gift to the world.

"Dorian, you're amazing at what you do. Your voice, your songs, the way you take control of the stage. I couldn't tear my eyes from you."

"You might be a teensy bit biased." I'm about to protest when he shrugs, adding, "And it didn't always come this easy. Practice makes perfect."

But I insist, "No, seriously. You were incredible."

"You should've seen me when I started out."

It pains me that I didn't know him back then.

Dorian pops a mini pretzel in his mouth and speaks between chews. "The first time I opened for another band in a stadium filled with thousands of people, I almost peed my pants."

I can't help but grin. "So, is bladder control the secret to stage presence?"

He laughs, a rich sound that ricochets down my spine, sparking little bursts of happiness. "Don't tell anyone, or I'll have to kidnap you and take you on tour with me."

The idea of being whisked away by Dorian, of spending long days and nights on the road with him, has all kinds of sensations zigzagging through my stomach. I act bolder than I feel. "Is that a threat or a promise?"

His eyes darken, and he leans in closer. "How about both?"

I study the spread of assorted provisions. "If the snacks are always this impressive, count me in."

He grabs another mini pretzel. "Should've known food was my best way to here." Dorian pokes a finger over my heart. The touch is brief, gentle, barely there... but it prompts shortness of breath and palpitations. Either I'm having a cardiac arrest, or he doesn't need any food to get into my heart. He's already lodged in like a stubborn fragment of glass. Every glance, every touch cutting deeper, hurting sweeter.

"Food is the way to anyone's heart." I attempt to sound like his hand on me didn't almost make me collapse.

"Is that so? I always thought the way to a woman's heart was something more complicated. Like poetry or, I don't know, writing *a love song*?" He arches a seductive eyebrow at me.

"Are you only listing things you excel at?"

He drags his teeth over his lower lip, sucking it in while shooting me a playful, heated side look. "I thought muscles and tattoos were my best flex."

And as much as I want to tease him back, this time, I don't. "Except they're not."

"No?"

"I love the smudges of ink on your fingers after you write lyrics more than I love your abs." I drop my gaze to his waist-band. "Which is saying something because that is a pretty perfect six-pack. And I love the absorbed look in your eyes when you're creating. The best parts of you are the ones you don't let everyone see. How you notice the little things, like when I need a hug but I can't talk about what's making me cry."

The playful spark in his eyes dims, replaced by something more contemplative. I carry on.

"And how you remember the stupid details I tell you, like my secret dream of being an extra in a movie that you made come true. Those are the parts that matter."

Dorian's eyes darken at my words and his throat bobs, but he doesn't acknowledge what I said. Instead, he says, "Have dinner with me tonight. I'd like you all to myself for one evening."

"Meeting the family was too much last night?"

Dorian shakes his head. "Not at all. I just want more silly things to remember. Learn more of your dreams to make come true. I want in here." He pats my chest again, unaware that his hand is the flint and my heart the steel that strikes against it. "I'm greedy," he confesses, "for every piece of you, the shy smiles and the cutting comebacks. You were the only person able to pull a laugh out of me when I thought I had none left. I want to be with you *always*. I want to be at your family dinners, and I want your solo nights. I want everything, Josie."

Another word and I'll give it to him. Even what I don't have.

"You know there are less intense ways to ask a gal to dinner."

Dorian throws his head back and laughs. "Right, I shouldn't take myself too seriously."

But as he looks at me it's clear he's still waiting for an answer.

I hesitate, my expression apologetic as I explain, "I can't tonight. I'm watching Penny while Lily works a night shift at the hospital."

"Can I have tomorrow night, then?"

I agree, relieved that he's not put off by my responsibilities. "Tomorrow is perfect."

Just then, Dorian is called back to rehearsal. He walks on stage while I return to the empty first row.

And as Dorian takes his place behind the microphone once more, I brace for my soul to get a little more scorched.

27

DORIAN

I stand in the stillness of my kitchen, waiting for her. The staff have been dismissed for the evening. Everything is ready. I check my watch again. She's not late, but the anticipation gnaws at me.

I walk to the French doors leading to the back patio and pull them open, welcoming the gentle breeze that rustles my hair. The table is set, understated but elegant. The appetizers arranged with care. I considered lighting a hundred candles, but in the end, decided to keep it simple. I don't want to overwhelm Josie.

The fairy lights strung above twinkle like distant stars. *They're enough*, I tell myself. I straighten a fork, making sure everything is perfect. Even if perfection isn't what she's after. It's not what I'm looking for, either. I tilt the fork back at the previous weird angle.

Before I move more stuff that doesn't need readjusting, I return to the kitchen and lean against the counter, arms crossed. Checking my watch again, I fight the urge to pace as the minutes crawl by with agonizing slowness until finally, security alerts me my guest has arrived.

I practically skip to the other side of the house, drying my palms against my jeans. One last inhale, and I swing the door open.

Josie shifts shyly under the warm porch light, stealing the ability to speak from me. She's breathtaking. Her hair is in her favorite style, half up with loose waves cascading over her shoulders, and she's wearing a simple white dress that cinches at the waist, falling above her knees. The fabric sways in the breeze, held up only by maddeningly thin straps. I'm transfixed.

The lingering scrutiny must give away my thoughts seeing how she's blushing when I finally meet her gaze.

"Hi," Josie says, eyes sparkling.

I step forward and wrap her in a hug. She leans into me without hesitation, her arms sliding around my waist, and I allow myself to inhale the salty, floral scent of her shampoo.

"I'm glad you're here." My lips graze the shell of her ear. "I missed you."

"Me too," she whispers, looking up at me. "I couldn't wait to see you."

"I might need to give you more work," I tease, dropping my hand to the small of her back as I guide her across the house. "I can't go another day without an excuse to see you."

Josie beams up at me, her smile radiant. "Are you canceling the last part of the tour and haven't told me?"

"No. But it's the least excited I've been to be on the road in a long time. I hate that I'm leaving right after the VMAs, so soon after reconnecting with you."

A small, shy nod is her only response. As we step on the patio, Josie's eyes light up even more as she takes in the romantic setting.

"Dorian, this is…" She trails off, seemingly at a loss for words. I pull out her chair, and she sits, smiling as she surveys the spread of appetizers. "This is amazing," she finally manages.

"I have to turn on the oven for the main course." I step back. "Don't steal the good stuff while I'm gone."

Josie's answering laugh follows me into the house. When I return a few minutes later with a pitcher of iced water, I stop mid-step. Josie freezes, wide-eyed, caught red-handed with a half-eaten stuffed mushroom in her hand.

"I couldn't help it," she mumbles around the bite, her cheeks adorably puffed with food. "I'm starving."

I set the pitcher down, shaking my head in mock-disapproval. "Did you eat something sensible for lunch, or was it snacks out of your bag again?"

Josie swallows her bite, her expression shifting to sheepishness. "Guilty," she admits. "I wanted to catch up with my tech clients and didn't take a lunch break."

"One day," I say, sitting by her side at the round table so we both have a view, "I'm confiscating the purse food. Consider it an intervention."

She laughs. "Good luck prying it away from me. I might bite."

"I might like it." I wink at her, then pour her a glass of water she looks like she could use, seeing how she's coughing after my teasing comment.

Once she's recovered, I move the appetizers closer to her. "Let's make sure you don't starve tonight, at least."

Josie pops another canapé in her mouth whole, moaning as she bites down on it. That sound does weird things to my chest, and I grab the table so hard my knuckles turn white.

It's good to wait, I remind myself. Not to throw the entire

spread of food on the floor, sit Josie on the table, and feast on her instead.

I shake the mental image away, not what tonight is about. Tonight is about getting to know each other better.

"Tell me about your art." I take a sip of water to cool the heat spreading through my body. "Have you always had a passion for drawing? What were you illustrating the other night when I called?"

The question earns me a big smile and a dance of freckles. "After telling Penny a bedtime story, I went home and felt this urge to bring it to life. The characters were begging me to give them form."

"For me, it's the same with songs. What was the story about?"

She glances down at her plate with a nonchalant shrug. "Merpeople."

"Ah. Was a tattooed merman included, by any chance?"

Josie groans, covering her face with her hands. "Ugh, Penny and her big mouth. I swear, that girl…"

"I should spend more time with your niece." I wipe my mouth on the cloth napkin before taking another sip of water. "Get all the dirt on her favorite aunt."

"Do you really mean that? My family wasn't too much the other night?"

I take her hand in mine, my thumb caressing her knuckles. "Josie, it was great to meet everyone. Honestly, I didn't realize how much I missed being part of a family until I was with yours." I pause, unsure if I should go on. But that's why we're here. To learn these things about each other. The good. The ugly. So I give her everything. "The past two years, I've been pretty lonely."

Her expression softens, and she squeezes my hand. "I'm sorry, Dorian."

The timer on my phone sounds, reminding me it's time to take the main course out of the oven. Reluctantly, I stand up, but not before leaning in close to Josie. With a gentle tap on her nose, I whisper, "I'm not lonely anymore."

As I walk towards the kitchen, I can sense her gaze on me. Knowing she's here, in my space, feels dangerously close to the thing I didn't think I'd have again... a home. I turn my head over my shoulder and find her eyes glued to my—*ass*.

So much for my soppy nonsense. Trust her to knock me off balance with a look and somehow make me enjoy it.

I swivel my hips in an exaggerated shimmy. "You like the view, Monroe? Should I give you the full show?"

"Woo-hoo," she cat-calls. "I'll be waiting with my one-dollar bills."

I spin around dramatically. "One dollar? I'm worth at least fives."

"I'd tip more, but I hear you're already rolling in platinum records."

I'm smiling like an idiot the entire time I'm in the kitchen.

When I take out the potato-crusted halibut, the aroma of herbs and garlic follows me outside. I set the dish on the table and scoop a generous portion for Josie.

She laughs as I hand her the plate. "Dorian, I'm not *that* starved!" Despite her protest, she devours the first few bites like a castaway on a desert island.

"Good, huh?"

"Terrible," Josie says around a mouthful. "The worst thing I've ever eaten. You should fire your chef. And I should take any leftovers off of you, for your well-being."

I chuckle. "I'll pass along your harsh critique."

As we eat and talk about all and nothing, Josie's gaze keeps drifting to the tattoos on my arms.

It happens again, and again, each glance lingering longer. Is she fascinated? Does she find the ink excessive? Or maybe... she's turned on?

"You really have a thing for my tattoos, don't you?"

"I'm obsessed," she deadpans, and I've no idea if she's joking. "I want to know the story behind each one."

Not joking, then.

And I want to share them with her. Each tattoo is a piece of me, a visible timeline of who I am and what I've been through. "We might not get through them all tonight, but we can start. Which one do you want to know about first?"

"What does the line of text on your ribs say? I've wanted to read it since the photoshoot."

Ah, she always goes straight for the throat, catching me at my most vulnerable.

I lean back and lift my T-shirt, revealing the inscription. Josie's eyes snag on it, drinking me in more ravenously than when she was staring at the food.

"It's a lyric from the song I wrote about my mom," I explain softly. "'You let me borrow your wings, so I could fly.'"

Josie's fingertips trace the words. The unexpected contact sets my skin on fire, and it takes every ounce of my self-control not to start purring like an overeager tomcat.

"That line is beautiful," she whispers, slowly retreating her hand.

I let my shirt fall back down, the fabric a poor substitute for her electric touch. "Which one's next?"

Josie shifts her chair to face me and reaches for my wrists. And I mirror her, angling my chair so the table is no longer between us. Her hand trails, featherlight, up my arms, exploring with both her eyes and fingertips. I struggle to keep still, caught between wanting the not-enough touch to end and wishing it could last forever.

Her fingers graze over my left forearm, following the dark, intricate linework that coils over my skin. As she moves higher, the design changes. The sharp geometry softens into curling vines, delicate leaves, and large, blooming roses.

"Why all the thorns?"

"Sometimes, my inspiration comes from things that cut deep."

"So tormented, rockstar. Do you ever sing about things that don't hurt?"

"Yes."

"Will I ever get a song?"

I laugh, not ready to tell her how many of my latest songs are already about her. "Be a good girl, and maybe you'll get an entire album."

She drags her nails lightly over my skin, just enough to turn me insane. "So, I can't be even a little bad?"

"Oh, you can. But then I'd have to write a very different kind of song. Not sure I could release it."

She shrugs. "I don't mind private performances."

"I know."

She blushes at that and looks away. I love how she's sassy but almost always falls back into shyness. Her attention drifts to my inner wrist, where she follows the loops of a small treble clef. "And this one?"

"It was my first tattoo," I confess. "A simple nod to music."

She keeps holding my hand and looks up at me. "I can imagine a younger version of you, impatient to get it done as soon as you turned eighteen."

"That's exactly what happened." I smile, the memory bittersweet. "My mom wasn't thrilled about it."

"Did she love it, eventually?"

Josie is the only person in the world I could tell without breaking apart. Mom would've adored her. "She always joked that it was my most tame one, and she should have appreciated it more."

Josie holds my gaze with a quiet understanding that makes it easier to talk about my mom. I don't have to explain too much. She already gets it, what it's like to carry memories that ache but are still good to share.

"She was right. It's angelic compared to some of these others." Josie chases the ink up my left arm, pausing on the minimalist infinity symbol. "Except maybe this one?" She flips my palms upside down, eyes searching. "Please tell me you have 'live, laugh, love' tattooed somewhere to go with this."

I mock-scold. "I don't."

Her lips part in a goofy grin. "One day, Phoenix. There's still time."

Josie's fingers continue their exploration, rolling up the short sleeves of my T-shirt and baring my shoulders.

I'm hyperaware of every point of contact between us, of the way her breath hitches as her fingertips graze over the faint ridges of an old scar hidden under the ink. She doesn't ask how I got it, and just as well. I don't want to think about Billie now.

Her gaze drifts lower, settling on my chest. "What's hiding under there? More ink I should interrogate you about?"

My smirk grows. "You'll have to see for yourself."

In one swift motion, I grab the hem of my T-shirt and tug it over my head, revealing the intricate tattoos adorning my torso. Josie gasps, her eyes widening as they roam over the newly exposed skin.

"Dorian! You should give me a warning before doing something like that."

I enjoy the flush of color on her cheeks, maybe too much.

"Still too hot for you?"

She shakes her head, exasperated, but her gaze remains fixed on my chest, a hint of hunger swirling in the whiskey of her irises. Her hand hovers above the intricate Japanese waves on my right side, hesitating before her fingertips make contact with my skin.

I inhale sharply at her touch.

"They're waves," she murmurs, more to herself. "I wasn't sure if it was a sea or a forest."

I have a sudden urge to pull her closer, to feel her body pressed against mine. But I hold back. She hasn't given me permission yet.

So I let her do with me as she pleases, surrendering to her examination as she charts paths I didn't know I wanted her to find.

And then I remember how to talk.

"The waves represent life's trials. The strength it takes to keep moving forward, no matter the challenges," I explain as I try not to shiver. "And the lost ship is a reminder that even through a storm, we can find a way back to shore."

"It's beautiful, Dorian. Not just the tattoo, but the meaning behind it." Her hands stop. "Is it okay that I'm touching you?"

Ah, I must've been not so good at hiding the shivers. "More than okay." I sound strangled. My vocal coach would call this a masterclass in how *not* to breathe.

Josie gives me a slow smile and her hand moves up, skimming over my skin until it comes to rest on the phoenix rising from flames on my left pectoral.

"No need to explain this one."

But I want to. I want her to understand every part of me, especially the parts I keep hidden from the world.

"The phoenix isn't just my name, it reflects who I am." As I talk, I wonder if she can feel the pounding of my heart under her palm. "Every time life burned me down, I found a way out of the ashes."

"You didn't just rise, Dorian. You took the ashes and turned them into magic for everyone else. It's kind of annoyingly impressive, you know?" She stares at me, worrying her lower lip in a way that drives me feral.

I lean forward, invading her space a little. "If you don't want me to burst into flames right now, please stop biting your lip."

"Uh, naughty. You're using your seduction voice again."

"Maybe it's just my lustful voice."

"Are you in lust with me?"

"Yes." I drop my hands on either side of her chair, pulling her close until her knees are between mine. "You have no idea of the unspeakable things going through my head right now."

Our faces are too close.

"Unspeakable?" she pants. "Don't tell me you're shy."

I nuzzle her neck. "Not shy, Monroe. Just thought it was against the rules."

Her chest heaves as she stutters her reply. "D-doing is against t-the rules... t-talking is allowed."

"Talking is allowed, huh?" I stare her down. "In that case, where should I start? By telling you how stunning you look tonight?"

Her breathing quickens, and her eyes become half-lidded.

"Dorian." My name on her lips is more of a plea than an objection.

"Or should I tell you about the way the thin straps of this dress have been taunting me?" I lift one, the material elastic, and let it drop back on her skin with a smack.

Josie gasps.

"I'm jealous of a piece of fabric, Josie. That should concern us."

"Maybe it should concern only you," she quips breathless. "I'm good."

"I'm not. I'm losing my mind. Having you this close. Do you know what you do to me?"

"Mmm... Unspeakable things, apparently."

I brace my hand on the back of her chair, my thumb brushing her shoulder. "More like unforgettable."

Josie's fingers grip the armrests, knuckles whitening. "Dorian, if you don't back up..."

I lean in until my forehead touches hers, the space between us a whisper of heat. "If I don't back up, what, Josie? You'll tell me the rules again? Or are you afraid you'll break them?"

Her breath hitches, and I recognize the conflict in her eyes, the push and pull between caution and desire. She doesn't answer, but the way her fingers tremble against the chair says everything.

I expect her to push me back. Instead, she surprises me yet again by moving her head to the side until her mouth is a breath from my ear. "You should put your shirt back on before I tell you how many times I dreamed of tracing your tattoos, not just with my fingers, but with my tongue, too."

I choke on the next breath and pull away coughing. "Are you trying to kill me?" I clutch my chest. "I just lost ten years of life."

Josie smirks, leaning back in her chair, the picture of innocence. "What? I'm following the rules. Talking is allowed, remember?" She pats my shoulder and offers me a glass of water.

I grab it and take a long sip to cool the fire she's stoked. Setting the glass down, I raise a hand in mock-surrender. "Truce. You win. I'll put my shirt on."

Her grin is triumphant, but her eyes flicker with disappointment as I reach for the T-shirt.

"Well, that's no fun," she quips.

"Right, it's self-preservation." I pull the shirt on. "Ready for dessert?"

Josie readjusts her chair. "After this, it'd better have a lot of decadent chocolate in it."

I stand. "Definitely going to fire the chef if it doesn't."

Josie opens her mouth to say something when a slow clapping sound cuts through the quiet of the dark garden. Both our heads snap in the direction of the noise. I peer into the darkness, stretching my neck as I scan the lawn, my muscles tensing. My brain immediately leaps to the worst scenario: a fan or a stalker has somehow breached my security. I fear the night is about to turn ugly and do the exact opposite of what I wanted to show Josie—that I can have normal moments.

My anxiety spikes as the sound grows louder. Josie's gaze darts between me and the shadowy edges of the garden. She yelps as a human shape takes form, confirming my worst fears. The home invader is lurching forward, listing like a zombie straight out of a horror movie. I put myself between the figure and Josie, pulling out my phone and pressing on the emergency app to alert my security team.

The silhouette keeps approaching until it comes into the circle of light on the porch, and Billie Rae emerges like a ghost straight from my past. Except she's real, flesh and bones, her features set in a mask of snarling fury. I suppress a groan in my throat, thinking I would've rather taken on an army of rabid zombies instead of having to deal with my ex-wife while on a date with my girlfriend.

28

JOSIE

At first, the figure emerging from the shadows is a blur, an indistinct outline against the backdrop of the night. But as it reaches the circle of light, recognition punches the breath out of my lungs. It's Billie Rae. My inner fangirl flares to life, and I have to physically stop myself from blurting out something mortifying like, *I loved your latest album!* This isn't a glamorous meet-and-greet. I'm not facing one of my favorite singers, she's Dorian's ex-wife. The woman who put him through so much, who hurt him so deeply. And she's pissed. If looks could kill, we'd already be making our way to the afterlife.

"Well, isn't this cozy?" Billie Rae sneers, her brown eyes flashing with anger as they land on me then Dorian. I swallow against my heart hammering in my throat. "So much for not having a side piece, uh, Dorian?"

He steps forward, jaw tight, hands clenched into fists at his sides. "Josie and I only work together."

There are a million reasons he must say this. The chief one that I asked him not to make our relationship public. But it still stings to be described as a mere professional connection in front of the woman he wrote countless love songs about.

"Do you think I'm fucking stupid?" Billie slurs, listing to the side and grabbing onto one of the pool chaises for support. She's visibly intoxicated. With what, it's hard to say, but Dorian wasn't exaggerating her problem. Still, I also can't help noticing how beautiful she is. His ex is jaw-dropping in a way I'll never be.

"You always lay out fairy lights for your 'employees,' Dorian?" She snickers. "Must be real tough business."

A muscle twitches in Dorian's jaw. "What are you doing here, Billie? How did you even get in?"

She tosses her blue-streaked blonde hair over her shoulder. "Oh, I have my ways. You should know that by now."

Every instinct tells me to go to Dorian, touch him, comfort him, but I'm afraid I'm only going to make things worse if I do, so I stay put in my chair.

The silence between them is thick enough to choke on. On Dorian's face, restraint is battling with frustration. Billie glares at her ex-husband and then fixates on me.

"Isn't she too plain for you, babe? Since when have you gone vanilla?"

Dorian squeezes his fists tighter and then releases them only to squeeze again, the movement causes the tattoos on his arms to move, the designs coming to life. "Watch it, Billie," he snaps. "You don't get to come here and insult—"

"Everything okay here, sir?" We're interrupted by one of Dorian's bodyguards stepping into the garden and placing himself between us and Billie Rae.

The man is tall, with dark hair, darker eyes, and clean-shaven. He's wearing an impeccable black suit and makes me wonder if Dorian shops for his security detail at the Elite Muscle and Charm Department Store. But then our guy takes in Billie Rae and his brows pinch in a scowl so fierce I'm sure Dorian must've found him at The Brooding Protector Emporium.

"Thank you, Nick." Dorian's voice is cold in a way I've never heard. "My ex-wife has decided to add breaking and entering to her track record."

Billie Rae's eyes narrow into furious slits, her lips curling back to bare her teeth. "You're such a piece of shit," she spits. "You want to erase me? This is my fucking house!"

She raises her voice with each syllable until she's screaming. In a surprisingly fast-moving blur for someone who was swaying on her feet moments ago, she lunges at Dorian, her fingers curved like claws as if she means to tear at his face.

But she doesn't get far. The bodyguard, Nick, steps in with deadly precision, intercepting her mid-flight. He pins Billie's arms to her sides and pulls her back against his chest, his grip unyielding as she thrashes against him. Billie fights like a woman possessed, twisting her body and flailing her legs. One kick lands on the bodyguard's shin, but Nick doesn't even flinch. Is he made of steel? Wearing shin pads?

"Get your damn hands off me!" she bellows, thrashing so violently that her hair whips in all directions. "Dorian, you coward. Fight your battles." Her screams are loud and jagged, her breath ragged and her movements growing more desperate. "You have no right!" she howls, her head jerking back in a fierce arc aimed at Nick's chin. But she's too short, and he dodges, taking the hit to the chest where it should hurt less. "You think you can throw me away? That you're better than me?" she snaps at Dorian, then yells at Nick again. "Let me go, you asshole!"

Seeing Billie Rae like this—a broken, furious mess—is gut-wrenching. Her rage is raw and tragic; blind fury seems the only way she can hold herself together. But the twisted helplessness that coats her anger is impossible to miss.

She's a stranger to me, and the sight doesn't leave me indifferent. How is Dorian even handling this? To see someone he once loved reduced to such a state. It must be heartbreaking for him, no matter how much time or distance he's put between them.

My heart twists as I glance at him; but his face is a fortress, his emotions locked behind high walls.

Billie starts to cry and that seems to break Dorian. His shoulders sag, the tension draining from him as if he's done, can't take any more. His voice softens, stripped of anger, pleading. "Billie, just stop. If you stop struggling, Nick will let you go."

Her thrashing halts, her body going slack as she glares at him through her tears, her chest heaving with exertion. For a beat, no one moves. Then Dorian gives Nick a small nod, and the bodyguard releases her cautiously. Billie crumples to the ground, folding in on herself like a broken marionette. She starts sobbing harder. Her cries are ugly and desolating, words spilling out between sniffles that make no sense. "I can't... You left me." She mumbles something else that disturbingly sounds like, "Alone."

Dorian turns to me, expression pinched. "Are you okay to drive home?"

I am being dismissed and I don't know how I feel about it. "Yes."

"We'll finish this tomorrow. I'll call you." He sounds distant, and I'm not sure if it's an act for Billie's sake, to pretend I'm just an employee, or if that's how he feels right now.

"Okay."

He nods with another look on his face I can't interpret.

I grab my bag with trembling fingers, and head for the

French doors. At the threshold, I pause, glancing back. Dorian is crouching next to Billie, his hands steadying her as if she's so fragile she could shatter. "Is there someone other than John I can call?"

Her answer is hollow. "You are my person, Dorian. I have no one else."

Tears sting my eyes, making my vision blur. I can't watch this —him comforting her, her staking a claim that burns through my skin. I've spent too many months haunted by their marriage to handle this. I know I'm being irrational. That Dorian is merely acting like a decent human being. But I have to remove myself from the situation.

I stumble into the house, choking back a sob.

Driving away doesn't calm me. The road blurs as I blink back tears, and I slow down, the taillights of the cars ahead turning into streaking smudges of red. Tonight started like a dream, a romantic dinner under fairy lights and Dorian looking at me as if I was the only thing that mattered. But it all feels so fragile now, like a crystal glass balanced on the edge of a counter, one wrong move away from shattering.

I want to believe this connection we have can be ours alone. But the truth is, Dorian doesn't exist in a vacuum. His life is layered, complicated, with pieces of Billie Rae embedded so deeply in it, they might never come out.

A part of me knows I shouldn't take it personally. Everyone has baggage, and I have mine too. But watching him comfort her, seeing her desperation, made me feel like the intruder. Like the one stealing someone who doesn't belong to me.

My knuckles whiten as I grip the wheel tighter. Love, or whatever this is growing between us, shouldn't feel this heavy this soon. And yet, when I think of walking away, invisible hands grip my throat, choking off the air, and something deep within me claws upward, primal and fierce, refusing to even consider letting Dorian go.

When I get home, I can't sleep. I brush my teeth, wash my face, and change into my PJs, but then I lie on the bed staring at the ceiling, my mind a blank space. I resist for an hour before I text him. He said he'd call me tomorrow, but I can't wait that long.

JOSIE

Are you okay?

As I hit send, I'm terrified he won't reply, or give me some curt response, a simple yes, or worse, a thumbs-up emoji. Instead, my phone rings.

I almost drop it in my hurry to answer. "Hi."

"Hey." His tone is subdued, bordering on hesitant. "Sorry for earlier."

"You don't need to apologize."

"I do," he counters, guilt edging his voice. "The way I said goodbye was cold. But I wasn't shutting you out. I just... I didn't want to rattle the cage. Billie was already unhinged enough."

I hesitate, biting my lip. "Is she okay now?"

A bitter laugh escapes him. "You saw her, Josie. She's not okay."

"I'm sorry. Is it always like that with her?"

"Yes. That's what she does—rage and insults one minute, guilt the next. She twists every interaction until it feels like I'm the one to blame. It's exhausting, and it tears at me every time. It's why I had to get away. I couldn't do it anymore... I couldn't breathe."

"I'm so sorry, Dorian." I pull my knees to my chest. "It's not fair for her to make you relive that pain over and over."

"Fair left the building a long time ago with Billie," he replies, his voice heavy with frustration. "You didn't see her at her worst, Josie. Tonight was tame."

"Tame? Dorian, she tried to claw your face off."

"Yeah. At least she didn't succeed this time."

This time? Has she hurt him before? My thoughts go to the thin scar I felt on his shoulder. How many more are there across his body? How many did she cause? And how many cuts did she make on the inside that are invisible?

"And now that she's seen us together, scratches are the least of our problems," he says grimly. "I wouldn't put it past her to go off the rails."

"Worse than this, how? Do you think she'll... escalate?"

"That's what worries me," he admits. "We'll have to be more careful. Billie's the type to hire a private investigator, tail me, you, your family. My security team is already sweeping the house to figure out how she got in."

I grip the phone tighter. "What do we do?"

"Don't give her anything to find. Lie low. Let her rage burn out and leave no fuel for it. If she got proof about us..." Dorian exhales, and I can picture him rubbing the back of his neck. "She'd start a press war."

"What can I do to help?"

"Just... be patient. I don't want to say this, but maybe it's a good thing I'm going back on tour after the VMAs. We'll be in different cities and Billie will have nothing to find."

"No, don't say that," I whine. "I'm going to miss you so much."

"I know, and I hate that she's stealing the last days we could've been together."

"It's not your fault. You didn't ask for this."

"That's the thing, though, at least in part, I did when I

married her. But you never asked for the drama. You're walking into a mess I should've cleaned up a long time ago."

"Dorian. I'm asking for it now. I'm here because I want to be. And I'm not going anywhere."

The silence on his end feels heavy, charged. "I can't tell you how much that means to me."

"Don't encourage me or I'll stick to you harder than sand after a beach day."

His laugh is low, warm. "Careful, Monroe. I might take you up on that."

"I'm counting on it. And you're not off the hook. Next time, I'm expecting fewer ex-wives and more chocolate."

"Duly noted." I finally hear a smile in his words. "Do you want to go to sleep? It's late."

"I'm too jacked up to sleep."

"Want me to sing you a lullaby?"

"Would you?"

"It worked last time." He means a year ago, and the fondness in his voice almost undoes me. "Any requests?"

"A song from your first album." I want something that he wrote before meeting her.

Dorian starts to sing, and I fall asleep to the sound of his voice, wishing I was in his bed, free to hug him all night.

29

DORIAN

On Saturday, I wake up restless. An entire weekend ahead, and I can't see Josie either day because of Billie. We can only video chat.

I toss and turn in bed a bit longer but I don't make it past 9 a.m. before I call her. I grin when her face pops up on the screen. Her hair's a wild mess, tumbling out of a lopsided bun, and she's wrapped in an oversized sweatshirt that swallows her whole, the cuffs covering half her hands. There's a window behind her. Is she in the kitchen? I hate that I don't know what her apartment looks like.

"Morning," she rasps, still groggy.

"Morning, beautiful," I drawl. "Looking cozy."

Her nose scrunches adorably. "Look who's talking. Is that bedhead I see?"

I run a hand through my mussed hair. "I *am* in bed, so technically, yes."

"Don't say you're in bed with that husky voice." She groans. "Please tell me at least you have your shirt on."

I dip the camera to show her my bare collarbones. "Err..."

"Oi." She theatrically puts a hand over her face, only to peer between her fingers. "Don't assault me first thing in the morning with all that sexy ink."

I bring the screen back up. "I thought looking wasn't against the rules."

"Should I leave my camera on when I go shower, then?"

I drop the phone on my chest and bite my fist.

"Hello?" she calls. "I'm seeing black."

"As you deserve"—I right the screen and glare into the camera—"after putting that image in my brain."

She grins. Goofy, unguarded, radiant. "Hey, I was only demonstrating the unfairness of subjecting me to extremely tempting skin art."

"Noted," I say pointedly. "Join me for breakfast? Virtually, of course."

"You want to watch me cut the crusts off my toast? You're weird, but okay."

I'd watch her clip her toenails if it meant spending more time together.

"What are you having?" she asks.

I glance at the breakfast tray resting on the mattress, holding a parfait of non-fat Greek yogurt, homemade protein granola, and mixed berries, alongside a glass of grapefruit juice. "My nutritionist is in cahoots with the chef so nothing wild." I show her the parfait.

She bites her lip in that maddening way, but her expression is serious like she's unsure what to say next. "Do you watch your weight, or—I'm not judging if you do but..."

"No, I don't. Not really. It doesn't help that whenever I put on a quarter of a pound, the press declares I've got a beer belly. But it's more a healthy thing." I mix the parfait before eating a spoonful. "After getting out of the relationship with Billie, I'm trying to follow a more balanced lifestyle."

"Makes sense." She nods. "Lily is my veggie police. She makes no distinctions between Penny and me."

"Should I tell your sister about the vending-machine purse?"

Josie points a finger at me. "Don't you dare."

She props her phone against something as she makes coffee and butters toast. I wedge the phone between my bent knees and eat my yogurt as we chat.

"What are you doing today?" I ask.

"Whine on the couch all day about not being able to see you?" Josie shrugs. "You?"

"Same." I lick off the spoon. "This may sound paranoid, but can I ask you to do something for me?"

She sips her coffee, scrunching her face. "I have no idea what you're about to ask."

"Nothing terrible. But I'd like you to bring your car to a shop and have them install darkened windows. If it's okay, I'll arrange everything."

"Why?"

"If Billie has someone watching the house, it's the only way your car can come and go from my place without anyone knowing if you're in it." I take a sip of juice. "Otherwise, if the rest of the team leaves and you stay behind, they'd notice."

Josie pulls a face. Good, bad? I can't tell.

"Too much?" I ask.

She shifts in her seat. "Can I make a confession?"

"Sure."

"All this spy-movieness is turning me on. Not the Billie thing, of course. But the sneaking around is hot."

I smile. "Do I get extra points if I start using code names?"

"You don't need extra points." Josie turns shyer as she adds,

"You've been back in my life only for a week, and I don't know how I survived the last year without you."

"Spotify?" I joke despite the heat flaring in my chest.

Her face gets emotional before she crumples, laughing. "You have no idea." Her eyes get shiny and she does that rapid blinking thing. I can't tell if she's about to joy-cry or just-cry. "It's so accurate, it's not even funny."

"I know." I sigh. "Let me arrange with the auto-shop. I'll send you the details."

She toys with the neckline of her sweatshirt, letting it drop off one shoulder. "So it's definitely camera off during the shower?"

I fix the camera and sing a line from one of my songs.

"Your breath on my skin leaves scars."

Her eyes go saucer wide, and her blush is glorious even through the screen. "That's—that's below the belt."

"Blame the muse." I use my "seduction voice," as she calls it. "She's very inspirational."

"Alright, I'm off to, uh... cool down. Talk later. Byyyeee."

She hangs up before I can reply. I toss the phone aside and sling an arm over my eyes, unable to stop grinning.

Mid-afternoon, she sends me a picture of her standing in front of her car with newly tinted windows at the repair shop. She's in a silly bodyguard pose despite her milkmaid dress: dark shades on, arms crossed over her chest, serious expression.

I trace her silhouette on the screen and am even jealous of the mechanic who must've taken the picture.

As I stare at the image, my heart turns into a glowing flare that sputters out too fast as I remember why she's there. This isn't the life I want for her—sneaking around, looking over her shoulder, hiding behind tinted glass. She deserves better.

But I'd do anything to keep her safe, to allow us to be together.

DORIAN

Totally badass, Monroe

JOSIE

I know. *cool emoji* Try not to swoon

Too late.

* * *

Later that night, I'm in my home recording studio. I'm still working, refusing to let the day be a total waste. I'm half-heart-edly composing the chorus for a new song when my phone pings.

JOSIE

Want to play a game?

A thrill crawls up the back of my neck, making the short hair stand to attention.

DORIAN

Sure

JOSIE

Are you in bed?

I rush out of the studio and take the stairs two at a time, launching myself over the mattress.

DORIAN

Am now

JOSIE

Did you run? You sound winded

I grin. Always with the sass.

DORIAN

How can a text sound winded?

JOSIE

Sixth sense

DORIAN

What's the game?

JOSIE

If I were in bed with you and you could look and talk but not touch, what would you do?

Ah. Fuck. I'd probably lose my mind and beg. How do I reply? She has no mercy.

DORIAN

Should we play on a call?

JOSIE

No, I'm too shy. I can only handle texts

DORIAN

Nothing about this game seems shy to me

JOSIE

Trust me

Just spill, what would you do?

I have to think. What would make Josie lose it? How can I

torture her back? My gaze lands on my nightstand and a slow grin spreads on my lips.

> I'd grab a fantasy paperback from my nightstand and read a fight scene aloud to you using my *seduction voice*

> I'd make the gore sound particularly dirty and bring the hero's sword thrusts to life so vividly, you'd feel each one

I hit send and, two seconds later, my phone rings.

I smile as I pick up. "I thought we weren't playing on the phone."

"You have a devious mind." Josie sounds parched. "I have a request."

"What request?"

"Would you—would you read me a bedtime story?"

"Let me guess, are we going for fantasy?"

"I believe I was promised a fight scene."

"What about me? Don't I get to ask a 'what would you do' question?"

"You will tomorrow night. Now read, please?"

I grab the book I was in the middle of, go back a few chapters, and, setting my voice extra low and coarse, I start reading. "Cassian didn't much care for mud, but the battlefield seemed determined to drown him in it. *Thick* and *sucking*, it clung to his boots like a jealous lover, slowing every step. He twisted his blade free of a gutted enemy, ignoring *the wet sound* it made, and stepped over the body, directly into more *muck*."

Josie groans on the line. "Oh my gosh, this sounds sooo dirty."

"Should I stop?"

"No, please, I'm already invested in this Cassian character. Go on."

I continue, "The *sludge* made every movement *treacherous*, but Cassian moved with practiced efficiency. His sword found purchase in *throats, bellies, and hearts* with grim regularity. He navigated the carnage, more inconvenienced than disturbed, his boots *squelching* with each step. Once, he nearly slipped on a severed arm, its fingers still twitching as if unwilling to accept their new situation.

"Still there?" I check on Josie.

"Yep." She yawns. "And I'm never falling asleep without a bedtime story from you again."

"Ah, enjoying yourself?"

"I'm so turned on, it's embarrassing. Is Cassian hot?"

"Dark, unruly hair, piercing blue eyes..."

She sighs. "Reminds me of someone. Keep reading..."

I resume from where I left off, taking my voice an octave lower. "Cassian brought his blade up in an arc, the point *slicing through* his attacker's abdomen. Blood *sprayed, warm and sticky, across his face.* He wiped it with the back of his hand, *smearing it* into the grime already caked there. 'Charming,' he sputtered. 'Really, this day just keeps getting better...'"

I keep reading without pause for an hour before checking again on her. "Josie, are you still there?"

She doesn't reply.

I close the book in my lap and listen to the soft, rhythmic sound of her breathing through the line.

"Goodnight, love," I whisper, knowing she won't hear me, and hang up with a smile.

Maybe today wasn't so useless after all.

* * *

The next day, I make it only until eight thirty before sending my evening text to Josie. We've been on multiple phone calls during the day, but this is the moment I've been looking forward to the most.

> **DORIAN**
> Want to play a game?

JOSIE
You're in bed already?

> **DORIAN**
> There are other places we can play

JOSIE
heart-on-fire emoji color me intrigued

> **DORIAN**
> What would you do if I told you I've never wanted anything as much as I want you?

I'd meant to be playful, but my brain went from zero to a hundred in less than a heartbeat.

JOSIE
I'd swoon

In fact, I'm swooning...

I live alone, this game is getting dangerous

If I face-plant in my living room, no one is going to find me for days

> **DORIAN**
> I'd come find you *wink emoji*

JOSIE
You're making me swoon again

Is that your question?

Is the game over?

DORIAN

No

That was a warm-up, here's the actual question:

What would you do if I asked you to pick something in your apartment and pretend it's me?

The dots signaling she's typing blink and blink until I'm bursting with impatience. When her reply comes in, it's a mile long. I eagerly scan the text, each word stoking the fire burning low in my spine.

JOSIE

I'd pick up the bottle of wine I left out on the counter earlier. First, I'd let my fingers slide around its neck, gripping it firmly just below the lip as I pop the cork with my thumb. Then, I'd lift it, watching the dark liquid swirl through the glass. Bringing it close, I'd let the cool rim brush against my bottom lip long enough to inhale the earthy flavor. Then, I'd take a slow sip, directly from the bottle, letting the rich, velvety red coat my tongue. I'd hold it there, savoring every bit of the warmth as it spreads. When I finally swallowed, I'd set the bottle back down, dragging a finger along the rim to catch the drop that tried to escape. And then, well... I'd stare at it, wishing it was something—or someone—else entirely

Fuck. *Oh, fuck.* I drop my phone and push both my hands through my hair, pulling at the roots until a new notification pings in.

JOSIE

How'd I do?

DORIAN

How you did?

I might never recover

Are you happy?

JOSIE

smug-face emoji so dramatic

DORIAN

Is there any of that wine left?

I need a drink

JOSIE

I can check if you want

Take another sip

Tell you about it in detail?

DORIAN

Please, don't

Nearly didn't survive the first text

Can't take another one

JOSIE

You're no fun

DORIAN

And you are all heart

JOSIE

I try

DORIAN

Try harder

JOSIE

Hey, shouldn't that be my line?

DORIAN

Trust me, baby, after I print that text, frame it, and put it on my nightstand you'll never need to tell me to try harder at anything

JOSIE

You called me baby, then put sexy visuals in my mind, and now my brain's mushed and I can't fight back

DORIAN

Truce?

JOSIE

Yeah

I can't wait to see you tomorrow, this has been the longest weekend of my life

DORIAN

Me too

Want me to read to you again before bed?

JOSIE

Would you? Really?

I was joking yesterday, you don't have to do it every night

DORIAN

I wouldn't mind if it became an every-night thing. Honestly, I'd look forward to it more than you would

JOSIE

You make it hard to say no

DORIAN

Easy pun there, Monroe, but I'm not gonna breach the truce

JOSIE

As long as no one's breaching

I chuckle but don't take the bait.

DORIAN

Call me when you're under the covers

JOSIE

Aye aye *military salute emoji*

I put the phone down and pace the room to shake off the restless energy buzzing under my skin. She'll call any second, and somehow that makes me feel like I've got everything and nothing under control.

30

JOSIE

I thought the weekend was going to suck, but with the text flirting, phone calls, and late-night reading sessions, it's been surprisingly romantic. The pull between Dorian and me doesn't waver, or need permission, or care how many miles or walls stand in its way.

As I park at his house on Monday morning and exit the car, my steps are lighter. Buoyant, even, despite everything that happened Friday night with Billie. The good mood carries me past the grand foyer, through the familiar hallway, right up to his home office—where it crashes headfirst into an invisible wall.

Something's wrong.

The atmosphere inside is tight. Not the entire team is present. Only Tessa, Bailey, and Dorian's lawyer sit stiffly at the table. And Nick is here. I almost missed him, standing guard by the door, still and imposing as if sculpted in stone or marble since his skin looks so flawless.

"Hi," I say cautiously.

Dorian lifts his head, making me forget about the tension

simmering in the room as he smiles at me in that slow, intimate, only-for-me way that speeds up my pulse faster than a triple espresso shot. But under the smile, his jaw is tight. His shoulders tense.

"What's going on?" I ask, sitting in my usual spot across from Dorian.

Tessa exchanges a look with the lawyer, then says, "We're discussing Friday night."

Ah, Billie's home invasion. I keep my face carefully neutral, determined to sell the "business dinner" story Dorian concocted as our cover.

Tessa turns to Marcia. "Is there really nothing we can do legally?"

"If you can convince him." The lawyer sighs as if she knows she's about to deliver a losing argument. "The best course of action would be to file a restraining order."

"You really should," Tessa presses, turning to Dorian.

"I said I won't do it." He slams a fist on the table. "Even if Billie crossed a line, I wouldn't call the police on my wife." A beat, then a guilty side glance at me. "My *ex*-wife."

"I hate what she fucking does to you." It's the first time I hear Tessa lose her professional composure, but I couldn't agree more. I loathe seeing Dorian like this—torn, caged, a little lost. "But I won't let you take it out on me."

"I'm sorry, Tess, I didn't mean to snap. You know she drives me up the wall."

I'm learning it too and hate how easily Billie can drag him into her chaos. But even more, I recoil at the question of *why* his ex still affects him so much.

That voice in my head, the one I've been trying to quiet since Friday, is getting louder, screaming the obvious: that it's because he's still in love with her—or at least with the person she was when they met. It's the only logical explanation. And no matter what my heart wants, how long can I ignore the warnings?

"You get one pass." Tessa stands, smoothing out her blazer. "I'll ask Alfred for one of his famous vanilla lattes." She scans the room. "Anyone want anything?"

I'd love a latte. But Tessa is being a little scary right now. I'm afraid she'd chew my head off if I asked her to bring me a coffee even if she's offered.

As if reading my hesitation, Dorian smirks and tells her to please get lattes for everyone. His eyes flick to me as Tessa leaves, and he gives me a small nod, silently confirming that yes, the lattes are for me. I mouth a quick, "Thank you."

"Well." Marcia stands. "That's all the advice I can give you. I'll draft the restraining order, anyway. If you change your mind, I'll be ready to file immediately."

"Appreciate it, Marcia."

"Sure." She snaps her briefcase shut. "And think about upgrading your security while you're at it."

With that, she strides out, stilettos clicking on the floor.

Tessa returns then, trailed by a maid carrying a tray of mugs. I accept mine and take a sip. Mmm—velvety smooth, creamy, perfectly frothed, the kind of coffee that makes you close your eyes to savor it. I get why Alfred's lattes are so famous.

Tessa takes a long sip, too, then flicks her gaze toward the empty seat beside me. Face grim. "I guess Marcia's exit means you're not filing the restraining order."

"I'm not," Dorian confirms. "I'd rather focus on how Billie got inside the house."

He turns to Nick. The only sign that the bodyguard is not, in fact, carved from stone is the fractional shift of his feet as he widens his stance before he speaks, eyes fixed straight ahead. "Sir, we've conducted a thorough sweep of the house—"

"Oh, for fuck's sake, Nick," Dorian interrupts. "Take a seat and stop hovering like a bat."

I would've compared him more to a vampire with centuries of honed discipline, but sure.

Nick approaches the table with the gait of a soldier ordered into unfamiliar terrain: rigid, measured, and painfully awkward to watch. He pulls a chair out and sits —ramrod straight, posture impeccable.

He's about to continue his report when Dorian slides a mug toward him. "And have a latte."

Nick eyes the mug like it's a radioactive water ration. "Sir, I don't really drink lattes."

Dorian nods. "You will after this."

The only outward sign of Nick's discomfort is the faintest flush creeping up his neck. Still, he stoically brings the mug to his mouth and takes a sip.

We watch, silent, waiting until Nick's eyes widen. Not even the most impervious man on the planet can stop his reaction to the most perfect coffee he'll ever have.

"Delicious, sir." When he lowers the mug, a white foam mustache clings to his upper lip, making him look unexpectedly human. He continues his report, saying there were no signs of a forced entrance, but we're all staring at his mouth. He doesn't notice at first.

I feel for him since I was in a similar position only last week with my Sharpie mustache.

It takes Nick a minute to catch up. The bodyguard stops, looks around, and exhales. "I have a foam mustache, don't I?"

We nod, biting back laughter.

Nick indulges in another, longer sip, this time deliberately swiping his tongue over his upper lip. "Worth it." He places the mug down with a satisfied grunt.

Ah. So definitely human.

Dorian turns serious again. "If there were no signs of forced entry, how'd she get in?"

Nick explains how an old garage fob was never deactivated, but that all access devices have been updated now so Billie won't be able to just use her old keys.

Dorian nods, satisfied. "Perfect."

Nick stands and makes to return to his spot by the wall, but before going, he stops and takes his latte with him. The rest of us share a quiet laugh.

After that, the meeting is adjourned.

As the others file out, Nick included, I sidle up to Dorian. He pulls me into a hug. His arms tight around me.

I breathe him in. "I missed you."

His chin rests on top of my head, his voice teasing. "Sure you didn't dream about Cassian last night?"

I sigh against his chest, letting the warmth of him seep in. "You two are the same in my mind. I even have the visual of you in full armor to go with the fantasies."

"Mmm... I want to hear in detail about these fantasies, but first, car keys." He extends his hand, palm up, expectant.

I hesitate, glancing at the door. "Dorian, I shouldn't stay. I have other clients."

His expression doesn't change. "Who, if I'm not mistaken, were reassigned?"

"Yes, but—"

"No buts. Give me an hour, please?"

The way he says *please* dissolves my spine.

Defeated, I go back to my chair, snatch my keys from my bag, and toss them to him. He catches them effortlessly, already moving.

Dorian vanishes down the hall, reappearing minutes later

with a satisfied look. "My driver is taking your car for a spin. He's an expert at shaking a tail. Ned will know if anyone's been following you."

I blink. "Are all your employees ex-special forces?"

"What? No, don't be ridiculous. Some of them were in the CIA."

I want to keep the banter flowing and the mood light, but my brain is throwing every red flag it can find at me.

Dorian notices instantly. "Uh-oh. Am I in trouble? What'd I do?"

"Nothing, but... can we talk?"

He tilts his head, studying me. "Yeah, but not here."

He slides his hands in his jeans pockets and guides me to what can only be described as a cozier alternative to the main living room. With oversized armchairs, a deep-set couch, and a central coffee table stacked high with books about musicians, it feels less of a showroom and more like a private space.

Dorian gestures to the couch, and we sit side by side but facing each other.

"What is it?" he asks.

"It's about Billie." Gosh, we spend more time discussing her than we do us, but I need to get my doubts off my chest.

"Billie. Of course." Dorian shifts, that hardness returning to his posture. "What about her?"

I look in his beautiful, expressive eyes, willing myself to be brave. "The way she makes you angry... it's visceral. And the only people who have that power over us are the ones we love..." I pause, holding his gaze. "Are you... is there any part of you that's still in love with her?"

His knees bounce as he stares past me. Dorian presses his lips together, and I fear he won't answer. But then, he rubs a hand over his jaw. "Josie, come on." He shakes his head. "That's not—" He stops himself. "You think I want that?"

"Wanting it and feeling it aren't the same thing."

His fingers tap restlessly against his knee, a quick, uneven rhythm. "She broke me. I should hate her." His voice drops and becomes conflicted, like he's fighting with himself. "But on some level..." He trails off, then looks at me, guilt heavy in his eyes. "I can't pretend Billie didn't matter once. That she didn't shape parts of me." His gaze is steadier now, less torn. "She is my past, Josie. A messy, complicated past that I can't erase." He reaches for my hand. "But that's all she is—past."

"Are you sure? Because I can't let myself fall for you if you aren't over her."

"I am." He shifts closer, his knee brushing mine. "I don't know how to explain it, but when I'm with you, she's not even a thought in my head." He chortles out a small, breathy laugh. "You make me want to move forward, Josie. Not look back."

The words settle something inside me. The alarms finally go quiet.

Dorian searches my face. "You believe me?"

I nod, smiling, because I do. "Can I ask another question before we get to the fun stuff?"

He pushes my hair back on my shoulder and leans in. "What fun stuff?"

I shift, gathering my thoughts, but it's impossible with him this close. "You're distracting me."

He grins, tilting his head. "That's the idea."

I nudge his shoulder. "Is your plan to keep me flustered so I never ask you the tough questions?"

He backs off. "The opposite, I want you to ask all the hard questions. But I also love messing with you."

I shift closer, pressing my hand flat on his chest and tilting my chin up, my lips a whisper from his. "What if I mess with you in return?"

His eyes darken, his fingers flexing. He looks two seconds away from grabbing my face. "Josie."

I let my lips part, wetting them. "What?"

His gaze drops to my mouth before bouncing back. Then, with visible effort, he pulls back, dragging a hand through his hair. "Alright. You win. Let's get through the hard stuff first."

I swallow, letting the teasing slip away, because the words I need to say are not that fun. I straighten up. "Earlier, you got furious with Tessa. It wasn't simple frustration, it was... more."

"I'm stressed, I snapped. You never snap?"

"I do." I watch him, weighing up how much to say. "It's not just today. I've heard things over the years. At the agency."

Dorian's hand, which had been resting loosely on his thigh, now closes into a fist.

"The night we met..." I swallow, forcing myself to continue. "You were there because a video of you punching a guy went viral."

He keeps his body very still, but tension ripples under his muscles. "What's the question?"

"Do you always carry this much anger and struggle to manage your temper or is it just Billie who turns you like that?"

"It's her. That night was about her, too."

My insecurities crawl back out of the dark as he tenses at the mere mention of his ex. Fucking Billie. I've never agreed more with Tessa.

He says she's the past, but then—

"That night." Dorian's gaze gets distant as if he is staring *through* the floor, replaying something only he can see. "You want to know why I punched that guy?" he asks, still not looking at me.

"I do."

Dorian drags his hands over his face, as if wiping away a memory he'd rather leave buried. When he speaks, his voice sounds like it's being dragged out of him through broken glass.

"When I was in New Orleans with Billie, things were already bad. We were staying in separate rooms. Fighting all the time. But I hadn't given up yet. I thought if we got through that tour, we'd figure our shit out." He frowns as if looking directly into the past. "That day, she'd missed rehearsal before our show. No texts, no calls. She wasn't answering her phone, so I went to her room to check on her." He huffs a short, humorless breath. "I had a key. Walked in. And she was in bed with someone else."

Nausea rolls through me. "Who?"

His mouth presses into a tight line. "Another woman I'd never seen before."

I'm not sure what reaction to have.

He glances at me now, his expression unreadable. "But that's not what fucked me up."

I want to hug him, but I let him continue without interrupting.

"I still thought we were monogamous," he says simply. "We hadn't had sex in forever, but I never strayed. And that day, she looked me in the eye and invited me to join them like it was nothing. And when I didn't, she threw a shoe at me and called me a pussy."

My stomach twists.

Dorian leans forward, elbows on his knees, studying his hands like they hold the answer to something. "I was hurting like hell. I didn't go to my room because I couldn't bear to be alone and went to get a drink at the hotel bar instead. And that's when some asshole comes up to me, already half-wasted, grinning like we're old pals, and says, 'Man, your wife has the best tits I've ever seen.'"

I flinch.

"He told me I needed to keep her on a leash. Because the night before, Billie was flashing everyone in the lobby for beads." Dorian pauses, considering. "The next part might be hard to hear. Do you still want it?"

I nod. "Always."

His jaw works, but then he speaks. "The first time we went to New Orleans together for a concert was right after we got married. That night, a fan threw a string of beads on stage. I caught it." He rubs his thumb along his palm as if remembering the sensation of the cheap plastic. "Back in our room, Billie wanted it. But I made her earn it."

I don't want to hear this. I'm gonna get sick. But I don't stop him.

Dorian keeps his eyes on me. "She flashed me for it."

The nausea turns to a lead weight in my stomach. I don't even know why—it's his past, I have no right to feel this way. But I do.

He notices. He always notices. "Josie—"

"Keep going," I say with a dry mouth.

A beat passes before he nods. "That was... one of our best nights. She still has those beads. I saw them in her car the other night."

I don't speak. Can't.

"So I was in that bar, having just walked in on her cheating, realizing it probably wasn't even the first time, and now I've got some guy in my face, talking about my wife's tits, destroying one of the last good memories I had of us." He lets out a bitter laugh. "I lost it. I forgot someone is always pointing their phone at me. Hell, I didn't even care." The memory plays behind his eyes. "I hit him once. Broke his nose."

"I'm sorry."

Dorian rubs the back of his neck, tipping his head up toward the ceiling. "That's Billie's special power. She makes me go nuclear." His gaze shifts to me, steady and certain. "And it's not because I'm in love with her. It's that she made me question who I was. My instincts. My judgment. And for years, I defended her. Gave her the benefit of the doubt. Told myself she was going through something, that we'd figure it out. And every time I thought I was making the right call—sticking by her, believing her—it turned out I was only the biggest fucking idiot in the room." His throat works, swallowing down the bitterness. "I hate that she still has the power to make me doubt myself. That's what pisses me off. Not her." His jaw sets with conviction. "I'm over her. But I'm still trying to unlearn the damage."

I want to reach for him, but I don't know if he'd welcome it right now. "Can I hug you?"

Dorian's lips twitch like he's surprised I even had to ask. "Josie, I'd love nothing more."

I shift closer, slipping an arm around his back. He does the same, pulling me against him. At first, it's a chaste side hug, I don't notice the shift, but gradually, the angle changes. I move without thinking, climbing onto his lap, my knees bracketing his thighs. His hands slide down to my waist, steadying me.

"Thank you." I rub my hands up his arms, over his shoulders, feeling the tension still knotted in his muscles that he doesn't know how to let go. "For telling me this."

His fingers dig into my hips as if he were holding onto something more than my body. "I don't talk about it. Not like this. Not with anyone."

I thread my fingers into his hair, pushing it back from his

face. He closes his eyes at the touch, exhaling slowly, his shoulders finally relaxing.

I trace small circles over his temples with my thumbs. "I'm sorry that happened to you."

His lids flutter open, gaze locking onto mine, not searching, not uncertain, just present. Just here.

"But," I continue, my lips curving, "if you hadn't punched that idiot, we wouldn't have met."

Dorian releases a breath that's almost a laugh, shaking his head like he can't believe I said that. "Silver linings, uh?"

I lean in, letting my forehead rest against his. "The best ones."

Dorian's hands slide up my back, his touch light at first, testing the shape of me, then firmer, as if he decided to hold on. "You're trouble, you know that?"

I smirk, brushing my nose against his. "You like trouble."

His fingers press harder into my skin, just enough that I feel it everywhere. "I like *you*."

I groan, straightening up. "I've never hated the rules more." I push his hair back again, fingertips dragging through the strands, slower this time, loving the way he shudders under my touch.

"Agreed," he croaks. "But you're enjoying this," he accuses, voice rough. "Torturing me."

I smirk. "And you're not?"

His jaw tics. "This is dangerous."

I hum, threading my fingers deeper into his hair. "For who?"

His breath stutters. "For both of us."

And yet—neither of us moves.

I want to kiss him. I crave to taste him. My gaze drops to his mouth, avid, and he notices. He, too, fixes on my lips and then looks back up at me, a question swirling in his eyes.

I'm not sure what my answer is, but it's leaning dangerously close to, *Fuck the rules, kiss me.*

I experimentally rock my hips on his lap, and a choked, inhuman sound rips from his throat. His hands drag down my thighs. They skim over the fabric of my dress, creating the slightest friction, a whisper of pressure that makes my skin prickle underneath.

I shouldn't push this. But I do.

I shift again, rolling against him just to see what he'll do. His breathing is shallow, and he drops his head back against the couch, exposing the line of his throat.

I watch, fascinated, as his Adam's apple bobs.

"Josie," he warns, voice wrecked, breath jagged, like he's wrestling the last thread of control and it's slipping fast.

I smirk, dragging my nails lightly over his scalp. "Problem?"

His eyes snap to me, dark and glassy, while his hands skim lower, tracing the hem of my skirt on my thighs, but staying rigorously on top of the fabric.

It's not enough. I don't want him tame. I want to feel him on my skin.

I push into him again.

"You don't want to test me right now," he rasps, the sound a growl, a warning—or a plea, I can't tell.

I kiss his neck. "Then stop me."

He doesn't. His fingertips sneak under my dress instead— *finally*—dragging up my thighs, stopping before he's where I need him most. I could scream with want. But I'm not the only one suffering. His fingers spasm. He could wreck me so easily, and just when I think he might—

A knock comes. Loud. Invasive. Reality barging back in.

We break apart too fast, two guilty teenagers caught doing

something they shouldn't. He lifts me and sets me up on my feet, standing next to me.

Tessa's voice filters in from the hallway. "Dorian? You in here?"

I'm not sure if I'm more relieved or disappointed by the interruption. "Saved by the bell, Phoenix."

Dorian lifts my hand and kisses the pulse point on my wrist. "For now."

And that single, tender gesture unravels me more completely than if he'd ripped my dress clean off.

31

DORIAN

After Tessa interrupts us, and Josie goes home, I'm still keyed up, my body tight with unspent tension. Every inch of me she touched refuses to forget, it craves more. I regret nothing— except maybe stopping.

I pace the length of my living room, replaying each second of our almost-moment.

Would a kiss really have been that reckless? I ask myself, knowing full well the answer. If we cross that line, everything changes. But right now, the thought of her parted lips is driving me insane. I can't hold out much longer.

At least my driver reported that no one tailed Josie's car when he drove it around town earlier. And it seems my house is not being monitored either. Maybe I've become paranoid where Billie is concerned. But my ex-wife did things I would've sworn she'd never do, so now I've learned to be overcautious.

Later that night, I should be asleep. Instead, I'm lying in bed, staring at my phone, waiting for Josie to text me.

She doesn't. Did I scare her off? She was pretty complicit, but maybe now she's regretting it?

I should show more restraint. Keep my white gloves on. But that was before she crawled onto my lap and nearly undid me.

I type a message and hit send before I can second-guess it.

> DORIAN
>
> I can't sleep after what you did to me today

> JOSIE
>
> I have no idea what you're talking about
>
> I am a professional rule-follower

I scoff.

> DORIAN
>
> Right. And I'm a Buddhist monk

She sends an angel emoji—the little halo over the yellow face—but the way my brain is wired now, it's the equivalent of throwing gasoline on an open flame.

> DORIAN
>
> Now I'm imagining you in a short angel costume

> JOSIE
>
> You have a thing for feathers?

> DORIAN
>
> I have a thing for you

> JOSIE
>
> Josie can't come to the phone right now 'cause she swooned to death
>
> P.S. Sophomore year of college, I dressed up like a sexy angel for Halloween, want a picture?

This is going to make my night so much worse, but I'm a glutton for punishment.

DORIAN

Yes, please

My phone pings. I keep my eyes glued to the screen as the image loads, and when it comes into focus, I regret asking for it because now I'm definitely not sleeping.

Josie is in a short white dress with feathery trim and high heels that make her legs go on forever. The wings are innocent. But not her pose. She has one hand on her hip, the other resting against a doorframe, head tilted as if she's deciding whether to let me into heaven or send me straight to hell.

JOSIE

Sweet dreams

smiley devil emoji

DORIAN

Don't tell me you also have a red version of this because I can't take it

JOSIE

Now I know what to buy for Halloween

I toss the phone onto the pillow beside me and stare at the ceiling.

Tomorrow. Tomorrow, I'll be normal again.

Or something close enough to fake it.

* * *

The next day, I bury myself in rehearsals. Josie already checked the VMAs setting, so she doesn't have a plausible reason to be here. And just as well. I don't think I would've been able to function if she were.

I plow through soundchecks. Wardrobe fits. And production meetings.

I should stay focused. I try to be.

But my phone is never far away.

Josie texts between whatever she's doing, keeping the conversation light, teasing, as we always are. But every time her name pops up, all I can think about is yesterday morning. The weight of her on top of me. How she moved against me.

That I could've kissed her right then if I'd let myself. She would've let me.

I roll a bottle of water between my palms to shove that thought into some deep, unreachable part of my mind. It doesn't work.

By the time I get back to my place, my body is exhausted, but my brain is wide awake. I scroll through emails, skim a few VMAs-related articles, open the Notes app to add a last-minute idea for my acceptance speech in case I win, then delete it.

Then I call her.

Not because I have anything specific to say. Just because it's become second nature, and I want to hear her voice before going to bed.

She picks up on the first ring. "I was about to sleep."

I smirk. "Liar. You were waiting for me to call."

She huffs out a laugh. "You have a high opinion of yourself, rockstar."

"And yet, here you are, still singing along."

She doesn't argue.

We talk about the VMAs and how excited Josie is she'll see the event live. I only got her a backstage pass. I could have gotten her a front-row ticket next to me. But we discussed the risks. The VMAs are a televised event, and we didn't want to attract attention to her. Not yet.

"Are you sure you don't mind being backstage?"

"No, I'd rather be where the free alcohol is," she jokes, making light of a situation that we can't change for now.

There's a pause where neither of us speaks. The silence is not uncomfortable, but long enough for me to be aware of it. And in that moment of suspension, I want to tell her things I shouldn't.

How much I feel for her. That what happened yesterday wasn't just sexual tension—it was more. Something bigger that I'm struggling to contain. Instead, I only wish her goodnight and read to her until she falls asleep.

32

JOSIE

A frenzied energy thrums through the backstage corridors, pulsing like a second heartbeat under my skin. The VMAs are about to start, the air buzzing with anticipation. My talent liaison pass dangles from my neck, a flimsy, laminated reminder I don't really belong in this world—at least, not the way Dorian does. But tonight, I'm here. And he's about to sing. Nothing else matters.

I smooth my hands over the fabric of my backless slip dress, my fingers tracing the silky material at my sides. The deep plunge in the rear feels like a secret hidden under the oversized cardigan I draped over my shoulders. The dress is sexy, but the covering and my low-heeled ankle boots tone it down. It could still pass for a semi-professional, big-event-appropriate attire.

When I reach the backstage area, I spot Dorian at once, my eyes zeroing in on him even in a small crowd. My chest reacts first with a jolt, then warmth floods in—a thick, liquid heat that spreads through me.

He's standing with his band in a loose circle a few feet away, the final moments before his performance ticking down.

I pause, taking him in. The way he runs a hand through his hair, the casual yet charismatic posture of his body, the focused expression on his face as he talks to his musicians. His outfit from rehearsal is back, the intricately embroidered black velvet vest hanging open over his chest, leather pants laced tightly along his thighs—dark, sexy. An aura surrounds him, a palpable energy that draws everyone in, making it impossible to look away. He was born for this.

As they do their pre-show ritual, Dorian claps his hands together and says something I can't hear. The band responds in unison, then they break up and get to their respective positions to make their entrances. Dorian stays.

My eyes trace the lines of his body, remembering how it felt to be pressed against him, the heat of his skin, the tension in his muscles. A thousand what-ifs flood my mind, each one more dangerous than the last. What if we hadn't been interrupted? What if he had kissed me? What if *I* had kissed *him*?

As if sensing my gaze, Dorian looks up and his black-rimmed eyes find mine. A slow, knowing smirk spreads across his lips, and my heart becomes a squirrel in my chest, scrambling madly.

"You made it." I read the words on his mouth more than hearing them over the crescendo of the crowd.

I lift my backstage pass in silent acknowledgment as I step closer so that we can hear each other talk. "Perks of being your PR handler. The job comes with all-access privileges."

His gaze drags over me, heat flashing in his eyes at the short hem of my skirt. Dorian takes a slow step forward. "Since it's no longer a rehearsal but the actual show, do I deserve a good-luck kiss?"

He's messing with me. He wouldn't kiss me here. But we haven't been alone since Monday morning on his couch—we're not alone *now*—and kissing him is all I've been thinking about since I left his house. How his full lips would feel against mine, the taste of him, the electric shock that would undoubtedly course through me. Every text, every call since then has only fanned the flames higher. The rational part of me knows that crossing this line could complicate everything, but the rest of me is screaming to just go for it. To hell with the consequences.

I bite my lower lip, torn. The noise of the arena fades into a distant roar, drowned out by the pounding of my heart. All I can see are his eyes, bright and dark at the same time and inviting—challenging. He's testing the waters, seeing how far I'm willing to go, and a part of me wants to dive in headfirst.

"Can't," I breathe.

His lips twitch, amusement dancing in his expression. "Aww, merciless." He glances toward the wings where a stagehand is holding up fingers, counting down to his cue. Then he turns back to me, gaze playful. "You sure you don't want to join the fans below the stage? Throw your bra at me?"

I narrow my eyes, then lift a single finger, curling it in invitation, beckoning him closer. Dorian leans in, his breath warm against my cheek as I whisper into his ear, "Sorry, I'm not wearing a bra."

Dorian goes still.

Then he stumbles back as if I've shot him in the chest, clutching his heart like he's been fatally wounded. His mouth parts in silent devastation, his entire body teetering as if he were about to collapse onto the floor.

For a moment, I believe he might actually fall on his ass. But at the very last second, he pivots, spinning on his heel and launching himself across the wings toward the stage right on cue with the music—but not before blowing me a kiss.

And then he's running across the stage to the roar of the

crowd, disappearing under the blinding spotlights, swallowed by thousands of screaming fans.

My heart screams with them.

The music explodes through the venue, the deep bassline reverberating through my ribs as the crowd erupts in even more enthusiastic cheers. I watch from the sidelines as Dorian takes command of the stage, his voice wrapping around the audience like a living thing. The sheer energy is intoxicating. It's a performance that will be replayed for years to come.

The crowd is a single, writhing entity, hands in the air, bodies swaying in unison to the rhythm he sets. It's a sea of adoration, and he's the undisputed king.

I can't take my eyes off him. Sweat glistens on his skin, catching the light as he works the crowd into a fever pitch. Each song flows into the next, a seamless medley that takes the audience on an emotional rollercoaster. They scream the lyrics back at him, their voices cracking with the intensity of their devotion. Even the other famous singers in the first rows can't sit still.

After fifteen minutes of pure adrenaline, Dorian bounds off the stage, still breathless, sweat glistening down his sternum. His smirk is exultant as he heads straight for me, his chest rising and falling under the open vest. "Not bad, huh?"

I cross my arms, feigning nonchalance. "You were okay, I guess. But I didn't see a single bra thrown."

He grins wider, stepping closer. "Tragic, really."

"What do you have to do now?"

"I need to change before heading into the audience." He sighs, tilting his head toward me. "You have two choices. Stay here and keep watching the ceremony like a responsible professional." His voice dips lower, teasing. "Or... you could accompany me to my dressing room."

"And watch you strip? How scandalous."

"I promise to be very professional about it." He cocks an eyebrow. "If you can do the same."

It's a slippery choice. I shouldn't go. But it's been two days of wanting to be alone with him and not being able to. The smart thing would be to stay here, to keep things in the safe zone, to avoid any more temptation than I can handle. And yet... I want to go.

My mind races through the potential outcomes. If I go, we'll be alone in an enclosed space. The tension between us is already at a breaking point; one wrong move and it could snap. But then again, one right move and it could be everything I've been imagining. Every rational thought is drowned out by the way he looks at me.

I think about the kiss he asked for that I denied, no matter how much I wanted to give in. I pretend to consider for another second, then sigh dramatically. "Well, someone has to make sure you don't wear your T-shirt backward on national TV."

He grabs his chin, mock-pensively. "The risk is real."

With one last glance at the screen broadcasting the ceremony, I let him take my hand and lead me down the hallway, away from the flashing lights, the screaming fans, and straight into trouble.

33

DORIAN

We stumble into my dressing room and I push the door shut behind us, the thud cutting off the sounds of the ceremony. Josie is hugging herself, her back turned as she scans the limited space. In the vanity mirror, her face looks like she's questioning every life choice that brought her here. She's maddeningly innocent and sexy as hell.

My pulse is loud in my ears. I should have thought this through.

I stay with my back pressed to the door, afraid of what I might do if I get close to her. "Sorry, no free alcohol back here."

She lets out a breathy laugh, shaking her head as she turns to me. "As long as there's a floor show, I'll survive."

I adore her sass, but I also enjoy calling her out on it. So I unhurriedly detach from the door and drag off my vest. Her cheeks flush, but she doesn't avert her eyes.

Her gaze follows my hands as they slide over the fabric, her lips parting in anticipation. I take my time, savoring being the sole focus of her attention.

I shrug one shoulder off, then the other, letting the vest hang loosely. Her eyes are drinking me in with a thirst I recognize too well—because I share it.

"Have I earned a twenty yet?" I go back to her joke of last week when she told me I was only worth one-dollar bills.

"Keep going and I'll slip you a hundred."

I give her a slow, seductive smile and get closer, invading her personal space a little as I shake the vest off. I catch it with a quick flick of my wrist, then break the tension with an exaggerated hip roll. It should be ridiculous, but she soaks it in, biting her lip. I twirl the garment over my head and throw it at her.

Josie catches it mid-air with a swift motion, her fingers curling around the luxurious fabric. She holds it, studying the intricate embroidery and the texture of the velvet. Then she does the hottest thing I've ever seen: she pulls it to her chest, inhales deeply, and closes her eyes, letting my scent wash over her.

Her lips curve into a subtle, guilty smile. Watching her savoring something so intimately connected to me sends a rush of blood through my veins. I imagine her wearing the vest with nothing else underneath.

She'd be perfect, she'd be mine.

Her eyes flutter open, and she catches me staring. I don't even try to hide it. She knows. We both know. But she has to be the one to decide. I promised her I'd wait. And I will, for as long as it takes.

"I'll be passing with a tip jar later." I wink at her and break the moment by bending to open the small suitcase pushed against the wall. I grab a fresh T-shirt and a pair of jeans. "I'll wash up real quick."

Josie nods. She drapes my vest on the chair behind her and turns to examine the stack of water bottles on the floor, as if half a striptease was already too much for her. I take that as my cue and move to the small sink in the corner to wash off the sweat from the performance. The cool splash against my chest is an instant relief. When I'm done washing, I grab a white towel and drag it across my skin.

I glance behind my shoulder as I dry off. Josie is standing stiffly, her back turned to me as she studies the ceiling.

I smirk. "You know, I'm not naked."

"That's great news," she says, voice more high-pitched than usual. "I was admiring the, uh, structural integrity of this room."

I chuckle, shaking my head as I toe off my boots and swap out my leather pants for jeans. Once I pull my clean T-shirt on, I walk up to her in my socks, dropping my hands onto her shoulders. She jolts at the contact, spinning so fast she collides with my chest.

She narrows her eyes. "Are you a panther?"

I blink. "Come again?"

"The way you move, silent on your feet."

I dip my head. "I only took off my boots, hardly makes me a ninja. Besides, it's not my fault you're so easily startled."

"Maybe I wouldn't be so jumpy if you weren't so..."

She trails off, circling a hand over me as if to conjure the right word.

I take a step closer, our bodies almost touching. "So...?" I tease.

She shakes her head.

"Josie—"

"I'm just saying," she cuts me off. "It would help if you warned me before you pounced."

"I didn't realize I was pouncing." I *so* was.

Her gaze dips to my chest, and I don't know if she's relieved or devastated it's covered now.

She tugs at my T-shirt, assessing my work. "Well, you put it on straight. You're good to go."

"Not so fast." I rest my hands on her shoulders, feeling the tension in her muscles, the rigid anticipation. I slide my palms down her arms, catching the edges of her cardigan. "We've got five minutes. And I have something to verify."

Her eyes widen, and her usual confidence falters. "W-what?"

I don't answer right away. Instead, I let my fingers linger on the soft fabric of her cardigan, taking my time as I ease it down her left shoulder. My gaze locks onto the strap of her dress—and the complete lack of any other band under it. Josie shivers, I can hear her heart pounding, or maybe it's mine.

My fingertips brush her skin as I let the cardigan slide down her arm. Josie doesn't stop me, but she doesn't encourage me either. Are we both waiting to see who will blink first?

Her eyes are searching mine, looking for clues, for intentions. Whatever she finds, I know what I'm feeling—an unbearable need to erase the short distance and taste the uncertainty, turning it into something real.

I lean in, catching the faintest hint of her perfume. "Josie," I croak, my voice betraying the storm inside me. "Are you really not wearing a bra?"

"My dress has no back." Her pulse jumps at her throat. "So, no."

A low, involuntary groan rumbles out of me, and before I can stop myself, I drop my forehead against hers. "Are you trying to kill me?"

Her lips part, and in the gentlest, most cruel voice, she whispers, "You're still breathing."

Barely.

I lift my head, taking in every detail of her. The cardigan is skewed now, slipping seductively off one arm, revealing the smooth, tantalizing expanse of her back in the mirror. The sight wrecks me.

Her skin taunts me, flawless and exposed.

I spin her so she's facing the mirror as I keep standing behind her. "Can I see?"

She meets my gaze in the reflection, her throat working as she nods. I lower the other side of the cardigan and let it slip down her arms, easing it off her until it pools on the floor. She grips the back of the chair for support.

For a beat, I just stare. At the knots of her spine, at the shadows that curl and play along the curve of her back. My fingers hover near her skin, trembling with restraint, aching to touch. When I finally give in, it's the barest graze of my knuckle down her spine.

Josie shudders under the touch, her whole body reacting as if I've sent a current through her. Her head tilts back, her eyes fluttering closed on a sigh.

I push her hair to the front and trace the path again, slower this time, feeling the contours of her vertebrae. I lean in and inhale the scent of her shampoo, savoring the sound of her unsteady breathing. My hands itch to explore more, to slide around her waist and pull her close, to feel her heart beat against my chest.

I want to kiss her nape, to taste her skin, and hear her gasp. I want to undo her, but if I start, I won't be able to stop.

Her eyes open slowly, meeting mine in the mirror. They're dark with desire, but also swirling with a thousand unspoken questions. She's letting me call the shots—decide whether we leap or stay on solid ground. The trust in her gaze is unbearable.

Her lips part as if to speak, but no words come out. Instead, she leans into me, her back pressing against my chest, her warmth seeping through my T-shirt. I wrap my arms around her, holding her gently, as if she might break—or to stop me from breaking. Her hands soon cover mine, and we stand like that, swaying slightly.

I close my eyes and let myself feel everything: the tickle of her hair against my chin, the rhythm of her breathing, the dizzying pull of her presence. We can't keep playing this game without tumbling over the precipice. I won't have the strength to whip us back if we go any further. Tomorrow, I'm leaving. I'll be gone for the best part of the next three months. I don't want to force a step forward when we'll have to take three back.

"Josie." I open my eyes, looking at her in the mirror. "I don't want to rush this. Rush us."

She nods, her head saying one thing while her eyes tell a different story. She wants this as badly as I do, and knowing that makes it even harder to hold back.

"We'll have our time," I promise. "I need you to be sure."

Her fingers grip me tighter.

"I know. I just..."

Whatever she was going to say is lost as a voice crackles over the speaker system, announcing that the Best Rock award is coming up soon and that I need to be in the audience.

Josie trembles in my arms. If her skin is burning like mine, then we're both seconds away from going up in smoke.

I squeeze her to absorb some of that heat, that tension, as if holding her tighter could somehow make it easier to walk away. "Saved by the bell again," I murmur against the side of her neck, pressing a featherlight kiss below her ear before stepping back. I force myself to be responsible. "I'll see you later?"

She nods, still staring at me in the mirror, her lips parted.

I beeline for the door, but as I pull it open, she calls me back, "Dorian."

I turn, expectant.

She has kept her back to me, only watching me through the mirror.

She tilts her head, her expression unreadable, then pants out, "You might want to put your shoes on before you go."

I glance down at my socked feet.

I curse. She smirks.

34

DORIAN

October

Being on tour rewires me. The second my boots hit the stage, I become a live current, buzzing, too charged to think about anything other than the beat, the melody, and the thousand voices screaming my name.

But then the shows end. And the energy doesn't know where to go.

That's how I feel stepping off the plane, back in LA after weeks of back-to-back concerts, my body still thrumming, my mind not sure how to shift back into normal mode. If I even have a normal mode anymore. My break is only four days. If it were a regular tour, I wouldn't even have come home to LA. But if I can steal even only a night with Josie, it'll be worth it.

As I get off the jet, it's already dark outside. I take in a lungful of air. The city smells the same—heat, concrete, and the faintest trace of salt from the ocean in the distance. I pass security and emerge on the other side of the terminal for private flights where Ned, my driver, is waiting for me.

I slip into the back seat of the dark SUV, stretching my legs out, silence creeping in. After weeks of city-hopping and being swallowed by the noise, the sudden quiet makes me too aware of what's missing. I haven't seen Josie in too long.

The VMAs were the last time we were alone. She came to the airport to say goodbye the day after, and this is my first break since then.

Despite the miles traveled and commitments keeping me busy, I thought about her non-stop.

And we talked. Constantly.

Texts between soundchecks. Calls squeezed into time zones that made no sense. She'd text me ridiculous things—articles about how fish can recognize themselves in mirrors, debates over whether a hot dog is a sandwich, pictures of Penny's latest art project. I called her every night, before her bedtime because I enjoy hearing how soft her voice gets when she's tired. Even if I had only a few minutes before going on stage. And she made sure I'd find a good-morning text when I woke up.

The distance has been hard but for the best. We need to learn how to be close and whether we can survive when we're apart. She can't follow me around the world every time I go, so we need to test this aspect of a future relationship, too.

I tell myself that, anyway.

As if on cue, my phone buzzes.

A picture.

It's a close-up of a red sequined fabric. The caption below reads:

JOSIE

I have a proposition

I smirk, thumbs already moving over the screen.

> **DORIAN**
>
> If it involves you and red sequins, I'm in

JOSIE

You should ask what you're getting into first

I settle deeper into the seat, tapping the side of my phone with my finger, already too invested in whatever game she's about to start. No point in playing it cool.

> **DORIAN**
>
> Alright, what am I getting into?

JOSIE

A mix of carrot and stick. Want the carrot first?

My mouth goes dry.

> **DORIAN**
>
> Sure

JOSIE

The dress is going to be short, and the horns sharp

I bite my knuckle, grinning like an idiot. If she keeps this up, I might tell Ned to make a U-turn and drive me to her place when I can't be seen there. Not yet. The weeks apart, if nothing else, must've thrown Billie off our case. But we can't go public yet.

> **DORIAN**
>
> And the stick?

JOSIE

We won't be alone

I shift in my seat, gripping the phone harder.

DORIAN

Explain

JOSIE

Tomorrow night I have to take Penny trick-or-treating. I was thinking you could come... wearing a mask, so no one recognizes you

She wants me to be with her and her family. Even if it's just to run around the streets collecting candy.

DORIAN

Sure Penny won't mind?

JOSIE

Are you sure *you* won't mind?

Penny is relentless on Halloween

She'll want to hit every house in the neighborhood

You'll be begging to go home before she does

DORIAN

I don't scare easy

JOSIE

Also, prepare for sugar-related crimes

DORIAN

Noted. Should I come armed with candy bribes or accept my fate?

JOSIE

Accept your fate. She's going to wear us down then be high on sweets and impossible to put to bed

DORIAN

Wow, you really know how to sell it. Total exhaustion and the risk of being held hostage by a tiny sugar gremlin

JOSIE

So a definitive yes?

DORIAN

Yes. I have a high pain tolerance. And an even higher appreciation for short red dresses

What about tonight? What are you up to?

JOSIE

Just finishing Penny's mermaid story on my tablet

Hopefully, it'll help sedate her tomorrow night

DORIAN

Could I tempt you with an adults-only night?

Her name flashes on the screen a second later.

I tap the green button, and she doesn't even let me say hello. "You're home early?"

I let my head fall back against the headrest, closing my eyes, picturing her on the other end of the line. "Yeah, a flying slot cleared tonight, and we took it."

"Is it safe for me to come over?" Her voice dips, cautious but hopeful.

"You want to?"

"Dorian." She exhales a soft rush of breath into the receiver that makes my grip tighten on my phone. "I haven't seen you in six weeks; I'm dying to be with you."

"We'll be alone," I clarify. I don't want to dance around what nearly happened the last two times we were by ourselves. "No Tessa to interrupt. No awards to get."

"Do I have to bring handcuffs?" Her tone is light, but there's a breathless edge to it.

"Kinky. I like where this is going." I grin, adjusting the AC vents as the car grows hotter—or maybe it's me.

"Wait, that did not come out right. I meant so that you'll keep your hands to yourself." She rushes to correct herself, her words too fast and flustered, and it makes my smirk widen.

I straighten, rolling my neck, the tension not entirely from the flight. "I know what you meant, but what about *your* hands?"

"I've been working on impulse control. Worst case, I'll sit on them."

I laugh. "Can you be ready in thirty?"

"Yeah?"

"I'm still on the road. I'll come pick you up."

I signal to Ned. Turns out, I will ask him to make a U-turn after all.

35

JOSIE

Dorian's SUV is already parked at the curb when I exit my condo. It's dark and inconspicuous, no one would guess who's hiding behind the tinted windows. The moment I exit the pedestrian gate of my building, the back door cracks open for me to slip in. Dorian doesn't get out, he can't. Someone could recognize him.

So I slip in and pull the door shut. And then it's just us. No screens, no cities separating us, nothing to diffuse the electric pressure knotting between my ribs. The car's cabin isn't small, but with him in it, it feels like a trap. Not one I want to escape from—one I want to get caught in forever.

"Hi," I manage, linking my hands in my lap to physically stop myself from reaching for him.

"Hey," he greets me, his gaze dragging over me, warm and amused. "You look cozy."

The SUV glides into traffic, but it might as well be floating from the way my internal organs lose sense of gravity.

"I thought you liked cozy."

"Oh, I *love* cozy," Dorian hums, leaning a fraction closer. He traces the hem of my sleeve with the tip of one finger and mutters, "Nice sweater."

I *knew* walking into this car was a mistake.

"You like the spooky cats?"

His thumb brushes a tiny, embroidered black cat on my side. It's the gentlest motion, a slow, lazy drag. But my body reacts as if he's touching skin.

"Soft," he murmurs, to himself.

I don't know if he means the fabric or me, but it doesn't matter because I'm already melting, muscles turning into something traitorous and pliant.

"This is bad," I whisper.

He sighs, while his palm hovers near my waist like he wants to touch me but thinks better of it. "I know."

"We should keep some distance."

Neither of us moves.

His eyes flick to my mouth, just as mine linger on his. I should sit back. Instead, I drop my head on his shoulder. He catches me, shifting so smoothly it feels inevitable. His arm hooks around me, pulling me in until my face ends up tucked into the crook of his neck.

"I missed you too much," I admit.

His head tips forward until his lips are brushing my scalp. "Me too."

His fingers skim higher, tracing my ribs through the fabric, not close to anything scandalous, but somehow burning worse than if he had.

"You realize this sweater is goofy, not sexy," I mutter. "It wasn't supposed to turn you on."

His laugh is low, rough. "You're terrible at *not* turning me on."

I hug him tighter, saying, "Pot, meet kettle," and enjoying the rumble of his laughter against my body.

We pass the rest of the ride in silence. Dorian caresses my back until the SUV slows, and the secondary gate of his house slides shut behind us, locking the world out.

I straighten up, and Dorian looks down at me because even seated, he's so much taller.

"Last chance."

"For what?"

"To be smart about this."

I should make a joke, but I can't find anything in my brain that isn't him—the weight of his stare, the way his body is angled toward mine, those damn tattoos on his forearms.

"You want me to be smart?"

Dorian's lips twitch. "Absolutely not. I'm depending on your terrible judgment right now." But then he becomes serious and cups my face, brushing his thumb over my cheek. "I don't *want* you to be smart, but I need you to be. I want this to be right. To be something you'll never regret, promise?" He tucks my hair behind my ear, his fingers combing through the locks.

I am putty under his touch. "Could you... err..." I can't think with his hands caressing my hair. "Could you not use your seduction voice when you ask me to be sensible?"

Dorian pulls back, laughing, and opens the car door on his side. "I told you that is just my horny voice." He gets out and circles to my side, opening my door for me and gallantly offering me a hand. "I can't help it around you."

I take his hand and, after we say goodnight to Ned, I let him lead me through the back entrance. The hallway opens into the main part of the house, where he hesitates.

Dorian clears his throat and gestures vaguely ahead. "Which living room do you want? The small one or—"

"The big one." I don't let him finish. The last time we sat in the small living room, I ended up in his lap, and I wouldn't survive a repeat performance.

His lips twitch like he expected that, and he keeps walking. We reach the main living room, and I wander to the massive windows overlooking the city. The view is too dark to see much, but the lights below shimmer in long, golden veins, stretching toward the hills.

Behind me, I hear him drop on the couch. "Josieee?" he calls.

I turn and watch him pat the cushion next to him. Then he stretches his arms over his head, muscles flexing. I hate that I don't even pretend not to ogle. I go to him and, kicking my shoes off, sink into the oversized sectional, curling my feet under my thighs.

Dorian throws one arm over the backrest, legs spread.

"How was the concert last night?" I ask.

"Wild." His face lights up as it always does when he talks about his music. "The crowd was insane, and we played three encores. I'm still buzzing from it."

"Sounds incredible," I say a little dreamily. "I don't know how you switch from that high to, well, everyday life."

"It's a balancing act." He shrugs, eyes crinkling as he cuts me a side glance. "The day-to-day can be as exciting, depending on who you're sharing it with."

Damn me, I blush. Dorian in real life is nothing compared to video-call Dorian. I haven't forgotten how it is to be face to face with him because I could never. But after several weeks apart, I'm feeling his proximity extra hard tonight.

"Right."

"What about you?" Dorian sprawls deeper into the couch,

one arm still draped along the back, fingers idly tracing the stitching. "Anything new?"

"You mean since we spent three hours on the phone two days ago?" I tilt my head, raising a brow.

His lips curve. "A lot can happen in forty-eight hours."

I grin wide because something has happened, and I've waited to tell him in person. "I have news, actually."

Dorian leans in. "Should I be nervous?"

I shrug. "Depends. How good are you at writing heartfelt recommendation letters?"

His brows pull together. "Who am I addressing them to?"

I wave a hand. "My potential new employer. I have a job interview on Monday."

I've spent the last month and a half sending out applications. After the VMAs, I knew I couldn't wait a year—technically, eight to ten months now—to be with him. I want it sooner. I want it yesterday. If my sister's tragedy taught me anything, it is that life is short. Shorter than we think.

Dorian blinks, processing, then gasps dramatically. "You're leaving me PR-less? Just like that?"

I smirk. "I figured you'd manage."

"Unbelievable. I open my home to you, I offer you a couch—and soon, a movie—and this is how you repay me?" Dorian drapes himself across the couch, pretending I've ruined his life. "Leaving me a struggling musician with no media shield."

I lift my eyebrows. "Struggling?"

"Emotionally," he deadpans. "Now that you're abandoning me."

I nudge his thigh with my foot. "Only professionally."

He catches my ankle before I can pull back, his palm warm where it wraps around me. Dorian rubs a slow, absentminded circle over my sock. "You're sure about this? The job?"

I nod. "I don't want to wait."

He searches my face, probably wanting to double-check I'm really okay with the potential career move, then nods too. "You'll get it." He squeezes my ankle before letting go. "They'd be idiots not to hire you."

I silently hope he's right and clear my throat. "So. Movie?"

He grabs the remote from the coffee table. "What are you in the mood for?"

"Something funny—Will Ferrell?"

"Yeah, come here." He opens his arms for me and I scoot closer.

As the movie starts, I nestle into Dorian's side, thinking how perfect this is. How perfect *he* is. I wonder if—and hope *that*—soon we'll be able to be together most nights, in the open, without worrying about me losing everything if we get discovered.

After we take Penny trick-or-treating tomorrow night, I'm going to spend the entire weekend prepping for my interview. If I get the job, we can try this for real, without sneaking around. I'll also be changing my entire life for a man I've never even kissed. That should terrify me. Instead, it feels like the only thing that makes sense.

* * *

When the movie ends, I'm already half-asleep. I'm not looking forward to the drive home, even if Ned will take me. But above everything else, I don't want to leave Dorian. Not so soon after getting him back.

I pull myself up anyway. "I should go."

"Do you *want* to go?"

"Eh, not particularly, but..."

"Then stay."

I freeze. "Here?"

"Yes, tonight." He pulls my hands in his lap. "No pressure. Take the guest bedroom. We can have breakfast together tomorrow."

I nod, relieved. "Okay," I agree too quickly, but the thought of staying longer, of not cutting tonight short, is too tempting.

He squeezes my hands. "I'm glad."

We rise from the couch, and he leads me up the grand staircase.

In the upstairs hallway, he pauses at a linen closet, pulling out a stack of fluffy white towels.

"If you want to shower." He hands them to me. "And here." He fishes out a spare toothbrush from a drawer.

"Thanks," I say, clutching the items to my chest.

He walks me to the guest bedroom at the end of the hall. The room is enormous, with a king bed wrapped in luxurious linens. I take a step inside, and the plush carpet sinks under my feet.

Dorian stops at the threshold, leaning against the frame with one arm braced on the top beam, looking hot as sin.

"Goodnight kiss?" he asks cutely.

It's become a new game for us. He pleads for kisses he knows I can't give, and each time, I struggle with the desire to say yes. And he knows. He's giving me sad-puppy eyes, but can't hide the spark of mischievousness. Dorian is testing me, teasing me, and I wonder who's going to break first. Maybe I should mess with him in return, give him a taste of his own medicine.

"Sure."

He frowns, his face a mix of feral longing and hesitant caution, which makes me smile inwardly. But I keep my features serious as I walk up to him seductively, swaying my hips. Hope flickers in his eyes, and his lips part ever so slightly in anticipation.

I stop just short of him, close enough to feel the heat radiating from his body. My hand comes up to his cheek, and I study the thousand thoughts racing behind his eyes. He's wondering if I'll do it, if I'll break our rules. I rise on my tiptoes, bringing our mouths less than an inch apart. He goes still, holding even the air in his lungs.

I close my eyes and savor his breath as it fans on my lips, warm and inviting. Every cell in my body is screaming at me to go for it, to take what I want. But at the last second, I brush to the side, my mouth landing on his cheek. I linger longer than I should, enough for the sexy scrape of his stubble to ruin me, enough to make him groan.

"Goodnight, Dorian." I pull back.

He drags a hand down his face, shaking his head with a helpless grin. "Guess I deserved that. Night, Josie."

Dorian leaves, closing the door behind him. I brush my teeth in the adjoined bathroom and then sag on the giant bed, still clothed, staring at the ceiling. I'm wide awake. The tiredness from before gone.

I don't know how long I stay in this position. But it feels such a waste to be here when he's just in the other room. My skin itches. I'm never going to sleep. On impulse, I get up, pad down the hall, and hesitate only a second before knocking on his door.

It flies open immediately, and my eyes widen. Dorian is on the other side in only black boxer briefs, a white T-shirt, and his ink. His hair is more tousled than usual. He's so breathtaking, I forget how words work and just stand, blinking like an idiot too long before I recover.

"Did you fly here from the bed?"

"No." He smiles. "I was pacing."

Ah. He must've been as restless as me.

"Can I sleep here with you? Only sleep," I add, even if I don't really need to specify.

Dorian doesn't hesitate. He grabs my hand, lacing our fingers together. He pulls me toward his bed with no urgency, just a slow, steady tug, as if leaving room for me to change my mind.

I don't.

When we reach it, I slip off my sweater and socks, ending up in just a tank top and leggings. He pulls back the covers and slides in, holding them up in invitation. I climb in beside him.

We don't touch at first. We just lie facing each other, the silence heavy with everything we *want* to do but won't—*can't*.

Then, slowly, carefully, he pulls me against him. I bury my face in his chest, and he rests his chin on top of my head.

His voice is a whisper against my hair. "We'll get there."

I nod, my fingers curling into his T-shirt, as he holds me closer and we fall asleep.

36

DORIAN

Early on Halloween night, I sneak up to Josie's sister's house looking like a B-movie Dracula, complete with a black mask and a red-lined cape. I'm hoping the disguise will keep me anonymous. I should've gone for a more foolproof costume with a full-face disguise. Kylo Ren, Dr. Doom, or a traditional Ghostface. But Josie has a thing for vampires, so here I am with my chin and mouth exposed—ready to sink my teeth in.

A wicked grin spreads across my face at the thought of grazing my fake fangs over her neck. The smile fades as I glance around the busy street where Ned dropped me off. A few kids in costumes run from house to house, their parents trailing behind, and I pull my cape tighter over my shoulders. Following Josie's instructions, I hop up a flight of steps to the second story of her sister's housing complex. I adjust my mask, schooling my features in a look as menacing as possible before I ring the bell.

Footsteps approach from the other side, prompting a warm friction to rise in my stomach.

The lock clicks, and a second later, Josie steps into view—or rather, her evil twin does.

My jaw hits the floor as I take her in. She's wearing the sequined dress I was promised, the skirt criminally short, exposing miles of long, toned legs. Her lips are painted a sinful red, and her dark and smoky makeup, much heavier than her usual, gives her an unrecognizable, sultry edge. Her hair is loose and wild, tumbling over her shoulders. A pair of horns peeks through the messy waves, and it's absurd how badly I want to let her be the devil on my shoulder.

Josie twirls the pitchfork in her hands with a wicked grin. "Trick or treat?" she purrs.

"You're stealing my lines." *And my heart. And my soul.*

"Answer me."

Bossy, I like it. I let my eyes trace the curve of her thighs before meeting her gaze. "What happens if I pick wrong?"

She leans against the doorframe, one leg crossing over the other, striking a pose that would make any mortal man weak in the knees. "You'll suffer."

"And if I pick right?"

Her lips curve wickedly. "You'll suffer—but enjoy it."

"So I suffer either way? You're not presenting my options very well. Shouldn't there be some seduction before the torment?"

"Didn't you read the fine print before promising your soul away for tonight? I told you it wouldn't be easy."

"My kind doesn't have a soul to sell."

She frowns adorably as she takes in my costume. "Why, who are you supposed to be?"

"A brooding immortal. A seductive creature of the night. Your pick."

"So vampire." The way she says *vampire*—silky, teasing, an invitation and a dare—grazes against my ribs like a wooden stake, poised to pierce my heart and end me. "Do I need to invite you in, Mr. Immortal?"

"You do. But if I were you, I'd think real hard before letting me cross that threshold."

She doesn't even blink. "Come on in."

Before I can even take her up on the offer, Josie catches me by the cape and pulls me inside.

The house is decked out in simple Halloween decorations—cobwebs crafted from cotton, paper skeletons dangling from strings, and a few carved pumpkins with friendly faces. It has a charming, DIY feel that speaks of a family's touch, not the kind you get from clearing out an aisle at the Halloween superstore. It reminds me of the ornaments my mom used when I was a kid, the sort that held more sentimental value than aesthetic.

"You've been merciful with this costume. I expected something much sexier," Josie teases. "You in superhero spandex, leaving nothing to the imagination."

"That's because you haven't seen my fangs yet." I flash her a slow smile, letting the porcelain props bite into my lower lip.

Josie's jaw drops, her eyes doing that dangerous sparkle thing. "You're really cruel, you know that?"

"Just trying to fit in with the other monsters."

She opens her mouth to say something, but a small figure barrels into the room. It's Penny wearing a mouse costume, complete with oversized ears and a golden crown. She's clutching a plastic sword and waving it around like a tiny menace.

"Aunt JoJo! I vanquished the dragon!" the mouse declares.

"Penny." Josie adjusts the mouse's ears. "Are you sure you want to trick-or-treat in your Mouse King costume? You'll ruin it before the recital."

"Mom said I could—" Penny doesn't finish, she gasps as she

spots me, then bolts straight for my legs, wrapping her tiny arms around my knees. "You came!"

I pretend to wobble under the impact. "Whoa, your Majesty, I didn't know I was getting escorted by royalty tonight."

Penny leans back, grinning up at me. "I'm the Mouse King," she declares, swishing her tiny plastic sword through the air. "We're gonna get all the candy."

"All of it? That's ambitious. What's our competition like?"

"Lots of kids, but they don't have a knight. We're unstoppable."

Josie lets out an exasperated sigh. "He's not a knight, Penny. He's a vampire."

Penny gives me a once-over. "Then you can scare the other kids away while my auntie turns into a human heart-eyes emoji. Cool."

Josie groans, rubbing her temples. "I regret everything."

I grin. "Too late. I'm committed now."

Penny tugs at Josie's dress, then at my cape. "Come on, let's go! We're wasting time!"

The three of us set out into the neighborhood. Penny is bursting with excitement, skipping ahead and waving her sword at imaginary foes with one hand while she carries a plastic pumpkin basket in the other. The warm evening air smells of dry grass and it's filled with the shouts and laughter of kids in various costumes scurrying along the sidewalks.

Josie walks beside me, her low-heeled ankle boots somehow sexier than stilettos. I should keep an eye out for anyone who might recognize me, but I can't look anywhere else.

"Lily's really bummed she had to work tonight. But she promised Penny she'd take her to a pumpkin patch tomorrow."

"Penny's lucky to have you."

Josie's face turns sad. "Penny was so happy when I told her

you were coming. Holidays like this are when she misses her dad the most. Danny loved Halloween."

I glance ahead at Penny, who's darting from one side of the sidewalk to the other, her mouse ears flopping with each bounce. The thought of her losing her father hits me anew like a punch to the sternum. Grief this big shouldn't fit inside someone so small.

I lost my mother as an adult and it hasn't been easy. I'm in awe of that kid's resilience.

"I'm glad I could help." I fight to keep the emotion out of my voice. "She's a wonderful kid."

Josie's smile fades into something more contemplative. "Yeah, she is. We give her as much love and support as we can, but sometimes, I worry it's not enough."

"You're doing an amazing job," I assure her. "She's surrounded by people who care about her. That makes all the difference."

Josie nudges me with her shoulder. "You're so nice, Mr. Immortal, weren't you supposed to be a monster?"

I scoff. "Want to hear me roar?"

"I thought I made it clear from day one that all I want is to hear you purr."

"Are you trying to tame me?"

"Never." She laughs, then—without hesitation—takes my hand, her fingers slipping between mine like she's done it a million times before. My heart does some ridiculous taekwondo move in my chest, and I squeeze her hand back as we keep walking down the block, just a regular couple out on Halloween night.

At the end of the block, Penny turns to us, her eyes wide with anticipation. "Are you guys ready? This street is the best!"

We follow her from door to door, hitting every house in

quick succession. Orange-and-purple string lights flicker along porch railings, while inflatable ghosts sag slightly in the heat. Plastic skeletons dangle from second-story balconies, their joints clicking in the breeze. One yard has a dozen foam tombstones arranged in precise rows across drought-friendly gravel. Spiderwebs stretch between cacti, and glow-in-the-dark bats cling to stucco walls.

Penny barely notices the decorations. She's a machine, her energy boundless as she sprints from yard to yard, dodging other kids and parents.

Once we clear the first block, Penny grabs my hand. "One more street, please!" she pleads. "We can't stop now!"

"Sure."

Josie scolds me. "You didn't even negotiate that this would be the last one."

"Oh, well." I brush the back of my fingers against hers. "I can't say no to any of the Monroe women."

* * *

We end up hitting three more streets. When we return home, I take off my mask and wipe the sweat from my forehead. Penny is bouncing off the walls, her sugar rush at full throttle as she dumps her candy onto the dining-room table.

"We got way more than last year!" she exclaims, as the assortment of sweets spills out in a colorful avalanche. Penny sorts them with the precision of a miniature scientist conducting an important experiment.

"How good are you at math?" I ask, loosening the collar of my Dracula costume.

"I can already do fractions. Like, if I eat half my candy now, I'll still have... half left!" she announces with a big, proud grin.

Josie walks in, taking in our loot. "Penny, no more candies for tonight. You need to wind down. It's way past your bedtime."

Penny pouts. "But Mom said I could stay up late because it's a special night."

"How about this?" Josie crouches down. "If you brush your teeth and get into your PJs, I'll show you the story I've been working on."

Penny's eyes light up. "The mermaid one, you've finished it?"

Josie nods. "And if you go change, I'll read it to you."

Penny considers. "Okay, but only if he reads the prince's part." She points at me.

Josie pretends to think it over. "Well, Dorian has the best reading voice..."

Her eyes meet mine, and I nod. "You've got a deal, kiddo."

Penny runs down the hall, whooping, while Josie walks to the chair where she left her bag and pulls out a tablet. I stand behind her, draping her hair to the side and dropping a soft, open-mouthed kiss on the juncture between her neck and shoulders. "Do I get a preview?"

She leans into me. "Sorry, no spoilers."

"Always so strict." I let my vampire fangs graze her skin, and she makes a small, helpless sound.

"And you're always so... tempting." Josie sighs, tilting her head to expose more of her neck as she shimmies against me.

My pulse kicks up. Josie is a devil and she knows exactly what she's doing to me. "I won't be able to read anything if you keep moving like that."

Mercifully, Penny calls out before Josie can reply, sparing me from whatever wicked retort she was about to deliver.

"I'm ready!"

We walk into her bedroom and find her sitting cross-legged on the bed, still wearing the Mouse King cape over her pajamas.

"Make room," Josie says, and Penny scoots over. Josie climbs on and looks at me. "You joining?"

No way I'll fit in that tiny bed, so I grab a chair and pull it next to them. Josie loads the story, and, as the first page appears on screen, I'm struck by how breathtakingly detailed the illustrations are. A mermaid with long, wild hair sits perched on a jagged rock, her iridescent tail glistening with a thousand multi-colored scales. The ocean behind her doesn't appear painted; it's *moving*, the waves curling and twisting in a dreamlike illusion.

"Wow. These are amazing."

Josie shrugs but her cheeks become as red as her horns. "It's just a hobby."

Penny interrupts, "Read, Auntie!"

"Once upon a time..."

As Josie begins, I lean back in the chair, following the text on the screen and waiting for my lines. When the prince makes his first appearance, I have to stifle a laugh. He has blue eyes, tousled dark hair, and a series of strikingly familiar tattoos.

"Is it just me," I cut Josie off mid-sentence, "or does the prince look a bit like—"

"Pure coincidence," Josie says quickly, but she's biting her lip, fighting a smile.

"I'm still flattered."

Josie turns the page purposely.

I deliver my next lines in my "seduction voice" to mess with her. She notices and scowls adorably, but keeps on reading.

When the story ends, Penny is fighting to keep her eyes open. "That was the best," she says in a small, sleepy voice. "Will you write me a sequel, Auntie?"

"We'll see." Josie kisses her niece on the forehead. "Sweet dreams, bug."

Penny is out before we leave the room.

In the hallway, I turn to Josie. "You should publish it. The art is incredible, and the story is... catchy."

She waves it off. "I'm just doing it for Penny and because I like to draw."

"You could still send it to an agent. What's the harm?"

She hums. "Mmm, I don't know. I would have to research agents and write queries. I should focus on finding a new job that will allow us to date openly, not chase a unicorn."

Her answer isn't just something I hear. It surges through my hands, charging them with the need to reach for her and grab that something that keeps growing louder inside me. Josie is rearranging her entire life for me, and I don't know what I did to deserve it.

"Thank you." I pull her to me and kiss her forehead. "I know this is harder on you. And it means the world that you're doing it for me."

She drops her cheek on my chest, hugging me close. "You matter more to me than my job."

"I promise I won't waste what you're giving us." I rest my chin on her head, brushing my hands down her back. "I should let you go to bed. Tomorrow, you need to study for your interview on Monday."

She nods, her fingers curling around mine before she steps back.

After we say goodnight, I fasten my mask back in place and step out into the night, knowing that even if I'm walking away, every road still leads back to her.

37

JOSIE

November

I didn't get the job. I failed. The disappointment presses behind my eyes, thick and swelling, ready to split my skull in two as I walk into Dorian's home office.

I had my interview set for early this morning and drove straight here afterward. I'm the last one to arrive—*again*. A wave of inadequacy crashes over me. The other people in this room are competent, prepared, and never late. I used to be like them. To have my shit together. But now, they're a well-oiled machine, and I'm the squeaky wheel.

I've been so absorbed by him, there hasn't been space for anything else.

As I take my seat, my gaze drifts to Dorian, and the whiplash hits me. The hard yank I always get when I see him after being away—for an hour, for a week, it doesn't matter.

He's leaning back in his chair, the sleeves of his black Henley shoved up his forearms, hair mussed, jaw with a shadow of stubble, as if he couldn't be bothered to shave this morning.

I should be used to this by now. And yet, every time, it catches me unprepared. My body reacts before I do, recognizing him on some deeper level, and it's like every cell exhales in relief that we're close again.

He lifts his head and ticks up his brows in a silent question, *How did it go?*

His mouth is already tilting in the barest suggestion of a smile, as if he didn't even contemplate the possibility of my failure.

I give him the smallest shake of my head to let him know I didn't get it, then drop my gaze before I can see his reaction. Because if I do—if I catch even a flicker of his concern, the quiet reassurance he'd offer, the way he'd *mean it*—I won't be able to hold myself together.

I keep my head down the entire meeting. We're just discussing logistics—plans for Dorian's upcoming concerts, touching base on ongoing sponsorships. No crisis, no scandals, nothing urgent to force me to engage. I only speak when someone asks me a direct question and answer mechanically, a robot reading off a teleprompter.

I can feel Dorian watching me, but I refuse to look back. His fingers tapping against the armrest of his chair are the only sign of his impatience. He barely acknowledges questions too. Dorian isn't paying attention either. He's waiting. *For me.* To talk.

And I don't know what to tell him.

When the meeting finally wraps, people filter out, throwing back casual goodbyes. I stand, pretending I'm leaving with the others. But of course, I stay.

The moment we are alone, the energy in the room shifts from professional to personal, and I'm not sure I've got the bandwidth to deal with it.

But I can't just ignore him and leave.

Dorian stands, crosses the room in a few strides, and wraps his arms around me without hesitation. It's a hug that offers everything without asking for anything in return. I grip the fabric of his Henley, my fingers pressing into the warmth of his back, and allow myself a few stolen seconds of comfort before I pull away.

"I'm sorry it didn't go well," he says, voice comforting. And, gosh, I hate it. "Do you want to talk about it?"

"No." I step back further, needing the distance. "I shouldn't even be here."

His head tilts. "Why?"

"Because I didn't get the job," I snap, frustration bursting out. "Because I blew it. Not because I wasn't qualified, but because they asked what new clients I was working on signing, and the answer was none. I had no names, no strategies. Just a blank."

He listens patiently, and it only makes me more furious.

"They didn't expect me to bring in my current clients," I continue, voice rising. "That's standard with a non-compete clause. But they wanted to know what I was *building*. And I had nothing. Because for the last two months, I've only thought about you."

He opens his mouth to say something, but I don't give him the chance. I barrel on before he can be kind and convince me my lack of career prospects isn't a disaster.

"I've let you take up every inch of my brain, Dorian. And while you were touring, doing what you love, I was here, doing nothing. I should have been building something for myself, reaching out to potential clients, making connections, proving I still belonged in the tech industry. Instead, I spent my days drawing stories, hiding in some fantasy, like I wasn't a grown woman with an actual career to build. And I forgot to plan for a future outside of this."

A long beat of silence. Then, cautiously, he asks, "Are you sure PR is what you want to do?"

I scoff, shaking my head. "Don't."

"I'm serious." He folds his arms. "You've never said you love it. But you loved creating that story for Penny. Maybe the kids' book thing is worth exploring."

"That's not—" I pinch the bridge of my nose to rein myself in. "You have *rose-tinted glasses* on because you chased a dream and it worked out. But your story is one in a million. For every musician like you, there are another thousand waiting for a breakout that'll never come."

He listens patiently, doesn't contradict me. And then he does something that makes me irrationally angrier. He apologizes. "I'm sorry. I'll give you more space. More time to focus on new clients and prepare for the next interview."

"I won't get another opportunity like this." My hands curl into fists, my exhaustion turning jagged, scraping at my nerves. "This was *it*. This was the perfect fit for me."

"You don't know that."

"Neither do you."

"Okay." He nods. "Well, I'm here for you. No matter what."

"Don't make promises you're not sure you can keep."

He doesn't hesitate. "I am sure."

That's when I snap.

"Yeah? And did you make the same promise to Billie when you asked her to marry you?"

The moment the accusation leaves my mouth, I want to claw it back. But it's too late.

Dorian stiffens, his entire body locking up as if I've physically struck him. His face doesn't just fall—it shatters. And I hate myself. Because I know—*I know*—how much that weighs on him. The staggering guilt he carries over his divorce. I took the sharpest thing I could find and stabbed it right through him.

"I-I didn't mean—" My feet move on their own, wanting to erase the distance between us. I'm desperate to take it back, to smooth over the damage I inflicted. But before I can reach him, his hands lift like a barrier, palms out, fingers stiff. It isn't an angry reaction. Not even a rejection. But something much worse: self-defense. He's protecting himself from me. From his biggest vulnerability that I threw in his face in the middle of a tantrum because things didn't go my way.

The thought guts me. My stomach twists so hard, I nearly double over. "I'm sorry. I shouldn't have said that."

"We should hit pause before we say something else we regret." He sounds so *wounded*. And it's my fault.

I search his face and only find the slow retreat of someone who's just learned he can't trust me not to hurt him. His hands stay raised a second too long before he finally drops them and gives me a curt, "I'll call you."

I nod stiffly. "Yeah. Okay."

And then I leave. I walk out of his house, my pulse hammering in my throat, my hands shaking as I get into my car.

I don't go home. I stop at the office, sit at my desk, and stare at my screen without seeing anything for hours. How did it get to this? What the fuck am I doing?

Dorian doesn't call. Not in the afternoon, not at night. He misses the time of our goodnight call. I get that he's not in the mood to read to me, but silly as it may sound, I don't want us to go to bed angry.

At midnight, I crack. I grab my phone and start typing a long apology.

I did a shitty thing, and it can't be undone. But I have to fix it somehow. He's leaving again tomorrow morning. Dorian will be on the road again for weeks, and I fear that if I let him go like this, I'll never get him back. So I type and type and type, pouring my heart out as I apologize to him.

When I'm done, I re-read the message, squeezing my eyes shut as I hit send and praying he will forgive me.

38

DORIAN

I'm in bed, staring at the ceiling, my phone face down on the nightstand. The alarm clock blinks past midnight, and I still haven't called her. I should have. But I didn't. Because every time I reach for my phone, I hear her voice accusing, *Yeah? And did you make the same promise to Billie when you asked her to marry you?*

The words land like a fresh hit, even now, hours later. I've had people throw worse at me—strangers, the press, even Billie herself. But Josie? She knew how to cut deep. And she did. I want to believe she didn't mean it. That it was just anger, frustration. But I don't know how to look past it, how to make it sting any less.

Because what the hell was I supposed to say to that?

Defend myself? Tell her she was wrong? That I wasn't making empty promises to her the way she clearly thinks I did with Billie?

That wouldn't have mattered. She wasn't looking for reassurance. She wanted to push me away, to make her failed interview about something bigger than what it was. And maybe I should've called her out on it. Made her stay, forced us to talk it through.

And I—*fuck*—I just let her go without a word.

I drag a hand down my jaw. My eyes burn, and my body is keyed up and exhausted at once. I should sleep.

I've just closed my eyes, knowing I'll never be able to rest, when my phone vibrates against the nightstand.

I tense, sure of who it is even before looking.

She sent me a message. A long one.

I swipe it open, taking in the block of text without reading it yet. This is her reaching for me the way I couldn't for her.

And even after everything, I still want to be reached. So I read.

JOSIE

> I thought about calling you. I should have. But I didn't want to fumble through an apology with half-formed words and nervous pauses. You deserve better than that. And honestly? I didn't trust myself not to make it worse, not to push *you* to make *me* feel better when I'm the one who screwed up. So I'm writing instead. I don't even know where to start, but "I'm sorry" is a place. A pathetic, inadequate place, but the only one I have. I hurt you. What I said was cruel. I knew where to aim, and I still let myself fire. That's not something I can justify or excuse. Other than saying that I'm not perfect and I fucked up. Real bad. I take full responsibility. For being selfish. For taking my insecurities and hurling them at you. And for dragging up something I know still hurts you, something you never deserved to carry in the first place. I was frustrated with myself, furious at how I handled the interview, drowning in self-pity.

And you—you were calm and kind, and for some insane reason, that only made me angrier. Which makes no sense. None of this does. Instead of dealing with life like a functioning adult, I threw a tantrum and took it out on you for no good reason. I know you respect me, my work, my goals—and I twisted everything into something ugly because I was too caught up in my mess to see straight. The fact that I used Billie against you makes me want to crawl out of my skin. It was a cheap shot. And false.

The divorce isn't your fault. I've seen it. I keep thinking back to the moment you pulled away from me like you had to protect yourself from me, and it makes me sick. If I made you feel unsafe or like you couldn't trust me, I don't think I'll ever forgive myself. If you need space, I understand. If you need more than space, I understand that too. But I need you to know that I would do anything to take it back. A million sorries wouldn't be enough, but I mean every single one.

I stare at her message, my jaw working as I read it again. And again. It's everything she could say. More than I expected. More than I've had in the past. This is what makes Josie different. Not just from Billie but from anyone I've ever been with. The ability to look her mistakes in the face, to name them, to own them without hesitation or excuse.

Billie never did that. The closest thing to an apology I ever got from my ex-wife was a hand sliding down my stomach, followed by a low whisper in my ear, a distraction that had nothing to do with remorse and everything to do with avoidance. With making the problem disappear and pretending it never happened. I went along with it. I let myself be smoothed over and shut up because it was easier than fighting.

But I'm not like that with Josie. She lays it out. The guilt, the self-awareness, the bone-deep regret. And it gets to me, settles under my skin, because I know how hard it is to admit you've hurt someone, to resist the impulse to justify it, to sit with the discomfort of being wrong. And she's doing it. For me.

I run a thumb over the side of my phone, debating. A part of me wants to make her wait. To let her stew in it a little longer, to hold on to the anger because it'd be easier than forgiving her outright. But another part—one that's louder—reminds me I spent all night not calling her, letting the silence stretch between us like a bridge I was too stubborn to cross.

And I... I fucking miss her.

So I press call.

Josie picks up right away.

"Hey," she says, breathless, uncertain.

I swallow. "Hey."

"I'm sorry." I can hear she's fighting not to cry. "I didn't think you'd call."

"I almost didn't," I admit.

A slow, shuddering exhale on her end. "And?"

"And... I hate how good you are at apologies."

A small, wet laugh. "Dorian, I meant every word. I was awful to you."

"You were human," I tell her. "Not perfect, but real."

"I don't want to be human if it means hurting you."

"Well, I'm not really a vampire so I can't suck you dry and turn you into a monster."

"I already feel like one."

I close my eyes. "Josie—"

"I was horrible to you."

"But you're not now." I shift onto my side, pressing the

phone closer to my ear. "Even at your worst, you still texted a novel-length apology at midnight."

"I never want to fight with you again."

"But we will. This has been our first fight, but it won't be the last. We'll just have to get better at it."

"That simple?"

"Not even close."

"I hate that I hurt you," she says after a while.

I swallow. "I hate that I let you walk away."

"So what do we do?"

"We figure it out."

"Together?"

"Yeah," I murmur. "Together."

39

JOSIE

It's too early. Too cold even for Los Angeles. And I should still be in bed.

Instead, I'm here, crossing the private jets' hangar at the airport, watching as Dorian's crew makes the last checks before his flight. His plane is waiting, sleek and ready, the engines humming low in the distance.

I hold the folder in my hands close to my chest as I move along. Maybe coming here was a stupid idea and I should have left things as they were last night. Skip the goodbyes, let our phone call be enough without turning our fight into something bigger.

But knowing he'd leave with nothing but the memory of me shouting nonsense at him made my stomach churn. I couldn't let that be how we ended things before he left.

So I'm here.

The door to the private lounge opens, and Dorian steps out. I expected him to be here, but seeing him still makes my heart clench as if an invisible hand is squeezing it.

He is dressed in a fitted black hoodie and dark jeans, his

travel bag slung over his shoulder, hair messy from lack of sleep. His steps slow when he sees me, his brows drawing together in something between surprise and worry.

"Josie? What are you doing here?"

We're not alone. His tour manager, a couple of security guys, and a flight attendant stand a few feet away. I keep my face neutral and hold up the folder.

"I have some important documents for you to sign before you take off. Can you spare five minutes?"

Dorian's lips twitch, his gaze flicking to the fake papers, then back to me. "Yeah. Come on." He gestures toward the private meeting room at the rear of the lounge, and I follow him inside.

The moment the door clicks shut, I drop the folder on the table. "Okay, so there's nothing to sign."

He flashes me a lopsided smirk. "No kidding."

I step forward and hug him, pressing my face against his chest. Dorian doesn't hesitate. He pulls me in, holding me close like he needs this as much as I do.

"I'm sorry," I whisper against the soft fabric of his hoodie. "I... I didn't want our last in-person conversation to be a fight."

His lips brush against my hair. "Me neither. You don't know how many times I thought about driving to your house last night."

"Why didn't you?"

"Anyone could've seen me and it was late."

I squeeze him harder.

We breathe each other in, his fingers tracing slow, absent-minded circles against my back, my hands fisting his hoodie, memorizing the way he feels.

Too soon, a knock comes. One of his security guys letting him know it's time.

Dorian shifts to look at me. "You're sure you'll be okay while I'm gone? That the long distance is not an issue?"

I nod. "Doesn't matter what time zone you're in. You're always in my thoughts."

His throat bobs. "Same."

His thumb skims over my hip, not pulling me closer, not letting go, just holding, as if this moment could stretch forever. Then, he dips his head and presses a slow, lingering kiss on my forehead.

And then he's gone.

* * *

In the following weeks, I don't fall into the same trap of putting everything on hold while I wait for him to come home. Every spare minute I have, I put it to use, making sure I have something to show for it.

With Dorian away, my plate at work is only half-full. I still have to monitor and manage his press coverage. It's enough to keep me busy, but not enough to fill all the gaps. Nadine still doesn't let me touch my old clients, which leaves me stuck in limbo. So, I attend networking events, shake hands, make conversation, and plant seeds. But it's hard when I can't close anyone new. I don't want to sign them while still under my noncompete clause. But with no new firm to bring new clients to, all the professional shmoozing adds up only to a pile of maybes. A lot of possibilities with nothing concrete.

The headhunter I've gotten in touch with only has positions open in different cities. But I don't want to move. My family is here. Dorian is here.

He doesn't bring it up again in our calls, the thing he said before he left—about publishing my children's book. But it stays with me, lodging itself in the back of my mind until, one night, I finally do something about it. I research literary agents, read submission guidelines, and send query letters.

It's a small step forward. But better than nothing.

Two weeks later, Dorian returns home for Thanksgiving. We sneak him into my mom's house, and he spends the holiday with my family. It feels like he's always been one of us.

In early December, an agent I contacted replies, offering me representation. I'm giddy with excitement, at least until we jump on a call and talk numbers. She lowers my expectations on what I could realistically earn on a single book in my first years—definitely not enough to replace my current salary, but we click, and I sign with her. Dorian is so supportive when I tell him. He treats the news like I've landed a seven-figure deal with a movie option already lined up, not a cautious first step and a sobering call about numbers. His belief in my success is loud, immediate, and entirely unshakable.

He encourages me to work on the next story, and it's all I do for the next ten days, until, finally, Dorian comes home for good.

40

JOSIE

December

The last three dates of Dorian's world tour are here in LA, from Friday, December 12, through Sunday, December 14. We don't get much time together when he arrives. His plane touches down, and within minutes, he's swept into soundchecks, press interviews, and rehearsals that stretch late into the night. Even offstage, he moves in sync with his band, their rhythm ingrained from months on the road. They eat together, breathe the same music, and operate like a unit. Dorian is home, but not really. Not yet. But I don't mind. This is the last stretch before he gets to slow down, before we both can take a breath. Only three more nights and then his schedule will be relatively clear for the holidays. And with Christmas around the corner, I'll have time off work, too.

I go to all three concerts, this time as part of his staff. Each night, the venue is packed to the rafters with screaming fans, the energy so palpable, my skin tingles. I sing along, I dance, and I lose myself in the music. But more than anything, I admire him.

By the last night, the buzz is even more powerful. The fans are enjoying the final concert of his world tour, but also saying goodbye.

I follow the event from behind the main stage with the technicians, listening to him sing, feeling the bass vibrate through the floor and Dorian's voice ring through the arena, every note, every lyric, overpowering.

I have my eyes fixed on Dorian, following him on a mega screen when, in an instant, everything changes.

I catch a flicker of motion in the lower rafters above him. A blur in my peripheral vision that sends a jolt of fear through me.

One of the hanging set lights, a smaller fixture meant to cast a warm glow during acoustic numbers, wobbles, then breaks free from its rigging. My stomach lurches as if I were BASE jumping off a skyscraper.

I bring my hands to my mouth as the fixture plunges downward, swinging erratically on its remaining cable before it breaks free.

In the flattened image of the display, I can't tell if it's on a collision course with Dorian, but the screen makes it look terrifyingly close.

Dorian turns his head at the last second and stops singing mid-lyric, his sharp intake of breath cutting through the arena speakers.

He tries to sidestep, but he's not fast enough.

The metal housing scrapes across his face, clips his shoulder, and then crashes to the stage with a sound like a gunshot, shards of glass and metal exploding in all directions. Behind him, the band falters, the instruments trailing off, the sudden silence deafening.

The crowd gasps as one as we all stay suspended in a surreal stillness.

My eyes are glued to Dorian, my heart a wild animal in my chest, hoping against hope that he's not hurt.

Dorian touches his temple, and when he removes his hand, blood trickles next to his eye. His fans scream. I feel like I might throw up.

But Dorian, ever the showman, barely flinches.

He presses his fingers to the wound again and blinks at the blood as if it's more of an inconvenience than an injury. Then he turns back to the mic, his lips quirking up like nothing happened.

"Guess that's one way to keep things exciting," he jokes, voice steady despite everything. The crowd cheers—a few girls in the first lines cry while smiling and hugging.

Dorian raises a hand to calm the crowd. "I'm gonna take five to get this cut checked out, okay?" His question is met with a thunderous roar of approval, the kind that shakes walls. These people worship him; they'd wait all night if they had to.

Backstage, the technicians scramble, talking into their headsets, while Dorian's tour manager, Grant, looks like he's about to have a stroke. They're coordinating with the band who opened the concert, signaling for them to get ready to go back on stage.

The message is related to Dorian through his earpiece. He listens, then nods. He's unhurried, composed, every inch the seasoned performer. Dorian brings the mic back to his lips. "Looks like you're gonna get a few more songs from Velour!" he announces to the return of the opening band on stage, then waves and runs off.

The fans erupt, a sea of bodies surging with newfound energy.

But backstage, I'm still frozen.

Dorian appears from a hidden hatch, and my first instinct is to run to him. I lurch forward, heart hammering in my throat, but the medics reach him first. I stop, hovering nearby while they check him out.

They clean the cut and run a flashlight in front of his eyes, asking him to follow the beam, presumably checking for a concussion. I watch, holding my breath, my fists clenched at my sides.

Finally, they step back, satisfied.

Dorian rolls his shoulders, then he catches my eye and lifts his brows. "Hey, you look like you just watched someone get hit in the face with a light."

I don't laugh. I don't even breathe as I cross the distance between us.

"Are you okay?" I demand.

He shrugs, tapping the shiny transparent coating that covers his wound. "Yeah. They, uh, superglued me back together."

"You're going to have a scar on your eyebrow."

Dorian smirks. "Cool, right? I'll look extra rugged now."

I scoff, arms crossing. "Yeah, because you needed to get sexier."

Dorian pulls me under the stage, away from sight. "Sexy enough for a kiss?"

The substitute band is playing above us, the sound muffled but throbbing through the structure.

I ignore his question. "Are you sure you're okay to finish the show?"

"Yeah, I'll live. But you know..." Dorian runs a hand through his sweat-dampened hair, tilting his head, considering. "I could use a little something to make it better." He smacks his lips.

I exhale through my nose, unimpressed. "You really expect me to kiss it better?"

He leans in. "I am tragically wounded, have you no compassion?"

I roll my eyes but step closer anyway, rising on my tiptoes to press a featherlight kiss below the cut on his brow. I meant it as a joke, as a peck without consequences. But the moment our bodies are flush against each other, a spark ignites. The heat of his skin, the scent of his sweat and cologne, the rhythmic thrum of music from above—it collides in a dizzying rush. My lips linger longer than they should as his hands settle at my waist.

And when I slide back down to the flats of my feet, my chest drags against his. I don't pull away. I brush my cheek against his jaw, his stubble scraping against my skin, rough and heady.

His fingers dig into my flesh. His lips brush my ear. I lace my fingers through his hair, not caring that it's damp with sweat.

With him so close, every nerve in my body is on fire, sparking and crackling with an unbearable intensity. The pain of an entire year spent thinking I could never have him scorches through me, setting my insides ablaze. And the past three months of having him but in name only char my skin.

His hands on me are a matchstick, his breath in my ear the spark that sets me alight. I want to consume him, to be consumed, to let this fire burn us both to cinders. My lips part, and I can almost taste the salt on his skin, the metallic tang of the blood that's dried on his eyebrow.

I drag my mouth along his jaw, savoring the roughness, the tickle of his stubble.

I turn my face, my lips nearly touching his. His breath has turned uneven, his grip on me iron-tight.

When I brush my lips over his in a whisper of contact, Dorian goes still.

I lift my gaze, meeting his black-rimmed blue eyes, and in them, I see everything—the desire fighting with restrain fighting with... *love.*

He's never said it, but I've seen it. It's been there for a while.

And I feel the same. My heart pounds so loudly that I'm sure he can feel it even through our clothes. Every rational thought screams for me to stop, to pull back, to wait. My brain scrambles to douse the flames, but it's hopeless. The longing is too intense, the pull of him too strong. I can no longer contain the flood of feelings I have for this man. My senses are drowning in him— touch, sight, hearing, smell—the only one missing is *taste*.

A thousand reasons why this is a terrible idea race through my mind. He needs to get back on stage. We're in a crowded arena in the middle of *the last show of his world tour!* We don't have time. But neither of them is strong enough to override the singular, all-consuming need that's taken hold of me.

He looks at me, hungry and desperate, but he's already setting his jaw, bracing himself to pull back. And it's that hesitation, that moment of uncertainty, that undoes me. Because if he's holding back for my sake, I'm the only one who can tip us over the edge.

The dam of my restraint breaks. I can't contain it anymore. The rush of emotions is too strong, too overwhelming, washing away the doubts and fears in a tsunami of pure, unfiltered desire.

I pull Dorian down to me, and finally, *finally*, I kiss him.

41

JOSIE

Dorian goes rigid at first. But he's quick to catch up, and when he does, his own dam bursts, flooding me with his pent-up desire. Our mouths crash together in a collision of raw need. It's not a gentle kiss. It's urgent, reckless, an explosion of every suppressed feeling we've both been carrying. There are teeth, and there's tongue.

The world blurs. The muffled music from the stage above, the distant roar of the crowd, fades into a background hum as every one of my senses hone in on him. His hands move from my hips up my spine, pulling me closer, crushing me against him.

He's yanking and pushing, and we careen backward until my back hits something—poles? I can't tell, and I don't care. Because Dorian is kissing me.

I can feel the hard lines of his body, the rapid thump of his heart echoing my own.

Heat radiates from his skin, searing through my clothes, and I'm melting into him, losing sense of where I end and he begins. Each stroke of his tongue, each nip of his teeth sends shockwaves of electricity through me, short-circuiting my brain. Thoughts scatter, and emotions prevail.

Time stretches and distorts, an elastic band pulled to its breaking point. Seconds feel like hours, yet they pass in an instant.

Dorian growls low in his throat, and the kiss turns carnal. His hands find the hem of my dress, sneaking underneath. The rough, calloused pads of his fingers squeeze my bare thighs none too gently, and a shudder of pleasure and need rips through me.

I bite down on his lower lip, equally aggressive, and he responds with another growl that comes from deep in his chest, the sound so raw and animalistic that my grip on reality falters. Am I dreaming? But then he presses me harder against the poles, his body a solid wall of warmth and muscle, and I arch into him, craving more, remembering he's real. And finally mine.

Dorian shifts his thigh between my legs, creating a torturous friction. I gasp into his mouth, my entire body tensing and then melting against him. The unexpected pressure makes my knees buckle, and I clutch at his shoulders, digging my nails in, desperate to steady myself as a wave of heat crashes over me.

He takes advantage of my open mouth, his tongue diving in without mercy as his hands cup my face.

The world tilts as he grinds his thigh harder against me, and my hips move, seeking more of the exquisite torment he's inflicting. My head spins. My body loses weight. I'm flying... I'm being lifted into another dimension.

I levitate, my senses disjointed, each one firing in different directions. Air rushes past me, cool against the feverish heat of my skin. On the back of my brain, I wonder if I've died and gone to heaven, surfing through the clouds.

Until the jarring reality of our surroundings seeps in. Dorian's lips are still on mine, his hands still cupping my face, but the world is no longer a blur.

The music has stopped. And the crowd that was singing along a moment ago is now mute.

The poles digging into my back start to make sense. They're the bars of the cage Dorian uses to make his dramatic entrance for the second half of the concert.

We're no longer under the stage. We're kissing in front of a sold-out stadium for the entire world to see.

42

DORIAN

Josie tenses against me.

It's small—the slightest stiffening of her spine, a hesitation in the way her fingers grip my shoulders. But the movement sends a ripple of awareness through the haze of the kiss.

Then understanding rushes in all at once. The absence of music. The unnatural hush from the crowd. And the sudden brightness of the stage lights above us.

We're not hidden, protected in the darkness under the stage anymore.

My stomach turns to stone as my eyes snap open, my pulse hammering for reasons that suddenly have nothing to do with the kiss.

Fuck.

I wrap my arms around Josie, shielding her face, pressing her into my chest to block out the thousands of eyes staring at us.

"We messed up," I whisper against her hair, calm despite the static running through my veins. "But it's gonna be fine. I've got you."

Josie gives a small nod against my chest.

I keep one arm locked around her while I lift my other, signaling the techs to lower us. It takes a second—an eternity—but then, with a mechanical groan, the cage descends.

Josie stays tucked against me, her breath shallow, until we're under the stage again. The moment we're swallowed into the lower level, Josie pulls back, her breath coming in quick, uneven bursts.

"Oh my gosh," she whispers, her hands gripping the front of my leather jacket. "Everyone saw. They all—Dorian, we're—" Her voice hitches, panic widening her eyes. "Everyone knows."

I cup her face, my thumbs skimming along the edges of her cheekbones, grounding her. "No, they don't." My tone is calm—because one of us has to be. "They saw me, not you."

Her brows knit together, unconvinced.

I tilt my head toward the ceiling, where the blinding stage lights had been. "Your face was in my chest the second I realized. I covered you. No one saw you."

Behind us, the backstage is a battlefield. Crew members bark orders, radios hiss with frantic voices, while upstairs, the lead of Velour is making jokes, keeping the audience entertained. And then Grant comes shoving through the chaos with murder in his eyes.

"What the fuck was that?" My tour manager has aged a decade in half an hour. His eyes flick between us, recognition sparking when he sees Josie, then lock onto me with renewed fury. "First, you almost get your head taken off—"

"Arguably not my fault."

"—and then you make out with your PR rep in front of a sold-out arena like a horny teenager?" He looks like he's two seconds from quitting.

I shift, keeping Josie behind me. "Relax, Grant."

"Relax? Dorian, where the hell was your earpiece? We told you we were about to lift the damn cage, and you gave us a grunt we thought meant go. We didn't know your tongue was halfway down someone's throat!"

I blink. My earpiece?

Instinctively, I reach for it, only to find the cable hanging loose on my shoulder.

Huh. That explains why I didn't hear them.

Grant follows my movements, sees the earplug, and mutters something foul under his breath. "Unbelievable," he grits out. "We had this tour locked down tight for a hundred fucking shows. No glitches, no screw-ups. And now, on the last night—"

"It's not a big deal." I cut him off. "I'm going to handle it."

"You'd better dial up the charm before my career flushes down the drain," Grant barks. "You're up in five. Side fucking entrance, using your own legs."

And with that, he spins on his heels and goes yelling at someone else.

I turn to Josie. She's still tense, clutching her hands in front of her chest. She looks small in the chaos, her dress rumpled, her hair mussed.

I don't want to leave her like this.

But I have to.

"I have to go finish the concert," I say apologetically.

She nods. But her eyes are still wide and worried.

I tuck a loose strand of hair behind her ear. "Hey. It's gonna be okay."

She nods again, surer this time. "Go. I'll be fine."

I squeeze her hand before stepping away. Readying myself for my fans.

The stadium is still buzzing, the energy electric, not from shock anymore but from anticipation.

They're waiting. For me.

I give them what they want. I step on stage, microphone already in my hand. The second they see me, a sound wave crashes through the arena, a deafening mix of cheers and screams. I bring the mic to my lips and let the roar ride out before speaking.

"Well." I glance around with a grin. "A lot of excitement tonight." The crowd erupts again, feeding off my energy. "We're going out with a bang LA or what?"

The responding roar is deafening. Good. I need to keep them with me.

I touch the spot on my eyebrow where the cut is already stinging. "First, I get my head knocked in," I joke, "which, don't worry, is still attached."

A fresh wave of screams.

"But as you may have noticed..." I let my grin turn a little sheepish, rubbing the back of my neck, "...there's someone new in my life."

The arena explodes.

It's not just screaming—it's full-body, losing-their-minds chaos. People are jumping, hugging, crying. It's a level of hysteria I haven't seen since the first few appearances Billie and I made as a new couple.

I hold up a hand to silence them, smiling despite myself. "Listen, she got worried about the head bump and she wanted to kiss it better." More screams. "And, uh, she did a pretty damn good job."

More shrieking.

I wait, then add, "I get that you're curious, but we're not ready to go public. Not yet. So I'm asking you to please respect our privacy."

I hold my breath, waiting. Then stare, stunned, as a wave

starts in the far section of the stadium—fans rising, hands lifted high, before dropping back down in perfect sync. The wave moves, gaining speed, circling the arena like a living, breathing force of support. The message is clear. They accept my explanation. They accept *us*.

"Alright, alright. You guys are wild tonight." I glance behind me, where the band opening for me is still standing, watching me with open amusement. "Hey, Velour! What do you say we do a song together?"

The lead singer grins, stepping forward.

And just like that, we're back on track.

We give the fans an extra song. Then Velour leave, and I finish the concert like any other. Without any other surprises or interruptions.

And when the lights go dark on the last show of my world tour, a familiar ache settles in, the high of the performance dissolving into silence. But nothing about this moment feels like an ending. Because no encore, no standing ovation, no moment on stage will ever compare to what happened underneath it. Because tonight, Josie kissed me.

43

JOSIE

The morning after the concert, I should be focused on the meeting taking place in Dorian's home office, not glued to my phone, drowning in the digital disaster unfolding online. But everything is in disarray today: the universe, the internet, my life. Even the room feels like a contradiction. Someone has decorated the French windows with stick-on faux snowflakes, which I find hilarious against the backdrop of the sunny garden and towering palms beyond. The world can't decide what season it is, and I can't make up my mind whether to panic or pretend this isn't happening.

Instead of paying attention to the meeting, my eyes are locked on the unending feed of headlines and photos of Dorian and me on stage last night. Every single media outlet, gossip site, and blogger is fixated on one thing: the mystery woman Rian Phoenix kissed in front of thousands of screaming fans.

I shouldn't have been so reckless, so entirely without brain function. I know better. I berate myself as I keep scrolling the pictures. There are enough screenshots of us to wallpaper all of

LA and I still can't tell if it's possible to identify me. Panic bubbles in my gut as I zoom in on one of the pictures with a better resolution, trying to pick out the details of my face. Dorian's arms cover me, but I see a temple, the bottom part of my jaw, my hair.

Has Nadine seen this? Could she recognize me from these photos? The only person who knows for sure is Grant, and Dorian has sworn him to secrecy.

I reassure myself that my boss is away at a conference, too busy with meetings and presentations to be scouring tabloid headings. And even if she saw the news, Nadine's never been the type to micromanage. But this isn't a minor PR hiccup—it's a full-blown media frenzy. If Nadine recognizes me, will I still have a job when she comes back next week?

I push the thought of impending unemployment from my mind and keep torturing myself with new headlines.

Who Is the Woman Who Stole Rian Phoenix's Heart? one article proclaims in bold, accusatory letters.

Rockstar's Secret Romance—Exclusive Insights Inside! promises another.

The sheer volume of speculation is overwhelming. Some theories are so outlandish that I want to laugh. One story claims I'm a European model Dorian was linked to seven years ago. A different tabloid swears I'm an old flame from his pre-fame days, resurfacing at the perfect moment to reignite our passion.

I chuckle inwardly, thinking that Dorian's high-school girlfriend, Sandy Parker, and her mom, who still sends Dorian Christmas cards, must be really pumped about that last wild guess.

Victor's voice cuts through my haze. "Dorian, you can't let the press control the story. It'll only grow bigger if we don't get ahead of it," his agent insists, his tone all business. "You need to go public with her identity before the gossip sites decide for you."

Dorian leans back in his chair, his expression unreadable. "And if I don't want to?"

"Then be prepared for a media circus." Victor's eyes narrow. "They won't stop until they uncover who she is. It's better if it comes from you."

As they discuss, the million images and videos create a vortex in my mind—part longing, part regret, part I don't even fucking know. Each pixelated image, each slowed-down video clip, feels like a ticking bomb waiting to go off. How long until someone sharpens the resolution enough to make me recognizable?

Dorian's gaze meets mine across the table, his eyes concerned but also determined as he turns to his agent. "I'll handle it. But on my terms. Not theirs."

Victor pleads to the room next. "Do you all agree with this?"

As no one replies, I realize he must be the only one in this office who doesn't know it's me.

I'm sure Bailey knows. She keeps glancing between Victor and me, her eyes widening each time they land on my face. Tessa's gaze is more assessing and narrowed as she studies me. But she must know, too. I can't tell if she approves or not. She just makes me nervous, as usual.

Grant, of course, knows everything. He was backstage when it happened and saw us together under the stage. But this morning, he seems less incensed than he was last night. As he chimes in with his thoughts, I get the sense that he's relieved the "mystery woman" storyline has overshadowed the falling-fixture incident. It means he can deal with the equipment security issue more privately, without it becoming the headline that could ruin his production company and put the technicians who worked on the tour so tirelessly out of a job. He informed us earlier that they're still investigating what caused the light to fall.

My suspicions that everyone knows are confirmed when another minute passes and none of them reply to Victor. We're all tight-lipped and avoiding eye contact, but I can still feel their eyes on me as I struggle to keep my expression neutral, not wanting to give myself away.

Dorian clears his throat, drawing everyone's attention back to him. "Like I said, I'll handle it," he repeats, his tone leaving no room for argument. "But we'll do it my way, on my timeline. Understood?"

Everyone nods. And maybe that's it. I'm safe. I won't lose my job over this. Nadine won't recognize me as the mystery woman locking lips with her star client. Victor didn't.

The positive attitude lasts all of five minutes before the negativity pushes back in, reminding me that my entire career is hanging by a thread. Dizziness hits me, and I stand abruptly. "I need to use the bathroom."

I don't wait for a response before stepping out of the room, barely making it to the hallway before my breath starts coming too fast. I brace one palm on the wall to steady myself as footsteps sound behind me.

It's Dorian. He leans on the opposite side of the hall, watching me with those piercing eyes that see right through me. "Hey, you okay?"

"Yeah, I just needed a moment."

He tilts his head, his presence both comforting and unnerving. "Right, we haven't had *a moment... uh...* since last night."

Heat rises in my cheeks as I remember the feel of his lips on mine, the way his hands gripped my waist, and how he ground against me. At the end of the concert, I changed into unrecognizable clothes and hightailed it home. The last time we've been alone we were kissing. And now Dorian looks like he wants a repeat show.

He pushes away from the wall, closing the distance between us. "I never got to tell you, but I really loved kissing you." His breath tickles my ear, and my skin prickles with awareness, with recognition, as he grabs my hand, bringing it to his lips. Dorian plants a soft kiss on the inside of my wrist, his eyes never leaving mine. "I'd like to do it again soon." His voice is thick with something that feels too big for this narrow hallway.

I scoff, overwhelmed. "I don't know, Dorian, it almost feels like if we kiss again, the world will explode. The Big One will come and split LA in half or something."

Dorian raises his eyebrows. "So dramatic."

He's about to add more when Tessa clears her throat behind us. We jump apart like criminals hearing sirens approaching.

"There's something both of you need to see," his assistant says, her tone serious.

We follow her back into the office, where she pulls up Billie's latest Instagram post on the projector. It's a moody image of Dorian's ex-wife standing under a rainstorm, her blue-blonde hair wet and sticking to her face, eyes downcast. The caption reads:

SAD & MAD

Damn it. This is what we don't need piled on top of the already massive shitstorm we're in. Dorian is stone-faced, grinding his teeth.

That *SAD* part of the description is a clear dig at Dorian, but the *MAD* half also implies he's been shady, like she's accusing him of cheating. I want to snort. After knowing she's the one who's been unfaithful. That woman has no shame.

But what she has is millions of fans. And they eat up the drama, believing her without question.

Bailey delivers her analysis of the responses to the post on the fly. "Thousands of comments flooding in—showing support for Billie, people branding Dorian a dirtbag. Fans professing their love for her, telling her he doesn't deserve her." Bailey huffs as she scowls at Dorian. "You should have told us you were seeing someone so that we could've had a strategy ready."

"Fair enough, Bailey Boo." He smirks at her. "You can put me on your naughty list for Christmas."

I glance at Dorian to gauge his real emotions under the sarcasm, but he's keeping himself in check. I can't get a read. As for me, I'm seething. How dare Billie play the victim after everything she put him through? The cheating, the lies, the pain?

I shouldn't be getting indignant. I should run point on the situation. Damage control is my *literal* job.

I should be working the media to shift the narrative before it spirals beyond repair. Instead, I'm sitting here, useless, watching the headlines and the comments stack up. Standing by, powerless, as Dorian gets dragged in the mud. The story slipping through our fingers.

Missy would've never let something like this fester if she were handling it. But I can't draft a strategy when I *am* the crisis.

I'm failing. At my job. At keeping Dorian out of the storm. And at keeping our secret.

Dorian's eyes are on me. He knows I'm spiraling, that the pressure is crushing me from all sides. But I don't know how to contain it.

And if Nadine figures it out before I have a plan—then it's over. Career gone, future wrecked.

But how do we spin this?

Dirtbag. Cheater. Liar.

The words glare at me from the screen like flashing warning signs, piling up in the comment section of Billie's post, multiplying by the second. They're not true, but that doesn't matter. Not to the people who are eating this up, dissecting every frame of the kiss, every lyric Dorian has ever written, every moment of his marriage to Billie. The narrative has already run away from us, and I'm sitting here, watching it slip further out of reach.

I don't know what terrifies me more—the world discovering us or Dorian realizing how scared I really am.

Because I know how these things go.

Once the internet gets its teeth into something, it doesn't let go.

* * *

Hours later, once everyone but me has left, Dorian's house is quieter than it's been all day. The constant stream of meetings, crisis calls, and statements to be drafted has finally ended. I should be exhausted. Instead, the adrenaline keeps my pulse jacked too high, the excess blood fizzling under my skin.

In the big living room, I curl up on the couch, taking a second to breathe. A massive Christmas tree stands in the corner, glittering with ornaments and warm white lights. It's the third one I've counted so far in his house—one in the foyer, another outside in the garden, and now this. Because why stop at one when you can have three? Dorian doesn't do anything halfway.

He flops down beside me, stretching his arms across the back of the couch, too relaxed for someone who has spent the day putting out fires. Dorian nudges my foot with his. "You look like you could use a distraction."

I raise my eyebrows. "Mmm? What did you have in mind?"

He smirks, all lazy charm. "I bet I can make you laugh in under ten seconds."

I cross my arms. "You absolutely cannot. Not today."

"Oh, that's cute. You think you have a say." He clears his throat, straightens up, then looks me dead in the eye. "Picture me with baby bangs."

A laugh bursts out of me before I can stop it. "Damn it."

He grins. "See? Too easy."

The tension isn't gone, but it's softened under his ridiculousness. He knows what he's doing, peeling my mind from the spiral I've been stuck in.

And it works.

I shake my head, still laughing, and somehow my knee ends up brushing his. Dorian registers the change and he's not teasing anymore as he scoops up my legs and moves them on his lap, pulling me close so that I end up nestled against his side.

I don't resist the shift as his fingers hook around my ankle, his thumb circling over the bone and shooting tingles up my leg. Above, with the hand still draped over the couch, he catches a lock of my hair. He twists it once, then again. He keeps twisting my hair as if he isn't aware he's doing it. I wet my lips, and his gaze drops, tracking the movement. His fingers unwind from my hair only to skim lower, his knuckles grazing the side of my face, light as a breath. When he looks back up at me, a silent question swirls in his irises: *Will you stop me if I kiss you?*

I won't. I can't. Not now that I know what he tastes like, how his mouth moves.

I don't mean to, but I lean in closer. And so does he. His grip tightens over my ankle as if to say, *Stay.*

I'm not going anywhere. In fact, I keep still as his nose brushes mine. His lips part, and I tilt my head, ready to claim his mouth—when his phone rings.

Loud. Obnoxious. Crashing through the moment like a wrecking ball.

Dorian groans but doesn't pull back. His forehead drops against mine, with a frustrated, "Seriously?"

I bite my lip, exhaling. "You should take it."

"I'm a little busy right now."

"How many people have your personal number?"

He sighs, eyes half-lidded, mouth an inch from mine. "Only a few."

"Then shouldn't you answer, in case it's something urgent?"

"They can leave a message." The phone stops ringing, and he smiles. "See? Problem solved."

He hasn't even finished speaking when the ringtone starts again.

Dorian closes his eyes and curses under his breath. "This better be fucking life or death." Then he smacks a chaste kiss on my lips, and mutters, "Later."

Dorian grabs his phone off the coffee table, barking, "What?"

I hear Tessa's voice on the other side of the line, urgent and clipped, even before he puts her on speaker. "Billie just dropped a new single."

Dorian straightens, his face darkening. "So what?"

"It's a diss song. You should listen to it."

I stiffen.

"Okay, Tess, thanks. I'll let you know if I need anything."

Dorian and I exchange a look before he pulls up a streaming service. While he presses play, I pull up the lyrics to read them on my phone.

(Oh, you thought I was done?)

You traded fire for smoke, baby, look where you
    landed.
A shallow spark that fizzles—barely worth being
    branded.
Tried to paint your new picture, but it's cracking at
    the seams,
Your frame's all shiny, but it's holding broken dreams.

You said you found your better, but the better's all fake.
Keep telling yourself it's love—it's more like a mistake.
I leveled up while you're still stuck in the past,
With your just-see life—it's never gonna last.

She got a name that says just fine,
But I'm the rare find that you left behind.

Whoo-ooh-ooh

Whoo-ooh-ooh-ooooh

She got a name that says just fine,
But I'm the rare find that you left behind.

Just see through the lies you tell yourself now,
I'm the storm you couldn't handle, she's the drizzle
    you allow.
You're playing it safe, but safe's so dull.
Keep chasing shadows while I'm running the world.

She's a paperback story—nothing deep, nothing real.
An empty shell with a bargain-bin feel.

You put her on a pedestal like she's your queen,
But your crown looks crooked, and your kingdom's
  routine.

I'm the plot twist you never saw coming.
She's your quiet night; I'm the fire that's stunning.
So go ahead, settle down, play your role.
But you'll never find me in her paper-thin soul.

She got a name that's easy to rhyme,
But nothing about her's worth my time.

Just see through the lies you tell yourself now,
I'm the storm you couldn't handle, she's the drizzle
  you allow.
You're playing it safe, but safe's so dull.
Keep chasing shadows while I'm running the world.

This ain't me bitter; this is me free,
Living my best life while you're stuck on repeat.
Keep the drama, keep the games,
I'll keep shining while you throw out names.

So just see me now, higher than you could dream,
No regrets, baby—I'm the one and only queen.
You settled for average, but that's not my style,
I'm the one you'll remember, mile after mile.

Just see—oh, you'll see,

I'm the lesson you'll never be free.

When the song ends, Dorian shakes his head. "This is pathetic."

I don't respond. Because I'm too busy panicking.

"She knows," I whisper.

Dorian frowns. "What?"

"Billie knows who I am."

"Josie, it's just a bad pop song."

"No." I shake my head hard. "The title. 'Just See.' It's basically Josie. 'Your just-see life'?"

He blinks.

"And the pre-chorus—'She got a name that says just fine'— it's basically a different spelling of Josephine." I wave a hand. "Even if the pronunciation is different. She knows."

Incomprehensibly, Dorian smiles. "Wait. Are you telling me your real name is *Josephine*?"

I groan. "Dorian."

His lips twitch. "How did I not know that?"

I swat his arm. "Be serious."

He bites back a grin. "Okay, *Josephine*," he says, voice teasing but eyes soft. "I'm being *very* serious."

"No, you're not. And I'm worried. What is your ex-wife going to do?"

"Nothing." Dorian pulls me close to him in a side hug and kisses my temple. "I won't let her do anything to you."

This time, my phone goes off with an alarm, a reminder that I have to go pick up Penny from ballet practice.

We stand and Dorian walks me to the front door. "I'll call before bed."

I smile, the panic in my chest easing a little. "Okay. I'll text you when I'm home."

I turn to leave, but before I can go, he catches my hand.

"And Josie..."

I glance back.

He tugs me closer, his grip gentle but firm as he whispers, "I almost forgot this."

And then he kisses me. Thoroughly, unrelentingly, turning me into a wobbling, shaking mess as I walk to my car.

44

DORIAN

After a few hours of playing with the guitar in my home studio, I sag on the couch in the small living room, phone in hand, the screen dark. Josie said she'd text when she got to her place. How much longer before Lily's shift ends? Another hour, maybe two? Either way, I don't need to hover by the phone like a needy asshole.

I drop the device onto the coffee table and lean back, shutting my eyes.

Billie's song replays in my head, an irritating loop I can't turn off.

> *Just see through the lies you tell yourself now,*
> *I'm the storm you couldn't handle, she's the drizzle*
> *you allow.*

Josie is convinced Billie knows. That the title is a dig at her. That the lyrics are screaming her name.

I don't buy it.

It's a coincidence. Billie doesn't know a damn thing. And yet, something gnaws at me, a small crack of unease needling at my throat. Not because of the song itself—I can deal with my ex-wife writing a bitter, whiny break-up anthem. But because it's Billie, and with her, no blow is too low, no line too far to cross.

As if on cue, the app on my phone connected to the front gate rings, meaning security is trying to reach me.

I accept the call.

"Sir?" the guard says. "We have a situation."

I sigh, already bracing for whatever fresh hell is waiting for me. "What is it?"

"It's your ex-wife. She's at the gate. Demanding to be let in."

My head drops back against the couch. *Oh, for fuck's sake.*

I wonder if I should be glad or worried Billie used the front door instead of going straight for breaking and entering.

"Tell her to fuck off," I say, rubbing my temple.

The guard hesitates, but he follows my instructions. The intercom cuts off, and I settle back, forcing myself to relax.

Two minutes pass. Five.

Then Nick strides into the living room, looking serious and composed as he carries a manila folder. His expression is grimmer than usual, and the tension in his shoulders makes my stomach drop with a bad feeling.

I brace my elbows on my knees. "What now?"

"Billie left, sir. But left this with security and said you'd want to see it."

My gut twists. I don't want to give Billie the satisfaction of playing her games.

But do I have a choice?

My fingers are stiff as I take the folder and flip it open. And then my lungs turn to stone as I find photographs. Dozens of them. Of Josie. Where she lives. Her entering her apartment, leaving the office, driving Penny around. Us three walking the streets on Halloween. I'm not recognizable in the picture, but Billie must know it's me.

The next photos are even worse. Lily. Penny. Josie's mom's house. Me sneaking in at Thanksgiving, hopping up their front steps, oblivious to the camera snapping from fuck knows where.

At the bottom of the folder, I find a note in Billie's scrawl.

Dump her, or I'll leak to the press who your mystery woman is. B

45

JOSIE

Dorian doesn't call that night. My text telling him I got home sits on delivered but not read. Earlier, when Lily returned home after her shift, I left her house as fast as I could, dodging all the questions my sister had about the mystery woman saga and the kiss. She wanted to know if kissing Dorian felt as hot as it looked on the million videos of us—it did, but that's beside the point.

I made it home uselessly fast. And now, hours later, I stare at my unread text, fighting the urge to send another one. A second message would probably share the fate of the first. So I call him instead and get sent straight to voicemail. I call again twice, but his phone appears to be off.

I hate myself for what I'm about to do, but I'm worried sick. So I call Tessa despite the late hour.

"Hey," she picks up, her voice sympathetic.

Why does she sound like she pities me? What does she know that I don't?

"Hey, Tessa, do you—"

"He went to his recording studio." She doesn't let me finish.

"When he goes there, he turns his phone off and no one is allowed in until he's done with whatever creative shit he needs to cope."

"Cope with the press? I thought he was taking it well but—"

"It wasn't the media. From what I gathered, Billie went to the house earlier. It's always her. He didn't let her in, but something must've happened."

Billie. A pounding pressure builds in my temples. My skull is shrinking around my thoughts, squeezing them in while they're pushing to get out.

"And you don't know what?"

"No. I haven't talked to him. But Josie?"

"Yeah?"

"Don't sweat it. This is how he's been dealing with the emotional abuse for the past couple of years. He isolates, creates, and comes out regenerated. And for what it's worth..." A pause, then a sigh. "I think you're good for him."

Okay, so we're not circling around it anymore. And she approves? I wish I could be happier about the discovery. This morning, I would've been. Now, I'm just worried.

"T-thanks, I guess."

"No problem. Let him have his time, and we can manage the rest from the outside. I'll see you at the house tomorrow, okay?"

"Yeah, thank you again, bye."

We hang up and I stare at the ceiling of my bedroom, unsure how to feel. Regular boyfriends don't have gatekeepers. A security detail that can keep their girlfriends at bay whenever they feel like having a moment to themselves.

Is this how it's always going to be? Shit hits the fan, and Dorian becomes unreachable. What did Billie want? What did she do to trigger him? And how is being shut in a recording studio alone helping him?

I get the answer two days later—after endless hours of worrying and wondering—when I receive a Google Alert that Rian Phoenix's new single is out. He wrote a song?

But when I click on the link, it's even worse because he didn't write a song, he made a cover of Billie's: "Just See (Rian's Version)."

I play the song and it has the same lyrics, but it's rock instead of pop. Billie's version has a catchy chorus and that's about it. Dorian's take is a masterpiece. It's rough, sexy, raw—angry. In the outro, he uses his low, seduction voice, adding a gothic-rock edge and I almost have an orgasm just listening to it.

It's a brilliant cover and a total disaster.

His and Billie's versions sit at number one and two in the charts. This is only going to enrage his ex-wife, escalate things, bring even more attention to their public spat, and feed the media frenzy when we need the exact opposite.

What the fuck was he thinking?

The last report I got from Tessa was that he still hadn't returned home. The chances that he's back now are slim, but I don't care. I grab my keys and hop into my car without changing out of an oversized sweatshirt and crappy leggings with a hole in the butt but that I'm never throwing away because the elastic has gotten stretchy enough to be the most comfortable.

On the drive, I consider how ridiculously I'm acting. I don't even know if Dorian will be at his place. But if he released the cover, it's safe to assume he won't keep living in a recording studio with nothing to record. And even if he isn't back, I'll squat on his porch, seething in my rage and in my hurt until he returns.

Luckily, it turns out an occupation of his domicile won't be necessary because Dorian *is* home when I get there.

I find him sitting on the couch—big living room—a glass of

bourbon in one hand, the bottle next to him, his gaze fixed on some invisible point in the distance. He looks livid. His jaw is tight, and his shoulders wound up as if to contain whatever storm is brewing inside him.

He looks so scarily mad that I consider turning around, walking back out, and letting him sulk in peace. But then my own anger flares up.

I stride in, arms crossed. "Welcome back. Did you have a nice time on your retreat?"

Dorian doesn't even flinch. He lifts the glass to his lips, taking a slow sip before replying. "I needed time to think."

I scoff. "Oh, *you* needed time. Right. And I'm supposed to just sit around and wait, wondering what the hell happened? Wondering if you're okay, if you—" I cut myself off before I say something pathetic, like, *forgot about me entirely.*

Dorian stands, drink still in hand, and starts to pace. "I *needed* to be alone."

"For what? To get back at your ex-wife in the pettiest possible way?"

The vein in his temple jumps. "Billie came here..." He presses his lips together, gaze flicking to the floor before snapping back up. "...made threats, so yeah, I took her little song and turned it into a half-decent single."

I let out a hollow laugh. "Yeah, because *that's* what this situation needed—more gasoline. And I'm not sure calling Billie's music small is what you want to do right now."

Dorian's grip tightens around the glass, tension rippling through his forearm. "What the fuck do you want me to do, then?" His entire torso coils up as he hurls his drink across the room. Some of the bourbon slashes through the air in an amber streak until the glass shatters against the far wall in a violent explosion of liquid and shards.

I freeze, my lungs locking, but not out of fear or anger. Because for the first time since I walked in, I understand what's happening. His reaction isn't rage. Or his usual knee-jerk defiance against Billie's bullshit. Dorian is panicking.

As he looks at me now, his breath unsteady, his chest rising too fast in sharp, uneven pulls, his eyes are filled with fear— sheer, unfiltered, and *helpless*.

And that terrifies me more than shattered glass.

I take a step forward. "For starters, you could calm down and *tell* me what happened."

Dorian drags a hand down his face and meets my eyes. "Billie showed up here with a folder full of pictures."

"Pictures?"

"Of you." His jaw flexes. "Of where you live, where you work," he continues, voice tight, controlled, like he needs to keep a leash on it or it'll unravel. "Of you taking Penny to school."

My heart turns into an ice stone in my chest and the blood freezes in my veins.

Dorian hesitates, his throat working like the next words are physically painful to say. "She had pictures of Lily, too. Of your mom's house. From Thanksgiving."

The room tilts. I drop a hand on the nearest wall to steady myself, but everything inside me is collapsing, crumbling under the weight of this revelation.

"My family?" I choke the words out. "She has—she *knows*—"

"She's threatening to leak it to the press."

I gasp but can't get enough oxygen in my lungs. Fear uncoils inside me, slithering around my wrists and ankles like invisible restraints, squeezing my ribs, pressing icy fingers against my throat.

I take a staggering step back. "And knowing that, you

provoked her?" I raise my voice as my pulse pounds in my ears. "You still went ahead and made *that* fucking song? *You had no right.*"

The accusation snaps out of me, sharp and vicious, and I don't even care that I'm yelling.

Dorian's face drops. "I'm sorry, I—"

"I can't do this," I cut him off, my throat tight. My vision blurs as hot tears prick at the edges. "It was one thing when it was just me and my job on the line, but Lily? Penny?" My breath shudders. "I *cannot* drag my sister into this."

"Josie, the press won't be interested in Lily. And there are laws to protect Penny, she's a minor, I checked with my lawyers."

"What of Billie's fans? Can you guarantee that if your ex plays the wronged woman on all her socials, they won't harass me or my family? All it takes is one unhinged follower."

Dorian doesn't reply.

I stare at him, seeing only the impenetrable wall that has risen between us. Because no matter what, I'll never put Lily or Penny in a harder situation than they already are. They lost too much. Whatever implied threat Billie wanted to make with those photos, it worked. I have to give him up.

My heart breaks, and then I break, too. My hands fly to my face, my body shaking as the first tear slips down. Dorian's arms wrap around me before I can stop him, his warmth surrounding me, anchoring me.

I almost push him away. But then a crushing thought slams into me: *this might be the last time I can let him hold me like this.*

So I let myself have it and sink into the safety of him, savoring the steady beat of his heart, the solid comfort of his body.

"I know." His voice is rough, and his lips are pressing against my hair. "That's why I needed time. I think best when I'm making music."

I pull back, wiping at my face, anger seeping in through the cracks again. "And what *brilliant* conclusion did you come to?"

Before he can answer, my phone pings with the ringtone I assigned to Nadine's messages.

Dorian watches as I pull it out, his hand still resting on my waist. "Who is it?"

I stare at the screen.

NADINE FOX

Report to my office first thing Monday morning

"My boss, making an appointment to fire me."

"I'm going to fix this."

I meet his eyes, feeling only despair. "How?"

He hesitates. "I don't know yet."

"Great."

"But I *will*," he says, voice fierce as he takes my hands and holds them between us. "I *will* make it right."

I stare at him, at the determination blazing in his blue eyes.

I want to believe him.

But I can't. Not this time. If it comes down to choosing between him and my family, there *is* no choice.

I glance down at our joined hands, at the way his fingers curl around mine. I lift my gaze, ignoring the regret already sinking in, and kiss him.

It's different this time. Not playful or teasing, not desperate or rushed or even lustful.

It's slow, weighted, and *final*.

It's a kiss that tastes of goodbye.

A kiss that tastes of *never again*.

46

JOSIE

I spend the weekend in a stupor on my couch, avoiding my family. Like a coward, I don't tell them how serious the "mystery woman" situation is or the risk I've unwillingly exposed them to. I hate what's happening, but most of all, I hate that I have zero control over it. That no matter how much I squeeze my brain for a solution that will force Billie to leave me and my family alone, I can't find one.

On Monday morning, I'm tempted to not even show up at the office. I mean, what's the point? I honestly would rather be fired via email than have to listen to one of Nadine's sanctimonious lectures. In the end, I head in just on the off chance that I've become over-pessimistic and my boss only wants an update on her star client's latest negative press coverage.

But as I walk into Nadine's office, my suspicions that I'm about to get fired three days before Christmas are confirmed. Sitting next to her is the company's grim reaper—the HR director. Only one reason he'd be here, and it's not to wish me a good day.

"Josie." Nadine gestures to the chair across from her like this is a casual performance review and not an execution. "Have a seat."

I lower myself down, my posture stiff, hands folded in my lap like a schoolgirl bracing for a scolding.

Nadine shakes her head as if disappointed I forced her into this conversation. "I'll get straight to the point: I'm not a fool. I recognized you the moment the first photos surfaced." Her voice is clipped, efficient. "I know you're the mystery woman kissing Rian Phoenix at his last concert when you were supposedly working." She sighs, folding her hands on her desk. "You've shown an appalling lack of judgment, and now we're paying the price for it."

I could do without the condescending, fake-worry speech. I almost ask her to spare me but bite my tongue.

"My company's reputation won't be tarnished by your reckless actions." She leans back in her chair. "If Rian walks away from his contract over this mess, so be it. He's free to pay the termination fee and leave, but I won't let you drag this firm into his latest scandal."

I seethe in the satisfying certainty that Dorian's lawyer will find a way to evade that fee.

I'm heartbroken, Dorian is too, his ex-wife just ruined his life a second time, and all my boss can think about is money. Or how smarter she is than me. How much wiser. I almost tell her to go fuck herself, but I don't want to come across as unhinged. If Nadine can be cold, so can I.

"You had potential, Josie. But integrity is the foundation of good PR, and clearly, yours is... lacking." She lets the words settle as if waiting for me to protest, tell her she's right, or apologize. Whatever she's waiting for, I don't give it to her.

She tilts her head in mock-pity. "And I suppose you believe he'll stick by you?" Her lips curl into something that isn't quite a smile. "That a man like Rian Phoenix, a legend, will weather this storm by your side? Tell me, was it worth it? Throwing your career away for nothing?"

The worst part is that she's right. It will all have been for nothing. Not because Dorian wouldn't have stood by me. But because we don't have a choice anymore. Billie made sure of that.

Nadine watches me for a moment longer before dropping the ax. "HR will go over the paperwork, but as of this morning, your employment here is terminated."

I nod once and don't argue. I turn to the HR director and ask where I have to sign. He hands me the papers.

Ten minutes later, he's still explaining the specifics of my dismissal when the interim head of the celebrity division barges in, announcing that Rian Phoenix is giving a live interview.

Nadine's eyes narrow on me. "Did you know about this?"

I shake my head.

As one, we get up from our seats and move to the main office floor, where a giant TV is tuned in on the feed.

Seeing Dorian, even if it's through a screen, is a knife to the heart. He's dressed in a simple black T-shirt and jeans. He hasn't shaved. Dark circles rim his eyes. He looks tired—but still painfully handsome.

He and the host of the talk show—Lilo, another singer and songwriter—must've already circled through the greetings because she jumps right in. "So, Rian, have you requested this last-minute interview to reveal who the mystery woman is?"

"No, Lilo, sorry." Dorian turns to the camera, expression dead serious as his eyes pierce through the screen. "But this is about her."

My stomach drops. I stop breathing. He's going to talk about me? On national TV? While his ex-wife has a loaded gun pointed at us? Fear claws at my chest, fast and panicked, because I have no idea what he'll say. Anticipation tangles with the dread, twisting into something reckless and stupid—*hope*. But I know better. Hope has no place here. Whatever Dorian is about to do, it won't change a damn thing.

But even as the world falls apart around us, I believe in him. After what he did with the cover song, he wouldn't put my family at risk again for a petty revenge. He must have a plan. So, I sit on a desk, grab the remote, and turn up the volume.

47

DORIAN

The studio set is standard—warm lighting, a polished, wooden dais, two armchairs, and a sleek coffee table between them. The massive Christmas tree behind Lilo is overkill, blinking at me with blinding white lights, taking my focus from the cameras locked on me, ready to shoot at different angles. Lilo sits across from me, her striped dress flowing over the chair, making her look both polished and approachable. Her hair falls in warm waves over her shoulders, framing a face that's open, engaged, and genuinely interested. She's done a thousand interviews with as many other artists, but today, I'm flipping the script.

I clear my throat, shifting in my seat. "This interview is about her."

Lilo takes my declaration in stride, smiling into the camera. "Well, that certainly sets the stage." Then she leans forward a fraction, slipping into full interviewer mode. "How long have you and the mystery woman known each other?"

"Since last summer," I say, blinking against the Christmas lights. "But before you jump to conclusions, we met once, nothing happened, and we didn't see each other again for a year.

We only reconnected a few months ago, after my divorce was finalized." My jaw tightens. "That kiss on stage? That was our first."

Lilo chuckles. "Didn't go according to plan, huh? And I wasn't going to assume anything, but your ex-wife, Billie Rae, has been making some... not-so-subtle claims on social media. And, well, in her latest hit."

"I never cheated on my wife," I declare flatly.

Lilo tilts her head. "But the divorce came from you?"

I nod once, curt.

Fuck, this is excruciating. I hate interviews. I never discuss my personal life with journalists. But if baring my soul to the world is what it takes for me and Josie to have a chance at being together, then I'll sit here and lay it all out, no matter how much I loathe every second.

Lilo shifts in her chair, adjusting her line of questioning on the fly. Normally, her team would've prepped a list of approved questions, but I didn't give them time to script this episode the usual way. I asked her to do this last minute as a personal favor. So here we are, both winging it.

"Do you think Billie wrote 'Just See' because she's still in love with you?"

I sigh, running a hand through my hair. "I don't think Billie can love anyone right now. Not before she learns how to love herself again."

A flicker of discomfort crosses Lilo's face. "That's... a pretty dramatic statement. Why do you say that?"

"Our marriage fell apart mainly because Billie refused to face her demons and take the necessary steps to heal."

"What steps?"

I'm about to drop a bomb, but I don't see another way at this point. "Rehab, mostly. I begged, I reasoned, I fought. I tried dragging her myself more times than I can count." I grip my knee tighter. "Every time I thought I'd finally gotten through to her, that she'd be different, she'd find a new excuse. An extra reason she wasn't ready, why she didn't need help. And I swallowed it, let her string me along, convinced that if I held on a little longer, I could fix it, her—*us*. But you can't save someone who doesn't want to be saved. Billie wouldn't take the help. And in the end, I had to face the reality that no matter how much I loved her, or how hard I tried, *she* needed to want to be better first."

The tension in the studio thrums like a drawn bowstring. Lilo's expression is unreadable, but she treads carefully. "That's a serious accusation. Are you saying your ex-wife is an addict?"

Another curt nod. "Yes."

"And you think revealing this on national television will help her... how?"

My jaw locks. "Because she has to face it. Because it has to stop."

"Do you feel guilty about leaving your wife when she was in such a fragile state?"

The familiar spear of regret lodges between my ribs, pressing against a wound that's still tender. "Every day. But it was either leave or lose myself in her wreckage."

Lilo nods, absorbing it. "Okay. We are sorry about Billie, and if she would like to respond to your revelations of today, of course, we're always available." She hesitates. "This isn't how I saw this interview going. I thought we were here to talk about your new relationship?"

"We are." I bounce my knees, too agitated to keep still. "But I can't do that without bringing Billie into this."

"Why?"

"Because Billie knows who my girlfriend is," I press on,

doing my best to rein in my frustration, "and she's threatened to expose her and her family. To turn her fans and the press against us. And I don't want the woman I'm with to have to choose between me or seeing her loved ones under that kind of negative attention."

Lilo's face softens. "That sounds... awful. Is there anything we can do?"

I swallow, fists clenching and unclenching as I stare at the camera in front of me and make my appeal. "To Billie's fans, I ask you to believe me when I say I never wronged her. The help she needs from you isn't to make me miserable. She needs to get better, to take care of herself, and you can help her do that by encouraging her. I—" I pause, steadying my voice. "The new woman in my life, I'm in love with her. And even if Billie breaks us apart, I will never get back with her—"

Lilo taps her earpiece, frowning. "Rian, I'm sorry to interrupt, but Billie Rae is on the phone. She wants to respond to your comments."

My stomach turns to lead.

A red light blinks on the camera rig, signaling the live patch-in. On the large screen in the background, a stock image of Billie appears—pristine, airbrushed, a curated version of herself she shows the public and a stark contrast to the slurred venom spilling from the speakers.

"You have some fucking nerve." Billie doesn't even wait for introductions. Her voice cuts through the studio, distorted by static and thick with anger—a mockery of the polished persona staring down at us from the screen. "Sitting there with your holier-than-thou bullshit, acting like I was the problem. You abandoned me, Dorian. Left me to rot while you played the hero. Fuck rehab. You never wanted to help me. You only needed me to be your perfect, manageable, little wife. Well, newsflash, babe—I was never gonna be that. And now? Now you're crying on national TV because I wrote a song? Because I called you out? You're pathetic. Play the victim all you want, but guess what? The world knows who the liar is. And I'm coming, sweetheart. I'm driving right to that fucking studio to look you in the eyes while I say it. So, fuck you, you lying piece of shit."

Lilo's smile tenses as she casts an apologetic glance at the camera. "Billie, I understand these are deeply personal matters, and emotions can run high. But we do ask our guests to keep the discussion respectful."

Billie's breath hitches before she spits, "Shut up, bitch, I'm not talking to you."

My ex sounds deranged.

The room goes still. Lilo recoils, blinking, but she's quick to recover. "Billie, are you driving under the influence right now?"

A dry, humorless laugh crackles through the line. "I told you to shut your trap. I'm handling my shit just—"

In the background of Billie's call, we hear a sudden screech of tires. Then a sickening crunch, followed by a loud bang.

Then nothing.

Lilo sits up straighter, pressing her earpiece again. "Billie? Are you okay?"

Silence.

A beat. Then another.

A splintery pressure compresses my rib cage, a warning my body registers before my mind catches up to what's happening.

A producer in the control booth mutters something unintelligible into a mic, and Lilo's eyes widen. "I—We've received confirmation that Billie Rae crashed her car into the front gates of the studio. We have a crew moving into place right now."

I grip the arms of the chair, every muscle in my body coiled tight. They're going to air this. Turn her wreckage into a fucking segment. I should tell them to cut the feed, to have a shred of decency and give her privacy, but—

But the crew will get to her before I can, and I need to know if Billie is still breathing, if she's hurt, more than I want to protect her dignity.

The screen behind us flickers to a live feed of the entrance. Billie's car is crumpled against the gate, the hood smoking. Security guards rush to the driver's side, pulling the door open. Billie stumbles out, looking dazed, confused, completely out of it. A guard reaches for her to help, but she shoves him away, screaming, "Fuck off!" She turns in circles, unsteady, her words slurring as she hurls more insults.

An ambulance arrives on the scene. Two paramedics jump out. One approaches Billie to steady her, but she swings at him, missing by a mile.

That's enough.

I rip out my microphone and stand. "I have to go. And you should cut this—she doesn't deserve for the world to see her like this."

48

JOSIE

I watch as Dorian rips out his microphone and stands. He says something to Lilo that the discarded mic doesn't pick up. But I don't need to hear it. The disgust on his face is plain. His hand hovers in mid-air as if he's about to knock the cameras over. He's done with the show. Dorian turns and stalks off the set, disappearing out of the frame as Lilo pivots smoothly back to the camera, slipping into her role like nothing happened.

"Well." The host flashes a quick, broadcast-ready smile. "That was more eventful than any of us expected this morning. Our thoughts are with Billie Rae, of course, and we sincerely hope she's okay. We'll keep you updated." Lilo presses her fingers together in a composed gesture, her expression solemn. "In the meantime, how about we all take five? We'll be right back after a short break."

As the screen cuts to commercials, someone behind me says something, a chair scrapes against the floor, but I don't register it. Words filter in as background noise, distant and unimportant.

I'm still processing everything that happened—Billie, the scene she made, her accident, the chaos she left in her wake. It's shocking. But that's not what has my pulse hammering in my ears and my stomach clenching like a fist.

It's what Dorian said before any of that.

I'm in love with her.

The words play back in my mind on a loop. The way he said them. Steady. Sure. His eyes locked onto the camera like he was talking directly to me. Only to me.

I had sensed his feelings, of course I had. But we've never said I love you outright. And hearing him do it—for the entire world to hear, with no hesitation, no second-guessing—it landed in my chest like a punch and the gentlest caress at once. Because it's real now. And if I lose him, I'm losing something that finally has a name.

I let out a breath I've been holding since Dorian started speaking, only then noticing the muted attention fixed on me.

The entire celebrity PR department is still gathered around the TV screen, standing behind desks and along the glass-walled meeting room. Staring. At me.

Nadine is the first to speak, her voice slicing through the dazed silence. "Alright, people, back to work." She claps twice, jolting everyone into motion. "Rian Phoenix hasn't fired us yet. That means we're still covering this, so we need to get ahead of it." She flicks a look my way, assessing. "And since he announced to the entire country that he's in love with you, we can spin this."

I don't reply.

She turns to me, tilting her head. "Josie, start putting together a—"

"You fired me half an hour ago," I cut in, my voice surprisingly steady.

Nadine waves a dismissive hand, unbothered. "You're rehired."

Her offer lands flat, like a joke with no punchline—empty, meaningless.

Does she expect me to be relieved? To jump at her barked orders like a grateful puppy?

Should I?

I don't have another job lined up. Publishing is great, but even if it works out, it won't be a steady paycheck for a long time.

I should be relieved she's giving me my job back. But instead of relief, all I feel is revulsion.

The idea of staying in this office, working for this woman, acting as if she didn't tear me down thirty minutes ago or reduce me to nothing more than a story to spin, makes my stomach curdle.

Maybe Dorian was right, and my heart *isn't* in PR. I'd rather wait tables than this. I did it in college, I can do it again. It'll be enough to pay my student loans. And if I can't make rent, I'll move back in with my mom until I find a new job.

I glance around the open space, at the people I've spent years working alongside. Some of them look at me with curiosity, others with thinly veiled opportunism, as if I'm another messy celebrity scandal they get to work on.

I lift my chin. "I think not."

Irritation flickers in Nadine's gaze, but I couldn't care less. I turn on my heel and leave, heading straight for my old desk.

I grab the empty cardboard box I find there—clearly set out for my departure—and start packing my things.

A few picture frames. My favorite pens. A crumpled sweater I always forget to bring home.

I lift the box and enter the waiting elevator, pushing the LL button. As the floor count begins to drop, a thought wedges itself between the chaos of the morning—this is where I met

Dorian. Where everything started. And now's the last time I'll ever be in here. Shifting the box onto my hip, I brush my fingers against the metal wall. "Thank you," I whisper, saying another goodbye.

The doors ding and open directly onto the parking garage, where a cooler draft greets me, sending a small shudder through my body. The parts of the world buried in snow and having a literal white Christmas this December would laugh at this SoCal girl shivering in sixty-five-degree weather. But I still drop my belongings to the floor and tug on my spare sweater just as my phone buzzes in my pocket.

LILY

Dinner at my place tonight

There's no question mark—it's a statement. An order?

A small, tired smile tugs at my lips. I tap the thumbs-up emoji and slide my phone back into my pocket. I'll need to be with family tonight. My sister is going to roast me for everything I didn't tell her, but she's my steady place. I crave the comfort more than I want to avoid the interrogation that's coming.

At home, I don't know what to do with myself. I change into my comfy sweats and my leggings with a hole in the butt. Then stare around the apartment, a little lost. I have the whole day ahead of me, and nothing to fill it with.

I should be worried about money. About quitting a stable career without a back-up plan. But my mind is consumed by Dorian. By what he did. I wonder where he is now. Is he with Billie? But above all, I think about what he said. And where that leaves us.

I *don't* know.

Should I call him? To tell him what? My feelings and fears are too complicated to dissect right now, but the media's response to his interview won't be difficult to analyze. So, I do what I do best and slip into PR mode. I pull out my laptop and start tracking the press coverage.

Nadine may be a harpy, but she's good at her job. I recognize her fingerprints all over the steady stream of articles reframing the story, emphasizing Dorian's honesty, crafting a narrative that keeps public sympathy where she—*we?*—want it.

And even in the outlets Nadine can't control, the flood of support in Dorian's favor is overwhelming. His social media are filled with love. People standing by him. *Believing him.*

But that's only half of the coin. Dorian's truth is finally out there, but that doesn't mean Billie's most devoted fans will accept it. They could dig their heels in deeper, his admission that he is in love with someone else sending them on a crusade. They could call his appeal an excuse.

I switch to Billie's accounts, expecting to see the usual backlash. People screaming that Dorian is a liar, a cheater, a fraud. But they're not.

After Billie's meltdown, her intoxicated rant, and the accident, even the most skeptical, angry voices quiet down. No one is tearing Dorian down.

The comments—*all of them*—are for Billie.

Billie, please get help.

We love you. We want you to be okay.

Rehab isn't a bad word. It's a way out. Take it.

Everywhere, across platforms, it's the same. No one is defending her behavior or buying into her version of events. They only want her to get better. I could cry with relief.

It worked. The fans are on our side.

Despite what Billie did—the threats to me, to my family—her public implosion doesn't make me happy. It makes me sad. Because for all the fire and rage Billie threw at the world, this is all that's left. A mess of bad choices, of pain, of a woman who never figured out how to stop sinking.

I close my laptop and rub my eyes.

I've no idea what will happen next.

With Billie. With Dorian. With me.

Everything is a dumpster fire, but I feel finally free of all the secrets and the lies. I think of Dorian's phoenix tattoo and hope that our love, too, can rise out of the ashes of this mess. But it's not just me who has to make the decision. I need to speak with my family first.

* * *

When I arrive at Lily's house, I can tell that my sister has a few choice words for me. I'm positive they have to do with the interview. But I've no idea what her angle will be. Is she going to berate me for putting her and Penny at risk? Call me irresponsible? Demand I leave Dorian?

She circles around the topic as we cut vegetables for soup in the kitchen while Penny does her homework in her room.

Lily slices through a bell pepper, then lifts her gaze to me. "Guess what the nurses at the hospital couldn't stop talking about today?"

I freeze mid-chop. "What?"

She levels me with a look. "Rian Phoenix's interview about his mystery woman." A pause—pointed, loaded. "And the train-wreck of his ex-wife. Oh, and how this mystery woman can't be with him because said ex-wife threatened her family."

"Lily..." My eyes sting, and I set the knife down, pressing the heels of my hands against the counter. "I didn't know about the threats. The moment I found out, I told him that if I had to choose between him and my family, I would always pick you."

"Well, you'll have to call him back and tell him you choose him instead."

My head jerks up. "What?"

"You heard me." She tosses a handful of peppers into the pot like it's nothing and we're debating what spices to add to the soup instead of making life-changing decisions.

"I can't."

"Sure can."

"No. If Billie goes public, the press will hound you and Penny. This doesn't affect only me."

Lily lets out a short, unimpressed breath and waves the knife. "California has strict laws protecting minors from press harassment, I've looked it up." She gives me the same objection as Dorian. "If they so much as point a camera our way, I can sue them for enough money to retire early. And I bet your boyfriend has an entire team of lawyers on retainer just for that."

"They could still harass you, and mom, and Moira."

Lily scoffs. "Please, if they go anywhere near Aunt Moira, they'll be the ones running for their lives. And I'm really photogenic."

I gape at her. "You're serious?"

"Like a grandma at bingo night." My sister puts the knife down and wipes her hands on a dish towel. "I won't be the reason you're miserable, Josie."

I stare at her, struggling to process this shift, this opening where I thought the door was locked and bolted.

"I watched the interview." Lily's features soften. "The way he looked into that camera when he said he's in love with you..."

She swallows, blinking quickly, her thoughts must've inevitably drifted to Daniel. To the love she lost. "A love like that? It doesn't come around often. Once in a lifetime if you're lucky. And when you find it, you don't throw it away."

I'm ready to argue that I refuse to make her or Penny's lives harder. But before I can, the unmistakable sound of an electric guitar echoes through the courtyard.

I turn my head to the front door. "What is that?"

Lily smirks. "Why don't you go check."

I narrow my eyes at her. "What did you do?"

My sister shrugs, still smiling. "I only texted him, saying you'd be here tonight and—"

I don't wait to hear the end—I'm already running.

49

JOSIE

I shove the front door open so hard, it bounces off the wall, but I don't stop. I don't have my shoes on and my socks skid against the terracotta tiles of the gallery patio. I catch myself just short of slamming into the balcony railing.

I grip the metal barrier, eyes sweeping the courtyard below. Dorian is standing by the pool as if he walked straight out of an album cover—black leather jacket unzipped over a fitted tee, dark jeans clinging in all the right places. He has an electric guitar strapped across his chest. An adjustable mic pole in front of him. And a portable amplifier at his feet with wires snaking over the Mediterranean stamped concrete like veins feeding into the night.

Dorian looks unreal, a vision conjured from pure longing. But he's not a fantasy. He's here, his gaze locked on mine as if nothing else exists. Not the Christmas lights that wrap around the railings and wind through the low bushes in the flowerbeds, blinking lazily in reds, greens, and golds. Or the neon reindeer that flickers in someone's window, casting a pale-blue reflection on the pool's still surface. Not even Lily and Penny appearing beside me.

He isn't playing a song, but strumming absent chords, his fingers moving hypnotically over the strings.

When he sees me, he clamps the strings, killing the sound. Dorian smiles. "Hi, Josie."

Two simple words that ripple through the courtyard, amplified by the mic and inescapable as they land right in my chest.

Around us, doors creak open. Neighbors step onto balconies, lean against railings, peek out from ground-floor apartments, phones at the ready. A small crowd is gathering in from everywhere, murmuring in hushed excitement.

"Hey, what are you doing?" I yell, half-laughing, half-stunned.

Dorian's mouth tilts at the corner. "In case it wasn't clear, I'm about to serenade you."

A jolt of heat sparks through my veins, exhilarating. I clamp my hands over my mouth, biting back the grin that wants to split my face.

A few scattered cheers ripple through the complex as he adjusts the guitar strap, shifting his stance. "But before I do, I need to apologize."

I drop my hands from my mouth and clutch them to my chest.

"For shutting you out." His apology voice is too close to his seduction voice, and it's doing unspeakable things to me. "For letting my anger get the better of me. And for making that stupid cover song without thinking. I was selfish and impulsive, and I hate it could've ruined everything."

A lump rises in my throat.

His fingers grip the guitar's neck harder. "Once, you asked me if I was going to write a song for you." His gaze is unguarded, searching. "The truth is, all the songs I've written lately are for you."

The crowd collectively sighs. Someone claps. My knees buckle under me, and Lily wraps an arm behind my back as if to make sure I keep upright.

Dorian tilts his head. "But I have a new one. If you want to hear it?"

Lily elbows me. "Say yes, idiot."

The entire courtyard shouts it for me, but I can only nod, too choked up to speak.

Dorian smirks, tapping the pedal at his feet to start a bass loop. He grips the guitar, fingers poised, eyes locked on mine. And then he sings.

> *"Guess I got lucky when all went dark,*
> *A city gone quiet, two strangers, two hearts.*
> *We played our cards, and you stripped me bare,*
> *Left me gasping for air.*
>
> *"I don't do fate, but maybe I lied,*
> *Cause I can't forget you, no matter how I've tried,*
> *So please,*
>
> *"Love me now, love me loud,*
> *Take my hand, let the stars fall down,*
> *Rock my world, turn my silence into sound,*
> *Rock my Christmas, when there's no one else around.*
>
> *"You told me I was too out of reach,*
> *Lost in the clouds, a man no one keeps.*
> *But you're a rainbow cutting through the rain,*
> *Now I chase your colors I hope not in vain.*

"I never believed in mistletoe wishes,
But now I'm dreaming of forever in your kisses,
So please,

"Love me now, love me loud,
Take my hand, let the stars fall down,
Rock my world, turn my silence into sound,
Rock my Christmas, when there's no one else around.

"If I could go back to that night in the dark,
I'd tell you then what I know now in my heart.
So tell me, love, will you stay?
Keep me from washing to gray?

"Ooooh...

"Now I know I won't walk away.
So tell me, love, will you stay?
And...

"Love me now, love me loud,
Take my hand, let the stars fall down,
Rock my world, turn my silence into sound,
Rock my Christmas, when there's no one else
around...

"Love me now, love me loud,
Turn my silence into sound."

His voice is honeyed gravel, rough and rich. He poured so much of us into this song. The night we met, in the dark in a quiet city. Our game of strip souls. Me calling him too hot, too out of reach. Even my "all celebrity relationships are doomed" statistics. Him describing me as a rainbow…

I don't realize I'm crying until Lily hands me a tissue.

By the time Dorian strums the last chord, the crowd is a mess of applause, cheers, and whistles. But I don't hear any of it.

I gracelessly blow my nose and run.

My socked feet slap against the cool tiles as I fly down the steps. Dorian watches me come, slinging the guitar to his back and opening his arms, ready to catch me.

I crash into him, my arms winding around his neck. "Yes." I look into his beautiful blue eyes. "I will love you now. I will love you *so* loud."

His hands cradle my face, his thumbs brushing away the tears. "I love you."

I nod. "I love you, too."

Our faces draw closer, noses touching, breaths mingling. I'm not sure who makes the first move, but soon, our mouths are locked together in an urgent and hungry kiss.

His lips are soft yet insistent. On them, I can taste the sweetness of his apology, the depth of his love, the worry of the past few days when it all seemed lost. My fingers thread through his hair, pulling him closer, never wanting to let go.

Dorian moves with a desperate tenderness that makes my heart stutter. I taste the salt of my tears, feel the heat of his skin through the cool leather of his jacket. Time stretches, bends, then snaps back as we pour every unspoken word and promise in this kiss.

His love is a wave crashing over me, but I'm not drowning—I'm floating, buoyed by the strength of our connection.

As we pull back to catch our breaths, our foreheads resting against each other's, the sounds of the courtyard seep into my consciousness. Around us, the neighbors erupt in applause, a chorus of cheers and whistles filling the air. Someone shouts, "Play another one!"

I glance up at Dorian, who is grinning like an idiot.

He waves at the crowd, his grip firm on me, as he talks into the mic, "You'll have to forgive me but I gotta take my girl home."

A cheer rolls through the courtyard as Dorian swoops me into his arms, brushing a kiss against my temple. "It's a little early, but Merry Christmas, everyone. I just got the best gift. Hope yours will rock, too."

Lily's neighbors erupt in a final burst of applause, voices overlapping in playful shouts and whistling approval.

I bury my face against Dorian's shoulder, laughter bubbling up as the noise swells around us. It feels surreal—this moment, this night, this man who loves me so boldly, so unapologetically. A part of me wants to press pause, to hold on to the magic before reality remembers it still has a say. But maybe that's the thing about love. The real kind. It doesn't need perfect timing or quiet spaces. It crashes in, loud and reckless, and dares you to grab on. And I'm not letting go.

50

DORIAN

I lower my head to whisper in Josie's ear, "Is it okay if I steal you?"

She nods and turns toward the balcony, waving at Lily. "I think I'll skip dinner."

Lily laughs. "Don't you want to at least get your shoes?"

"No, thanks," Josie shouts, and I agree. I can't wait another minute to be alone with her.

"I'll get her new shoes," I yell, already walking out of the courtyard.

Josie pulls up in my arms and stares behind my shoulders. "What about your stuff?"

I shrug. "I'll send someone to get it." The only thing unique is the guitar strapped to my back. "Nick will stay here with the equipment."

Josie gasps, turning to the dark spot where Nick is standing. "I hadn't even noticed him. Your bodyguard really blends in with the shadows."

I carry her out of the courtyard, her legs curled against my side, the soft fabric of her leggings pressing into my arm. She has one hand hooked behind my neck, the other curling over my shoulder. At my truck, I reluctantly set her down and get the door for her.

Josie stretches her toes in her socks against the concrete, then looks up at me with a playful squint. "Where's Ned?"

I pop open the door. "Nick drove on the way here."

Her mouth pulls into an exaggerated pout. "That's a shame."

I smirk, tipping her chin up with my fingers. "Why's that?"

"Because that means we can't make out in the back seat for the entire ride home."

An electric heat shoots through me, setting every nerve on edge. My grip on the truck door tightens to metal-denting strength. My restraint is hanging by a thread, and she knows it.

"That's actually for the best."

Josie leans closer, lips an inch from mine. "Oh?"

"Yeah." I brush a strand of hair from her face. "We need to talk first."

Josie groans, but it's teasing, her hands falling dramatically to her sides. "Fine. Ruin my fun."

I chuckle, nudging her toward the seat. "I promise to make it up to you."

She slides in, flashing me a grin as I shut the door and round the hood. I pause at the back, unstrapping my guitar and placing it in the truck bed before heading to the driver's side. Once I'm behind the wheel, I shift the gear into drive, easing us onto the lane.

Christmas lights blur past the windows, the city shimmering in festive colors. Josie watches them for a while before turning to me.

"What did you want to talk about?"

I drum my fingers against the steering wheel, eyes flicking between the road and her profile. "Did you quit your job today?"

She blinks, surprised. "Why would you think I did?"

I give her a side stare, arching a brow. "The official email informing me that my previous PR rep had resigned and that I'd been assigned a new one tipped me off."

Josie snorts. "Gosh, Nadine is a piece of work."

"So, you didn't quit?"

"Technically, yes," she drawls. "But only after she fired me first and then tried to rehire me."

I glance at her again. "Are you okay?"

She shrugs, staring at the passing streetlights. "I realized I didn't really love my job. And the idea of going back and working under Nadine made my skin crawl. So yeah, I think I'm okay. A bit financially irresponsible, but otherwise fine."

I nod, processing that. "Want me to fire your old firm?"

Josie lets out a surprised laugh. "Tempting, but actually? No."

I study her out of the corner of my eye, mouth twitching. "Oh?"

"Nadine's a shark," Josie explains, shifting in her seat. "She's awful to work for, but she's incredible at what she does. For all her faults, she knows how to control a story. And after your interview, she had the press eating out of your hand."

I smirk. "Don't I get a little credit for that?"

Josie's eyes sparkle. "You were fantastic."

"So you're not mad I did it, the interview?"

"No." Josie shakes her head. "Do you know how Billie is?"

I grip the wheel a little harder. "She got out of the crash unscathed. Not a scratch on her."

Josie exhales, nodding.

I roll my shoulders, forcing myself to loosen my grip. "And she's going away, she'll no longer be a problem for us."

Josie's gaze snaps to me. "What do you mean?"

"Billie had so much crap in her system, any judge would've given her jail time. But her lawyers are negotiating a deal for rehab instead of prison." I don't know if this will change anything. If hitting rock bottom today will finally make Billie face what I couldn't make her see for years. But I want to believe she'll take the help this time. That she'll come out of this experience whole. "She'll be gone for at least six months. And hopefully, when she comes out, Billie will be ready to move on."

"Wow."

"Josie..."

"Yup?"

"I'm sorry I made our relationship public without asking for your permission." I keep my eyes on the road, but I feel her studying me. "But with the fans backing me, you quitting your job, and Lily's bossy text, I figured I could take the risk. That I could grand-gesture you."

Josie's smile really is a rainbow. "Feel free to grand-gesture me whenever you want, rockstar. I loved my song... You put so much of us in it..."

I look at her, then at the road, undecided.

"What?" she asks, because she always notices when something is going on with me.

"I really tried to put a lyric in there about how I'll always let you eat my fries, but couldn't find the right poetics."

She stares at me, stunned. "Did you have a microphone on you that night and record our entire conversation? How do you remember stuff like that?"

"I just paid attention. I always do when I care. And I know you remember everything, too."

"I guess we were both paying attention, then."

I chuckle. "Good to know."

Josie frowns. "Wait. How was Lily's text bossy? She swore she only texted you I was at her place."

"Yeah." I snort. "Your sister was a tad more assertive than that."

"What did she say? Can I read it?"

"Sorry." I make a zipper-over-my-mouth motion just as I pull up to my gate.

Josie narrows her eyes. "Dorian."

I kill the engine and turn to her, already undoing my seat belt. "That's classified information."

She's about to protest, but before she can, I step out of the truck and round to her side.

I open her door, offering my hand. Josie eyes me, still mock-outraged, but takes it anyway. As soon as she's on the ground, I scoop her up in my arms, pressing my lips to the shell of her ear.

"And we don't have time to discuss it now, anyway."

"Why?"

"Because now, *Josephine*, the time for talking is over."

51

JOSIE

Dorian takes the stairs two at a time, his grip on me secure, his breathing steady despite carrying me. I'd be impressed if I weren't distracted by the cage of muscles I'm riding in. His chest, arms, even his shoulders are firm. Every shift sends a ripple through him—biceps flexing, chest hardening—and it passes on to me as a shiver.

I secure my arms around his neck more firmly, breathless as the second flight disappears under us. "How are you carrying me as if I weigh nothing?"

His laugh vibrates against my side. "Adrenaline."

"That's not how adrenaline works."

"I don't care," he says as we crest the last step.

"You could have let me walk." I nuzzle against his neck.

"And miss the chance to show off?" His voice is teasing, but underneath, he sounds possessive. "Nah."

Dorian nudges his bedroom door open with his boot before striding inside and kicking it shut behind us. The room is dark except for the soft glow of the city filtering in through the floor-to-ceiling windows. The skyline stretches endlessly beyond us, but I barely notice it. Dorian is the only thing I see.

He lowers me to the mattress with a care that contradicts the heat simmering in his gaze. My breath stutters as I sink into the sheets and his weight settles between my thighs. His hands frame my face, warm and steady, thumbs brushing my cheek-bones as he looks down at me. I can read so much in his expression—his eyes say, *I love you, I want you, I need you.*

I love him, I want him, and I need him right back.

I curl my fingers into his jacket. "Kiss me."

Dorian doesn't hesitate. His mouth crashes down on mine, capturing my lips with a groan, his teeth dragging over my lower lip. We've kissed a bunch of times, and each one has been different. It's the same for this one. Because finally, we're not hiding, no one is watching. It's a kiss that's not stolen or forbidden. Something we have to pretend isn't happening. This is real, open, and ours. We're alone. Just us, together, finally free to want—no barriers, no limits.

His lips are fire, his body a heavy weight wrapping around me, staking his claim. I grab the lapels of his jacket, pushing it off his shoulders, and he shrugs out of it without breaking contact. Dorian kisses me deeper, making up for lost time.

His hands slide underneath my sweatshirt, palms skimming my sides. My back bows as if to help him remove the useless barrier faster, pressing me harder against him.

I want more, need more. But... Oh. *Oh.*

I freeze, my stomach dropping as a horrifying realization slams into me.

I shove his hands away, gripping my sweatshirt before he can lift it. "Wait—"

Dorian stops, his brows pulling together, breathing heavily. "What's wrong?"

I groan, covering my face with both hands. "I'm not wearing my best seduction outfit right now."

He stills, and I worry I've killed the mood. But then he crawls over me, prying my hands away from my face. "Are you serious?"

I wince. "Dorian, I'm literally wearing my oldest leggings with a hole in the butt and period-stained granny panties."

He stares at me, shocked, then his lips twitch before he's full-on laughing. The sound rolls over me, warm and tingly.

I glare at him. "This isn't funny."

"Oh, I think it's *very* funny." Dorian's grin is nothing short of wicked as his fingers skim the hem of my sweatshirt, toying with the fabric. "None of that matters to me."

I turn my head, a wave of embarrassment creeping over me, but he doesn't let me look away, he grabs my chin and turns my face to him. "Let me make one thing absolutely clear. Baby, you could wear a garbage bag, and I'd still think you're the sexiest woman I've ever seen."

I scowl. "That's a terrible analogy."

Dorian leans down, dragging his mouth along the column of my throat, pressing a kiss on my jaw. "And it doesn't matter what you're wearing." His hands slip under my clothes again. "Because I'm taking it all off anyway."

His palms skim up my sides. Heat pools low in my stomach as Dorian sits back on his knees, drags the sweatshirt over my head, and sends it flying somewhere. I'm done protesting or worrying he might be turned off by my crappy clothes. Especially as his eyes darken as they sweep over the old, unsexy bra I'm wearing, his thumbs teasing the strip of skin above my waistband.

"Fuck," he murmurs, voice rough. "You're so beautiful."

My face burns as he pulls my leggings down my hips in one tortuously slow motion.

Dorian leans back, still fully clothed, his hands settling on my bare thighs. "You have no idea what you do to me."

"Mmm." I might be losing the capacity to speak. But not the one to move, thankfully.

I hook my fingers into the hem of his T-shirt, desperate to feel him with nothing between us. Dorian lets me pull it over his head, and my gaze rakes over him, tracing every sharp cut of muscle, the expanse of tanned skin, and all that sexy ink. I trace the tattoos sprawling across his chest, the intricate details I've memorized, sketched on the skin of the princes in my stories, and dreamed of every night I spent alone.

"You're obsessed with these," he teases, watching me as I drag my nails lightly over his ribs. Finally, I can kiss the phoenix over his heart, lick the wave crests on the other side.

I stare up at him with my mouth still on his chest. "They're my favorite."

Dorian looks feral as he shifts his weight to press me back into the mattress. "Good. Because they're all yours."

We kiss again with no restraint. No teasing. Only heat and urgency, the kind that sinks into my bones and takes over. His hands are everywhere—skittering over my ribs, gripping my waist, mapping my body as if he's been waiting forever to do it. And maybe he has. Maybe I have, too.

I slide my hands up his arms, over his shoulders, nails skimming the back of his neck as he kisses down my throat.

I don't realize I'm trembling until his palm flattens against my stomach, grounding me. "Everything okay?"

I nod, tracing the curve of his jaw, the shadow of stubble rough under my fingertips. "I just... I don't want to wait anymore."

"I love you." He says it like it's the easiest thing in the world. Like it's always been this simple. "I'm never letting you go."

I smirk against his lips and undo the first button of his jeans. "Can you let go of these?"

Dorian shimmies out of his pants comically fast before he kneels back between my spread thighs—nothing comic about that. He slides a hand down my leg, fingers curling around my ankle as he lifts my foot, looping it over his shoulder. The motion stretches me with a delicious tension.

He smirks. "Socks stay on?"

I open my mouth to say something—something sarcastic, something teasing—but the way his fingers slowly peel the sock off steals the words from my throat. He takes his time, tugging it past my toes before tossing it aside, peppering my ankle with featherlight, open-mouthed kisses. Then he does the same with the other sock, his palm skimming down my calf in a touch so reverent, it nearly undoes me.

And then nothing is left between us except our underwear.

His mouth brushes the inside of my thigh. "Tell me you want this."

I don't hesitate. "I want you."

A muscle ticks in his jaw, his restraint fraying at the edges, but he keeps his movements measured. His fingers dip under the waistband of my panties, and he drags them down my legs, his knuckles grazing over sensitive skin.

And then I'm bare under him.

His gaze rakes over me, dark and hungry, his breath coming slower, heavier. My chest rises and falls in time with his, my pulse thrumming in my ears. Being laid out like this, exposed, makes me flush with heat all over.

"You're perfect." The words are barely a whisper, but they crash into me anyway.

Dorian moves over me, his body a wall of warmth, pressure, and friction.

I map his back muscles with my hands, every dip and curve, and the ridges of his spine. Then lower. I squeeze his round, perfect ass, loving the way he tenses under my grip before I slide his briefs down.

He dips his head, kissing me over my collarbone, across the swell of my breast. I don't know when he unhooked my bra, only realize he's tearing it off now.

His teeth scrape skin, sending a shiver rolling through me.

"Dorian—please…"

He hums against my skin as our bodies come together. And then there is no more him or me, we're an us locked in our movements—slow and tentative at first, then desperate, urgent. I gasp for air as he claims every inch of me, the sensation overwhelming and perfect.

His forehead presses to mine, his breath ragged. "You okay?"

I nod, arching into him. "More than okay."

Each slow roll of his hips sends heat ripping through me, winding me tighter and higher.

His name falls from my lips, a plea, a prayer, a promise.

He grips my thigh, his hand curling under my knee, lifting my leg higher against his waist. The shift sends a new wave of sensation crashing through me, and I gasp, fingers digging into his back.

Dorian's breath is ragged. "I love you."

The words unravel something deep in my chest, and when I tip my chin up to meet his mouth, I kiss him like I'm sealing a vow.

And then I let go.

I shatter underneath him, waves of pleasure pulsing through me. He follows me seconds later, his body tensing before he groans low against my neck. His hold on himself slips, and he collapses onto me.

We stay like that for a long time, tangled together, chests rising and falling in sync.

Dorian shifts, brushing the damp hair from my forehead, his lips ghosting over my temple. He watches me like I've undone him, like he's still catching up to what just happened between us.

I rake my fingers through his hair in a slow caress. "So, did I rock your Christmas?"

He grins, slow and lazy. "Christmas is a few days away, we still got some rocking to do."

"Already?" I laugh. "And here I thought Christmas only came once a year."

Dorian shifts over me, pinning my hands above my head. "Are you sure you want to tease me right now, baby?"

The smile dies on my lips. "You know my brain goes mush when you call me baby."

He arches a diabolical eyebrow at me. "Oh, I know, love." Then his mouth finds mine, and I'm his again—now, tomorrow, always.

52

DORIAN

We spend the next two days holed up in my bedroom, the world outside a distant memory. Occasionally, we venture into the kitchen to forage for food, raiding the fridge like a pair of sleep-deprived college kids. With most of my staff on leave for the holidays, the house is our own private sanctuary, giving Josie and me the extra privacy we crave.

The first morning she's here, I send someone to retrieve her phone and shoes from her sister's place and a change of clothes from her house—not that I'm letting her stay clothed for long.

We live in a perpetual state of sleeping in late, having each other for breakfast, and losing track of time in the best way.

We talk, we laugh, we make love.

I've officially lost my edge. Give it another week, and I'll have *Live, Laugh, Love* monogrammed on my pillows. At the speed things are going my obituary will read, *Here lies Dorian. He lived, he laughed, he loved. And Josie roasted him for it.*

On the second morning, Josie attempts to cook—burns toast —then declares we should stick to our strengths, which for her means looking devastatingly cute in my shirt, and for me means reheating the gourmet frozen meals my chef stocked in the freezer.

We stay wrapped in this cocoon made only for two until, on Christmas morning, she stirs beside me, her bare legs tangling with mine underneath the sheets. The room is still dipped in that early-morning winter light.

Josie's fingers brush my stomach as she sighs into the pillow. My lips curve into a smile before I even open my eyes.

"Morning," I mumble, pressing a kiss to her shoulder. "Merry Christmas, love."

"Mmm. Merry Christmas."

I shift on top of her, flicking my tongue over the hollow of her throat. "Got any Christmas wishes?"

"No, I already have everything I want."

I swallow, my fingers pressing harder on her waist, my pulse drumming against hers. "You sure about that?"

Her nails drag along my shoulder, her breath warm against my mouth. "I don't want to be greedy, but if you have something specific in mind, I can always be persuaded."

"Oh, I've got lots of specifics in mind, love." I kiss her deeply, unhurriedly, savoring every second like it's a gift. There's no rush, no urgency—just two people who finally have all the time in the world. I want her to feel how much I need her, how much I love her.

And I do. I make love to her slowly, tenderly, every touch and kiss a silent confession of my feelings. Her soft gasps and the way she clings to me the answer to a love so profound, it scares me. We move together. Breathe together. We give and take, we love each other until pleasure ricochets through us, leaving our bodies trembling and our minds dazed. We collapse into each other, our skin slick and warm, our hearts pounding in a shared, chaotic beat.

For a long instant, we simply lie there, entwined and silent, basking in the afterglow. I stroke her hair, kiss her forehead, and she nestles closer, her breathing calming. An overwhelming sense of peace settles over me—an undeniable rightness, as if every fragment of my life has aligned to bring me here, to this perfect moment with her.

I might drift back to sleep—I'm not sure—but when Josie's phone pings on the nightstand, it feels like a rude awakening.

She rolls over to check the notification, and I miss her warmth. I scoot closer, ready to convince her to drop the phone and love me some more. But when she leans against the headboard and pulls her knees up, worrying her lower lip as she reads the text, I panic.

Worst-case scenarios flash through my head. Something terrible has happened. A new reason we can't be together. Lily is tired of the paparazzi camping out of her housing complex after videos of my serenade went viral. Josie's sister has reassured us they are no bother, and the excitement should die down soon. But something could've changed. The attention becoming too much. The press not leaving Penny alone. My mind spins through every catastrophic possibility as I watch Josie read, the glow of the screen casting shadows on her face. She's too still, too quiet, and it's killing me. Not knowing is torture.

"What is it?" I ask.

Josie looks up at me, her frown immediately disappearing. "My agent. She wishes me happy holidays and asks if her Christmas present is that I'm Rian Phoenix's mystery woman."

My heartbeat slows down. "Oh?"

"She says that if I am, she's going to put my book out for auction." Josie winces as if discussing money with me is something she'd rather not do. "That publishers go nuts for celebrity books and with the attention we're getting now, I can hope for a high-six-figure advance."

"And you look so dejected about that why?"

"I don't want to piggyback on your fame, or exploit who you are."

"Josie." I pull her into my lap, doing my best not to get distracted by her naked chest until the conversation is over. "You lost your job for me, your career. If my fame will help you launch a new one, I want you to go for it."

"But—"

I press a finger to her lips. "Dating a celebrity has many downsides. I want you to also take the upsides. And, honestly, I'm just being selfish right now."

She pouts adorably. "Selfish how?"

"If you can be a full-time author, it's a job you can do from anywhere. You could come with me when I'm on tour, we could see the world together..."

"Ah." Josie beams at me. "Your long-standing plan of turning me into a full-time groupie."

I smirk, fingers tracing absent patterns over her bare thigh. "Groupie? No, love. I prefer the term 'traveling muse.' Much more poetic. You inspire, I perform, we make questionable decisions in every time zone."

Josie laughs, tipping her head back and exposing her long throat. I have to grind my teeth not to bite her. "Questionable decisions, huh? Like what? Wearing matching leather jackets?"

"I was thinking more... sneaking you backstage, kissing you breathless against a dressing-room door, giving you a beard burn so fierce the entire world will know who I'm singing about."

She presses a palm to my chest, pushing me back just

enough to study my face with a serious frown that doesn't match the teasing sparkle in her eyes.

"You realize that if I come on tour with you, you'll have to focus on performing? That you can't just spend your time keeping me entertained."

"Well, my last tour just ended, so for the next couple of years, I'll have nothing to do but keep you entertained, baby."

Josie's eyes smolder, turning molten, and it's the last straw. I flip her onto the mattress, pinning her under me again, her phone tumbles off the bed—neither of us so much as looks at it.

Her hair fans out across the pillow like a halo, and her lips part in breathless anticipation. I lace our fingers together over her head, studying her face, her mouth, the rise and fall of her chest.

She wriggles under me, testing my hold as a sly smile curves her lips. "Dorian." Her voice is a seductive challenge. "Are you going to just stare, or will you"—she sing-songs the next part—"love me now, love me loud—"

I cut her off with a kiss, swallowing the last of her teasing words as my mouth claims hers—hot, insistent, and entirely without patience. She meets me just as eagerly. Her hands are still blocked and the only way she can get closer is to arch her body into mine, torturing me with the soft press of her curves against me. The heat between us is a living, growing thing, all-consuming.

I trail kisses down her jawline and her neck, taking my time, savoring the taste of her skin. She tilts her head to the side, offering me more, and I oblige, nipping and sucking, leaving a trail of red marks that will fade too fast. I want to be on her skin forever.

I drop one hand on her hips, holding her steady as I shift my weight and make love to her again until the only words left between us are whispered pleads and gasped names.

Because here, in her arms, is where the song ends—and where forever begins.

* * *

MORE FROM CAMILLA ISLEY

Another laugh-out-loud, sparkling romance from Camilla Isley is available to order now here:

https://mybook.to/NewCamillaIsleyBackAd

NOTE FROM THE AUTHOR

Dear reader,

I hope you enjoyed reading *You Rock My World*. This was my first rockstar romance, and I had such a great time building up Dorian in my head—troubled, magnetic, secretly a golden retriever, the kind of man who looks like trouble and sounds like every dream you're not supposed to have. And then there's Josie, with her epic sarcasm and open soul. She's the one person who sees him for who he really is—and loves him more for it. I fell for them hard—maybe you did too.

But as it also happens while I write my stories, my heart went out to a supporting character: Lily. She's strong, struggling, battered down by life and grief, but still fighting. I couldn't stop my brain from wanting to give her an HEA, too, and I'm writing her story right now. I won't make it easy for her; I'll have her fall for the one man she isn't sure she could survive loving. This book will be emotional, fun, uplifting, heartbreaking, and heart-warming. I hope you'll want to follow Lily on her healing journey. (PS. The book-boyfriend I'm writing for her is so swoon-worthy I'm making my own toes curl as I write.)

Now, I have to ask you a favor. If you loved my story, please leave a review on your favorite retailer website, Goodreads, Bookbub, or wherever you like to post reviews (your blog, your Facebook wall, your bedroom wall, in a text to your best friend... a BookTok or Bookstagram video!). Reviews are the best gift you can give to an author, and word of mouth is the most powerful means of book discovery.

Thank you for your constant support!

Camilla

ACKNOWLEDGMENTS

Another book has officially seen the light of day, and I couldn't be more excited—or possibly more sleep-deprived. But it's all worth it when I think about how this story now belongs to you, the readers. Whether you devoured this book in one sitting or savored it over time, thank you for choosing to spend your time with these characters. I hope they've entertained you, kept you up too late, and maybe even made you smile when you needed it most.

A big, grateful nod to my family and friends. You somehow still ask me how the writing is going, even though you know the answer involves coffee, procrastination, and a lot of "it's almost there."

To my editor, thanks for having me focus on all the flirty banter moments. And to my proofreader for spotting all those tiny details.

To the production team for making this story the prettiest it could be.

To the marketing and sales teams for helping my story travel far and wide to readers all over the world.

To all of you who review and post about my stories, I can never express enough how much your support means to me.

ABOUT THE AUTHOR

Camilla Isley is an engineer who left science behind to write bestselling contemporary rom-coms set all around the world. She lives in Italy.

Sign up to Camilla Isley's mailing list for news, competitions and updates on future books.

Visit Camilla's website: www.camillaisley.com

Follow Camilla on social media here:

facebook.com/camillaisley

x.com/camillaisley

instagram.com/camillaisley

bookbub.com/authors/camilla-isley

ALSO BY CAMILLA ISLEY

Boldwood
EVER AFTER

x♡x♡

JOIN BOLDWOOD'S
**ROMANCE
COMMUNITY**
FOR SWEET AND
SPICY BOOK RECS
WITH ALL YOUR
FAVOURITE
TROPES!

SIGN UP TO OUR
NEWSLETTER

HTTPS://BIT.LY/BOLDWOODEVERAFTER

Boldwood

Boldwood Books is an award-winning fiction publishing company seeking out the best stories from around the world.

Find out more at www.boldwoodbooks.com

Join our reader community for brilliant books, competitions and offers!

Follow us
@BoldwoodBooks
@TheBoldBookClub

Sign up to our weekly deals newsletter

https://bit.ly/BoldwoodBNewsletter

9 781836 333739